STALLING IN LOVE

Rebecca Chase

Copyright

This ebook is a work of fiction. Names, characters, businesses, places, events and incidents are either the products of the author's imagination or used in a fictitious manner. Any resemblance to actual persons, living or dead, or actual events is purely coincidental.

Copyright 2023 Rebecca Chase

All rights reserved

Published by Rebecca Chase

All rights reserved. No part of this publication may be reproduced, distributed, or transmitted in any form or by any means, including photocopying, recording, or other electronic or mechanical methods, without the prior written permission of the published, except in the case of brief quotations embodied in critical reviews and certain other noncommerical uses permitted by copyright law.

To the women in my family, you taught me to dance and to never give up on my dreams.

PROLOGUE

Evie drew a deep breath and sighed—Josh's bedroom smelt of clean washing and the aftershave she bought him for helping her quit smoking. Sadly, the scent of spice with a hint of fruity zest ruminated from the carpet as, thirty seconds after she gave it to him, he managed to spill it all over his room. He paid her back, transferring the money from his phone within moments while blushing at his mistake, not that it was an issue. For a professional athlete, he seemed to have clumsy moments around her.

"This is the song that played the night in the pub. You know the one," she said, standing in her best friend's bedroom, flicking through Spotify playlists. More than a year ago, Evie apologised to her ex-boyfriend, Aidan, for her behaviour and admitted that she didn't want to be the fun-loving party girl known as Bianca anymore. Instead, she wanted to return to her original name, Evangeline Draper, or Evie.

Thighs she could barely wrap two hands around filled her view as he walked closer. Josh was her world and, unfortunately, a friend of Aidan, too.

"Can you believe that was the night we became friends?" Josh asked as he pointed out a song he wanted on the list. She rolled her eyes at his choice of a 90s boyband hit. But he nudged her playfully until she added it to his playlist for their late rugby training session. It would be just the two of them on the field in the darkness with her shouting drills as always. She loved every second of it. "And now look at us."

He had a point. They used to hate each other, but here Evie was, helping him improve his rugby skills to become the best player the Bulls team had.

Evie pulled her strawberry blond hair out of its messy bun and ruffled the frizz with her fingers, hoping he would watch, but as usual, his thoughts were on rugby plays. It was evident from the way his hands danced in the air as if he was positioning players around the pitch. "Why did you let me hug you that night? You hated me."

"I barely knew you. You were the woman who made my mate's life hell." Evie gazed at Josh, who blushed under her gaze. The flush was evident even under his messy beard. A fluttering filled her belly. That night was the first time they had a proper conversation. And now she was secretly in love with him. What a fucking mess.

"True," she announced, jumping up to her feet. "Are you sure you want to go to the field and practice drills tonight?"

"Definitely." Josh crossed his bedroom and filled his sports bag with things they might need for training. He held his hoodie aloft. It was his special one from playing in the World Cup for England. He often kept it hidden at the back of his closet. But why?

"Do you want me to help?"

He swatted her request away with his hand. "You lie on the bed while I do this. You look tired…" He left the comment open, but she didn't fill the space.

She couldn't tell him what was happening in her life, or he'd want to fix it. It didn't matter how often he fished because being with him meant she could forget the things outside their world. He was allowing her to relax in a way that no one else did. He glanced briefly at her, but she launched onto the bed and watched him instead.

"Right, cool," he said when the silence stretched too long. "You chill out, and then I'll make us dinner before practice. What would you like?"

No one else cooked for her, let alone asked for her thoughts. Why was this guy in her head? There wasn't anything sexual between them, which kept their friendship a safe space. She was the real her only with him. She didn't worry about his or anyone's expectations. The bedding smelt of his natural musky scent mixed with the fruity shower gel he often used, and her heart swelled. She gritted her teeth. She couldn't ruin this friendship with butterflies. Josh was the only true friend she had. Evie scrolled through playlists to find a song that would motivate Josh when he got low in that night's practice. He distracted her with his slow side-to-side neck stretches as he worried his lip and picked items for his sports bag. Her mouth temporarily dried up, and she swallowed a few times to regain control.

He needed motivating, not seducing. Rugby was his only love, and her aim to ensure he was the best he could be was the most important thing to her. Josh's friendship dripped confidence into her life every day and crushed demons from her past, not that he knew. Any way she could help him was important. His patience and support helped her quit smoking, and she was a self-confessed bitch during those months. But he took his time checking in on her, supporting her and ensuring she was never alone with her cravings. Josh's Adam's apple bobbed as he drank water from his Bulls rugby team sports bottle. He was so proud of his team. Evie wetted her lips as she stared. Fuck.

"Josh," she screamed, instantly drawing his attention. His eyes widened as he stared. Shit. What could she say to cover up her attraction? "Come listen to this song," she stuttered, holding out an earbud to him.

His eyebrows knotted as he strolled over. Josh joined her on the bed and placed the earbud into his ear. Her skin prickled with heat. They'd hung out on his bed plenty of times before. What was going on with her hormones? This attraction had grown over months but was in full force tonight. Maybe it was all the ballet she was doing in her spare time. It was helping her to find her true identity. Not that Josh knew about that, either. He'd want to watch her perform, and she wasn't ready. He was always trying to find new ways to support her. Evie stretched like a cat before silently reprimanding herself. Her body was in flirt mode, but she needed to calm it.

Josh shrugged. His thigh touched hers. Was she the only one sensing the heat? Her flirting was wasted on him. Neither dated since they became friends, but they also never mentioned partners. "It's the theme tune from the film Rocky. Haven't we used this one before?"

Evie laughed, but it was a hollow sound. "No, I, I'm not sure."

Josh side-eyed her. "Did you know I wrestled at school? I used to practice my moves in my bedroom to the Rocky soundtrack. I felt like The Rock." Josh showed her a bicep, and her stomach dropped. She slowly sucked in the air.

"The Rock isn't the same as Rocky. Sly–"

"I know that," Josh jumped up, and she took a long breath. They needed space between them. "But it was motivating. Add it to the list. I got my wish, though."

Evie tipped her head to the side. "Your wish?" She knew what she wished for.

"Yeah." Josh flexed his bicep again, and she pressed her thighs together. Maybe she should skip his practice that night and head home to relieve herself with her purple 7-inch friend. She'd taken a vow of celibacy, so sex with any of her exes was out of the question, not that she'd go back there. The only man she wanted underneath her was lifting his tee to show his six-pack. Fucking hell, he was all muscle, and there was a smattering of hair on his chest calling for her fingers. "I'm now stronger than The Rock. He's got nothing on me."

Evie choked, and Josh rushed to give her his water bottle. "The fuck you are," she replied between splutters as he patted her back and looked at her wide-eyed. "There's no universe where you're stronger than him."

That got a reaction. Josh patted his chest and shouted, "Hey. I'm a beast." His laughter was infectious, and her heart danced again. Why was everything about him endearing?

"Prove it," she chuckled. He'd back down like he usually did when she challenged him to anything that wasn't rugby-related. She'd challenged him to share his relationship history, and he wouldn't talk about those secrets, which was probably for the best. Her reputation didn't put her in good stead there either. When they were together, their past and families didn't exist. They lived in a friendship bubble.

She beamed her smile and beckoned him closer with her hands waving. As she leaned forward, her chest pressed against the v of her t-shirt, revealing the top of her breasts, but she knew he wouldn't notice. He didn't see her that way.

"Okay," Josh launched onto the bed and met her contest head-on. Evie gasped and pressed her lips together as Josh positioned himself above her. She was at his mercy. He held her tightly beneath him as her strawberry blonde hair splayed around her head.

"Do you surrender?" Josh asked breathlessly, replacing merriment with tension that made her belly pulsate. His nearly black eyes darkened as she wriggled and tested his strength. Evie's skirt rode up her thighs from the friction of his jeans. Her breasts peaked out of a low-cut T-shirt that emphasised her curves.

How did this escalate so quickly? Maybe she wasn't the only horny one, but what did it mean for their friendship if they crossed an unspoken line?

While Josh pinned her wrists above her head with one massive hand, the other gently moved down her body. Was he threatening to tickle or stroke her? The rough skin of his palm brushed her naked hip, the T-shirt bunching above her waist. Evie's tummy muscles tightened, preparing for his touch, as she tried to hold the lust flaring in her stomach. Her need for him rippled before taking hold of her core, which clenched tightly in anticipation. She held her breath and focused on each pulsation. Her skin seared as if she might suddenly combust. At that moment, her vow of celibacy heightened every sense. She was known for her unwavering cockiness, but suddenly she faced a situation that left her heart floundering. Josh leaned closer, his eyes holding hers. His body covered her completely, heating her and adding to the lust that transformed from ripples to quakes.

"Do you surrender, Evangeline?" he asked again. His voice deepened, saturated with a want she'd never heard from him. His lips teetered above hers while his hand settled at her hip. His grip had been soft, but his intention was clear. She wanted his hands clutching her tightly. The floor was hard beneath her back, but it was his erection inside his jeans, pressing between her thighs, that had her aching for more.

"Yes." The whisper left her lips, the expectation and yearning evident as her chest rose and breath escaped her mouth.

A knock at Josh's bedroom door made him move quicker than if a bomb had gone off in his boxers.

"Oi, mate," Max, one of his teammates and his housemate, shouted as he pushed through the bedroom door. "I need a power tool."

"You and me both," Evie grunted under her breath as a sweaty flushed Josh paced the room.

"Sure. There's one in the garage. I'll find it for you." Josh pushed Max out the door before turning to Evie. "On second thought, I'll get an early night and sack off training tonight." Evie held her breath. Was he going to ask her to stay? "Shall I walk you out?"

She gritted her teeth against the pain that radiated through her chest. It was a clear brush-off. He left her standing on his doorstep as the door closed in her face. What the fuck?

Chapter One

"Don't you know him? He's one of those rugby guys, isn't he? Bet he goes like a rollercoaster in bed," Maddie said with a wink.

Evie's stomach blistered. Yes, she knew him. It was Josh. He was the man who went from being her enemy to her safe space. Her fingers trembled against her legs. He was her everything and only friend until he ghosted her ten weeks earlier after their night wrestling, and she still didn't know why.

"Yeah, vaguely. A friend of a friend," she replied, hiding the despondency that clamoured through her words.

"I was talking to Jack." Her gaze swung Jack's way. "You know him, don't you? Wasn't he in our year at school and dated that girl you were mates with?" Maddie queried.

As one, they stared at the giant man commandeering the cinema's lobby. Solid thighs she knew were like steel girders caught her eye as her fantasies of the rugby guy clouded her consciousness. His looming body instantly demanded attention, though his slumped shoulders and drooping head suggested he was attempting to fade into the background. Ill-fitting clothes hid his straining muscles and well-defined torso, and the fuzz of hair springing from his face disguised the baby-face profile that Evie had spent hours studying. In the last year, they'd gone from enemies to friends to the brink of lovers. And now? Nothing.

Was it only a couple of months ago they lived in each other's pockets? They'd spent every day together, laughing and avoiding the rest of the world. But then they'd gone their separate ways, and each painful hour without him turned slowly into days and weeks until she'd built her barriers back up and blocked any man from getting close. But no matter how much she'd tried to erase him as quickly from her memories as he'd removed her from his life, every moment remained etched on her heart. He promptly became another reminder never to trust men, including the ones who seemed like good guys.

"Yeah, he's been kind of a friend since school. He's worked with my charity, too." Jack worked at a local charity for bereaved kids, and Josh helped at events. As a local premiership rugby player, his presence held the fascination and worship of some of the more complex and hurting kids. "I'll call him over."

"No, don't," Evie snapped, but her response was too quick. Immediately, Jack and Maddie stared at her. "He looks like he's on a date, and we'd hate to bother him."

A giggling blonde woman hung off his arm and tried to force her hand on any part of him. To Josh's credit, he gently tried to ease her away or remove her hands from his body. Evie rolled her eyes as Blondie flicked her hair before attempting to slide her hand beneath Josh's top. Jealousy ripped through Evie. What would a date with him be like? *I want to be the woman on his arm.* But she refused to set herself up to be rejected by him again. There was enough shit in her life already.

The panic radiating through her short outburst must have been enough to intrigue Jack. Within seconds, he'd called him over, "Hey, Josh. How're things?"

A gentle grin reached Josh's lips when he recognised his old school chum. How dare he look so cute. "Hey, mate. They're not bad. How's things with you?"

Thighs she intimately recalled, featuring in her fantasies as she brought herself to dull orgasms, brought him nearer. Blondie bounced against him, desperately trying to grip him between her pincher-like fingers and not be left behind.

His gaze flicked around the group. It darkened when he saw Evie trying to step back and hide behind Jack and Maddie. It reminded her again of their last interaction. Josh took in the entirety of her face.

Lips she'd longed to feel against every inch of her skin opened, but his words faltered.

"Oh my God, Jack, I can't believe it's you!" A piercing voice shocked them, although Josh continued staring at Evie.

"Tasha, what the hell?" Jack mentioned Tasha often enough at the pub where Evie worked. The "callous witch" also worked at the charity with Jack, although he often commented that work was a foreign concept to her. He said her priority was frolicking around the office while telling people how great she was and doing whatever it took to get their attention. "I wouldn't have put you two together. Not ever!"

Tasha screeched, "I know, but—"

"We're not together," a gruff-voiced Josh interjected quickly, his eyes never leaving Evie's.

"Oh, baby, not yet," Tasha replied, giggling. "But we will be. You'll be my King Kong, and I will cover your fur with my—"

"Tasha, for the love of God, stop," Jack spoke all their thoughts.

At Tasha's shrieks of laughter, Josh and Jack blanched. The synchronisation would have been funny if it had been for any other reason.

Josh prised Tasha's spindly fingers from his arm and stepped to the side. Even from this distance, his heat overwhelmed her. *Why can't I stop trembling?* Seeing him again without warning was too much, and her smart-ass mouth seemed broken.

Josh cleared his throat loudly enough to distract Evie from her panic and draw her attention to him. As if she could conceive of anything else. "Tasha won me at a charity auction last night. All she gets is one night at the cinema. She insisted we do it as soon as possible." He winced as he spoke the last sentence. "The cinema, I mean." Exasperation left his mouth in one long, painful sigh.

"So that you fall in love with me even quicker. Besides, baby is horny and needs some loving," Tasha screeched.

"You need to sort your shit out, baby," Evie snapped between gnashing teeth.

"Oh my God, you're Bianca. I can't believe I'm dating a celebrity and meeting another famous star in one night. Wow, a real-life glamour model." Tasha squealed, jumping like she had a pogo stick stuck up her arse.

Josh rushed to Evie's defence as he addressed Tasha succinctly. "You and I aren't dating. She's not a glamour model anymore, and her name is Evie, not 'Bianca.'"

"I don't need you being my knight in shining armour," Evie bit out in a display of hurt. "But Josh is right. I don't do glamour modelling anymore." Or as her nan called it, "Miss Playboy UK".

"And you date The Destroyer too, don't you, Bianca? That man has a body I would destroy. I would fuck him until he cried and then keep going." Tasha followed up with a cackle.

Evie responded quickly, "Don't you ever give it a rest? You're like a fucking harpy devil crossbreed!"

"Oh, you charmer," was the bizarre response from Tasha's blood-red lips. *Was I like that in my Bianca days? No wonder I had no friends.* As Bianca, Evie lived a life of raucous parties and drunk nights that lowered her inhibitions and offered her fake confidence. She did despicable things in desperation to help those she loved, including attempting to sell a sex tape. The shame and being on the brink of self-destruction forced her to change, although the guilt sat with her daily. About eighteen months earlier, Evie deleted her alter ego from her life. She'd ditched the outfits that forced her sexuality into strangers' faces; the same clothes hid her personality. Since then, the focus was reducing alcohol-related mistakes and trying to be her authentic self.

"It wasn't a compliment, Tasha," Evie added. "Not that it's any of your business, but I haven't seen The Destroyer—I mean, Gavin—for months, let alone dated him in that time." Evie refused to study Josh's reaction, though the words were for his benefit. There were still the best bits of Bianca inside her, but Evie didn't need to pretend to be someone she wasn't and didn't want to be. However, she wasn't sure who she wanted to be either.

Josh slipped closer to her. "Then where have you been?" he whispered.

As she stared at Josh's bear-like hands gripping his drink tightly, their last moment together forced its way out of the box where she'd kept it locked away. The attraction was still there even if she wanted to blank him like he'd blanked her for the last ten weeks. She'd desperately tried to lock her emotions away. Instead, she'd used an array of vibrators to satisfy the one need that refused to be ignored, but they'd barely touched the edges. She pushed her needs to the side after another empty and unsatisfying experience where if she did manage to orgasm, it was barely a footnote in her morning. She'd tried numerous times not to let Josh's toned body and thick thighs fill her head when trying to get herself off, but he always pushed his way in, making her fantasies better than porn. But her phone remained quiet, and her heart was cold. She'd set herself in a position where no guy could reject or break her again, yet he'd found a way past her barriers. Looking into his messy beard now, she hated herself for wanting him as much as she had that night.

Evie breathed deeply. She had too much to hide from him, including how much she wanted him. Out of the corner of her eye, she caught the uncertainty in Jack's gaze. He'd demand to know everything before the night was over.

"We should go in. The movie will be starting soon," Evie uttered with a mouth so dry that her tongue stuck to her hard palate. She gave Jack a warning look to keep quiet before walking in front of the group. Tasha continued to witter about her favourite rugby players and what they could do to her.

Evie swung her hips, and when she neared the big glass doors, she was rewarded with the reflection of a captivated Josh. Desperation disgraced her conscience even as she willed Josh to respond to her needs and touch her bottom. As if reading her mind, his hand accidentally brushed across her butt cheeks as they passed through the doors. As Evie turned and smiled, she saw Josh's raised eyebrows and a shy smile that had existed in her dreams laying down the gauntlet. *Do I accept his challenge, or should I walk away as the winner of this fucked-up game?*

CHAPTER TWO

What is she doing here? Josh contemplated in the darkness of the cinema. Jack had orchestrated that Josh sat next to Evie.

Was it possible that Evie wanted it too? Josh peeked at her face, but it was as unreadable as the last time they were together. Was she happy to see him, or did his presence piss her off? It had been precisely ten weeks since they'd seen each other, and he'd spent every one of those weeks remembering her body beneath his and her mouth declaring that she surrendered to him. The rosy hue of her lips had teased him closer in a sensual smile that no woman had given him before. If his eyes hadn't given away his intentions that evening, then his erection had. If Max hadn't knocked on Josh's door and broken the hunger ramping up with an intensity neither of them could control, he would have given her everything before regretting it for weeks.

It was impossible to believe he used to dislike and loudly insult Evie in public. Initially, when she'd been her alter ego Bianca, she'd dated his close friend Aidan, who played with him on the Bull's side. To say their relationship was fiery was a massive understatement. Not a day passed that they weren't trying to get a reaction from each other. He'd learnt Aidan's reasons: he'd thought he had a terminal illness and refused to fall in love. She'd explained that she'd tried to get pregnant because she was desperate to be loved by someone, but aside from that, she remained a mystery. Rejection had often brought out a dangerous side of her, and she had a reputation for rampaging when guys tried to split up with her. *She didn't do that when I stopped calling. I guess she wasn't that bothered about me after all.*

Josh needed to stop the friendship, or whatever it was, that existed between them again. He'd worked so hard to protect himself recently. Yet he pressed his thigh against hers as junk food munching and cheesy romcom lines echoed around them. Everything about Evie was dangerous, but even as his conscience lectured him, his heart sped up at the heat of her leg against his.

And what was that about Gavin? Josh's teammate with the Bulls, Gavin, aka The Destroyer, taunted him with stories of his conquests at every practice. He had to be referring to Evie when he shouted those stories, didn't he? Josh's stomach bubbled. The anger was back. *It's definitely anger, and it's not jealousy.* He'd read many articles on what might be causing his heartburn over the last months, and once he'd ruled out his diet, he'd conceded it might relate to his mental health. But any suggestion that he was jealous of someone like Gavin was ludicrous. Gavin was an arsehole that didn't deserve to be with Evie.

Josh attempted to spy her eyes to decipher her thoughts, but the darkness of the cinema hid her mood. She wasn't moving her leg away. His knee bounced in reflection of the busyness of his brain. Should he make a move? What if she didn't want him? His experience with women was limited, but he knew the importance of consent. He tapped his knee incessantly as his brain continued to storm.

Suddenly Evie's hand landed on his. His heart swelled

at the touch, although he reminded himself it was the start of something dangerous that he'd hate himself for. She wanted exciting guys like Aidan and Gavin. But what did he want? He remembered a list of qualities his type of women should have. It had branded itself to his conscience. He'd created it in pain ten years earlier to protect himself and everyone around him. In his loneliest moments, he knew it was a ludicrous list of ideals he probably didn't want, but if it stopped people from getting hurt like his ex-girlfriend had, surely it had to be a good idea.

I want someone who sticks to the rules and never rebels, who's quiet, doesn't hide things, is acceptable to my dad, won't bring out the side of me that hurt people during my teenage years, and someone safe. What did that last word mean, and in what context? Either way, Evie wasn't like that. And yet, as she grazed his hand, his heart beat faster. He wanted her, but he couldn't have her. Her skin felt soft against his, and he fought the temptation to bring her knuckles to his lips. He bounced his knee again.

Evie's breath stroked his skin, and her lips brushed his ear. "Josh, if you don't keep still, I will give your body something else to distract it."

Heat crawled up his neck. His following words surprised him as much as they did Evie. "Go on then. I dare you." A burst of joy hit his belly when she shivered.

His tapping knee pushed against hers, made her hem climb higher. She took his hand and placed it on her thigh. The temperature of her leg against his burned his insides with need. Night after night, he'd lain awake while imagining her in his bed. He fantasised about pleasuring her in every way. There hadn't been any indigestion on those nights. Instead, he'd run his lips against her breasts as his fingers explored her. But even though those moments were some of the few happy ones he had, he didn't call her. Josh had to avoid her because of his list and to heal from his past mistakes.

The irony of the situation wasn't lost on him. He was the one without self-control when around Evie, yet he blamed her for his actions. But what if he hurt her like he hurt his ex, Lulu? Sadness clouded his decision-making temporarily. But the smoothness of her thigh obliterated his conscience. With his finger, he slid the hem of her skirt higher and gently stroked her skin.

Josh tentatively slid his hand to the inside of her thigh. Evie opened her legs a little, giving him greater access. He stretched in his seat letting out the quietest pant, while at the same time his fingertips gently scratched her inner thighs. Her palm settled against his jeans.

"Don't stop," she whispered with a slight whimper. There was something so beguiling about a powerful woman like Evie betraying her need for him.

His fingers continued to travel higher. Would her knickers catch on his calloused hands? Would they be wet because of him?

Suddenly Tasha shifted in her seat, and both he and Evie froze. He let a deep breath of relief escape when he saw Tasha fully engrossed in the movie from the corner of his eye. She sat forward and jumped at the little action on screen. If this were a proper date with Tasha, he would have been so consumed with guilt that he wouldn't have tried anything with Evie, but this was different. For months he'd only had eyes for Evie, and no "win a date" competition changed that.

What if Evie wasn't wearing any knickers at all? Adrenaline rushed through him when his hand teetered higher. His cock quaked as aggressive need owned him. Evie's hand returned his gestures and rested on his thigh, stroking it gently, before sliding nearer to his crotch.

The cinema was crowded, and there had to be fans of his team in spitting distance. They were a premiership side, and the city regularly came out in support of them. What would his coach say if he got caught? Would he end up in the local papers for disgracing his team? Josh's conscience was fleeting, and instead, he dared higher. His cock juddered at the image of slipping his fingers inside her and finger fucking her until she came silently in her seat surrounded by strangers. His lips lifted in a devilish smile.

Suddenly she stilled and then removed her hand from his jeans. In the semi-darkness, she grabbed at something in her bag. He pulled his hand back as she jumped up and eased herself between the patrons to get to the aisle before striding towards the exit. Did he push her too far? He spied something that turned his fear into jealousy. Her phone lit as if it was ringing. Evie's lips moved when she brought the phone to her ear as she walked out. Who was she talking to? Had she been lying about Gavin? Maybe he'd made a booty call, which would fit something he'd said recently about his hook-ups. He announced to a changing room full of disinterested players that he always called his women when they were busy with friends, as it showed how desperate they were for him. "I always call on Thursday nights to fit a good fucking between practices and the big Saturday game." Gavin's smug voice churned Josh's stomach.

Quickly Josh made his excuses for leaving the screen.

"But, Kong, we haven't kissed and felt each other up yet," Tasha replied in a loud baby voice before the people behind them shushed her.

Battling past the bodies in his row raised his frustration as embarrassment latched on to his already destructive emotions.

Pushing through the doors, he spotted her by the refreshments. Evie held the phone so tightly that her knuckles turned white. The scent of popcorn and hot dogs swept deep into his lungs. Josh caught her last words of the call.

"You don't think I should come? Okay, if you're sure," she said softly, but her voice wavered. Evie was the most confident woman he knew. When they'd been friends, he'd hidden his erections when she sassed him or put strangers in their place. It was partly why he wound her up. There was something of a disciplining headmistress vibe about her when she gave him attitude. But one thing he rarely witnessed was her fear.

"You okay?" he asked. He wanted to kick himself when Evie jumped.

She whipped around and glared at him with green eyes that froze him in place. "What the hell are you doing here? You don't want your date to get cold," she bit back impatiently.

"She's not my date, not really. Besides, I'm not the one jumping out of the cinema to take a booty call." *Fuck, why did I say that?*

"Booty call? Firstly, that wasn't a booty call. Secondly, it's none of your business what call I was taking. You've not been in contact for months."

"Ten weeks." *Damn, she'll know you've missed her.* "I reckon."

"You've been avoiding me on purpose," she replied, pointing at him.

"You're the one avoiding me," he hit back.

"Whatever. How is your date going, by the way? It's not a good sign to leave her stranded in the cinema. You clearly don't understand how to treat a lady."

"You enjoyed how I treated you a minute ago." He kicked himself. Why couldn't he control his mouth when around her?

A flush of unbridled laughter caught him completely unaware. "I've missed you," Evie replied between her chuckles. "I've missed laughing at your cheekiness."

Evie knew how to disarm him with one phrase. She never stayed angry with him for long, so why did he continue to push her away? "I've missed you too. I wouldn't put up with your attitude from anyone else."

"You can't resist my charms," she joked. The air thickened between them again. Memories of their play from ten weeks ago reigned. Her chest shook as she laughed. Her breasts had pressed against his body that night, and he'd fantasised about pushing up her top and licking her nipples. Surreptitiously he sneaked a look at her chest. 32D. He'd found out her size on the internet late one night. There had been photos from her glamour modelling days on there too. That night he'd wanked so hard he'd almost burst a blood vessel.

"My eyes are up here, Romeo." Her raised eyebrows and smile convinced him she wasn't annoyed.

"I know where your eyes are," he stammered. "I was wondering what… what material your jumper was. Is it wool?"

She chuckled again, and his awkwardness was replaced with a smile. "Of course you were. You're a big fan of women's tailoring and a fashion icon yourself in that hoody and jeans combo you're wearing. Is that the best you can do on a date?"

"It's not a date. Not a real one. Besides, dressed like this, I'm ready for anything."

"So is your cock, or have you got a badly concealed weapon? I'd hate for it to go off at the wrong moment."

"Evie, do you have to be so direct?"

Her filthy grin made his longings to kiss her surge. Evie's gaze flicked to someone behind him, and she grabbed Josh's hand. "Let's talk outside. It will be less busy there." She dragged him across the sticky-floored foyer before he protested.

There wasn't the opportunity to turn and see what had spooked her before she whisked him out the wide glass doors into the warm evening, but he did hear what sounded like a child say, "She's amazing. I want to be a dancer like her when I'm older."

"What was that about?" Josh asked as she pushed him onto a wooden bench before throwing herself down next to him. At six foot five, he towered above nearly every person he met, but with Evie's four-inch leopard print heels and five nine height, she tried to match him. Sitting, he stared directly into her eyes. They were bold and beautiful, like her, and he eased a little closer to see what colours might be swirling in them tonight.

There was a slight chill in the air but a warmth too. It had been a long winter, but the yellow daffodils fighting for space on the little patches of grass around the lampposts gave hope that spring was finally here.

"I needed fresh air." It was a blatant lie, but there was no point in questioning her. Evie only shared the information she allowed people to know about her. It had taken six months of friendship and some ranting arguments to learn that. Josh wasn't sure if it was because she was secretive or trying to protect herself. Would he ever work her out? Secrets and lies. Another cross by her name for his list.

"You're not smoking again, are you? It's a shitty habit, and you were a mega bitch when you were trying to give up," he moaned. Those weeks of cold turkey had been unbearable. He'd tried to find new ways to take her mind off her addiction. He'd almost resorted to kissing her one evening to keep her busy. It could have ended with his name on her lips as a battle cry for more.

Her eyes dipped to his crotch before she turned so she was face-to-face with him. "Of course I haven't started smoking again, but I'll still be a mega bitch to you if you want," she teased. Josh's cock throbbed as he willed it to calm. It wanted something other than a safe woman, and maybe his heart did too. "And what are you thinking? That shotgun in your pants keeps getting ready to gun down me and anyone else in your sightline. So going on a date with Tasha gets you going, eh?"

"That's not it," he grumbled, shifting slightly against the wooden bench made for someone smaller.

"Then what has made you as hard as rugby post? I'm scared to get close in case I end up covered in your jizz."

"You really don't have to say everything you think," he muttered.

"I'm not the one with a major hard-on on a cold park bench."

He leaned closer even as his conscience tried to keep him still. Josh whispered in her ear, "No, but I bet your nipples are getting hard right now."

She stretched her arms up high, and her breasts pressed together. Josh caught the smug grin she gave him when his eyes dipped briefly to follow the contours of her curves. "Can't keep your eyes off me, eh? When will you learn that challenging me gets you into trouble, sweetie?" she teased. "That's what happened in your bedroom the last time we spoke, remember?"

"Your memory must be as fucked as you want to be." Everyone else had concluded he was shy and reserved, but bantering with Evie made him grin. "If I recall correctly, you were trying it on with me."

"You wish," she replied.

"You wish I'd fuck you," he countered.

Suddenly she was jumping up and straddling his lap. He grabbed her thighs beneath her skirt. "What the hell are you doing?"

"I'm recreating that night to prove that you tried it on with me first," she declared with a grind to his crotch.

"Whatever it takes to prove you wrong," he quipped as he held her thighs tightly and his thumbs stroked her skin. "Although this isn't what happened."

"I can't lie down on the pavement while you pin me," she replied. A yearning replaced her earlier confidence.

"Then maybe once we've proved you came on to me, we can take it somewhere you can lie down. I will ease myself on top of you before pinning your arms above your head."

Her hands cupped his face. Evie was the only soul in his existence. Her green eyes stared deeply into his, holding his focus and making demands it was impossible to keep up with.

"Then what would you do? I mean, what did you do that night?" she purred, grinding harder against him. His fingers pressed into her flesh as the scent of her perfume, a mixture of tropical fruits and flowers, filled his lungs. Was it lily or jasmine on his tongue?

"What did you do that night?" she repeated.

"I asked if you surrendered." He couldn't hide the gruffness in his voice.

"And what did I say?" Her mouth moved closer to his, their lips now inches apart.

"You didn't say anything. So I had to test your will with my hands." Josh's hand travelled higher beneath the hem of her skirt. He hesitated as his conscience fought with the desire coursing through his limbs. He brushed his fingers across her inner thighs. The groan that barely left her mouth was satisfying but not enough. "And then I asked again if you surrendered."

Her lips gently brushed his. It wasn't a kiss, not yet, but two people testing each other. "And what did I say?"

As she bit his lip, Josh remembered everything that had stopped him from calling her over the last ten weeks. The phone in his pocket vibrated. He hadn't answered the previous call from his dad about how he'd underperformed at practice that day. He'd enjoyed some of his practice session until his dad arrived to watch. His dad liked to remind Josh that he was letting the family down. If he knew he was spending time with someone like Evie and not practising his rugby drills, then it would lead to a lecture about how he'd protected Josh in the past and the mistakes Josh had made as a teenager. Was Evie another mistake? Too much hit his brain, like a ramrod crashing through a fortress, and his head reared back.

"I can't do this," he blurted as he pulled his hands away from her thighs.

Evie's brow furrowed, but the moment she realised he was uncertain about her was clear, and she jumped off him.

She turned away, but he caught the tears brimming in her eyes. Evie was the hardest woman in the world and didn't get upset, yet the way she brushed at her eyes as she tried to hide her face suggested otherwise.

Josh's words faltered as he attempted to explain. "Evie, I—"

"Yo, sexy tits, is that you?" a booming voice shouted. Josh's heartbeat skyrocketed as he turned to see Gavin "The Destroyer" Burke.

"Long time no see. I've missed that ass." Gavin leered.

"Fuck off, Gavin. We're in the middle of something," Josh snapped, standing between Evie and The Destroyer. They were equal in size and stature, but everyone knew Josh didn't fight other players. He still wanted to punch Gavin's smug hairy face though.

"No, we're not. It's obvious we've finished," Evie replied, stepping to the side and glaring at Josh before dismissing him. Josh gritted his teeth as she turned to Gavin and licked her lips before giving him a smile that didn't reach her eyes. That's one of her fakest smiles. "How about we get reacquainted, Gav? Got any plans tonight?"

"Nothing I wouldn't cancel for you, sexy tits. Let's head back to mine. I've got a mattress you need to try out and a couple of countertops too," Gavin added with a laugh that brought bile to Josh's throat.

"Laters, Josh. Make sure you enjoy the rest of your date," Evie called out before grabbing Gavin's arm. Josh stepped back and resumed his place on the bench, which was more uncomfortable without his partner in crime. Evie and Gavin strode down the road together as his booming voice reverberated off the pavement.

Josh ground his teeth and grunted as he struggled to take his eyes off them. Once they'd turned the corner, he held his head in his hands. Would he ever stop thinking about her and the version of him he was with her?

Chapter Three

"It's been a while, babe. Where have you and that perfect ass been?" Gavin asked as he walked arm-in-arm with Evie. She knew this road led to his bachelor pad. Nothing about him had changed since she'd fallen out of love with him several years ago, and it was unlikely his place had changed too. Every wall had been grey, and all the furniture was dark leather. Not long into what she believed was their relationship, he'd arrogantly laughed while winking at her and saying, "Easily wipeable leather." He was as tasteless as the painting hanging above his bed of a woman bent over and primed for sex. Her painted arsehole had often winked at Evie through the open bedroom door.

"The Trojan has been missing your hole," Gavin said as he swaggered closer to his apartment. He had to be kidding himself by calling it the Trojan.

"Sorry, what?" Evie asked, trying to ignore Gavin-induced nausea, which came at her in waves. She had no intention of going home with him. Instead, she'd grabbed the opportunity to extract herself from Josh's rejection in a way that would hurt him as he'd hurt her. Evie shook her head. That was Bianca's way of treating people. She was better than that now, yet her damaged alter ego reared itself every so often, adding to her regrets. And now she'd jumped out of the frying pan and into the fire and had to ditch Gavin too.

"You've heard the saying, 'any hole's a goal'?" Gavin smelt of sour musk and sandalwood, and she held her breath to stop gagging. "Your mouth was always my favourite hole. Especially when, this one time…"

She closed her eyes, as if it would block out his voice as she considered her options, but Josh's face was there. It was always there when she closed her eyes. His poorly styled beard and soft brown eyes that sparkled when he tried to cheek her were deeply lodged in her brain. But Josh didn't care about her, so why couldn't she forget him? She opened her eyes to Gavin's cocky smile, which instantly turned nausea into stomach cramps. "I remember that night too. As I recall, you kicked me out straight after sex. That was a dickhead move."

"What's up with you? Was Josh being a wanker? The guy is as wet as I used to get you." Gavin roared with laughter at his quip while Evie rolled her eyes so hard it was a surprise they didn't fall out of her head. Had she really loved this guy? It was at her lowest point when she didn't believe she deserved respect. Was he an adolescent lesson she'd learnt late? Either way, her feelings for him were so destroyed that every memory and moment associated with him was soiled.

"No, nothing like that. I've got a lot on," she replied. It wasn't a lie, but it wasn't the entire truth. No one got to learn the real her or her secrets, and she was better off that way. She'd trusted before and lost all the people close to her, apart from her grandma, who she couldn't burden anymore. They would have talked over gin and biscuits or tea and toast about why Josh had pushed her away, but that wasn't possible anymore.

She shook her head to return to this moment, but Josh clung tight to her thoughts. Their flirting was two-sided, his erection pressing against her while she straddled him on the bench. So why had he rejected her? Maybe she was out of practice. She hadn't been with anyone in a while.

"I'd say. You dress differently these days. No more boob tubes and mini skirts that I loved ripping off you," Gavin replied. "So do you want to hook up tonight? Because I can't work you out. If it's a no, no worries. I'm meant to meet up with a fan anyway." He leered at her and waggled his hands near her breasts.

"I'm not going to sleep with you."

He threw his hands in the air. It was embarrassing, the number of times he'd lied that he was good with his hands. "Alright, chill out, babes. Walk with me to the bar I'm meeting the fan at then. Maybe you'll change your mind after spending time in the presence of greatness."

"What shall we talk about?" she said with a low sigh. Maybe the chat would get Josh out of her head. And as much as Gavin repelled her, she could handle his weird version of seduction, and it was better than overthinking at home alone.

"My awesome cock?" he joked. Gavin's dick made most of his decisions, but it couldn't fill a conversation, let alone anything or anyone else.

"How about we talk about life and stuff? Don't you think there must be more to our cheap lives? Like, maybe, I dunno, don't you wonder if life has gone wrong, and maybe you need to change things to get yourself back on track?" she asked, fingering the silver bracelet she frequently wore around her wrist. It caught the glow from the streetlights and made little sparkles dance around them. She used Gavin's grunting response as a yes to push on. "Some days, it's like the world's spinning too fast. If I prevent it from turning for a minute, I'll catch up and make some good decisions, and then life will be better or have the chance to be. Do you get what I mean?"

Those thoughts entered her brain a lot at the moment. She rarely had time to think, but when she did, what-ifs consumed her. Her gran was severely ill, and it seemed to make her thoughts jump as much as her moods. Why else had she flirted with Josh when he'd ghosted her?

"No, I don't. My life is awesome. I'm either playing rugby, which I love, or fucking, which I really love." Several months ago, she would have shared these thoughts with Josh. They frequently talked about life and the myriad of possibilities it brought.

"Have you heard of the butterfly effect?" she tried again. Her heels tapped the pavement as they got further into town.

Gavin shrugged.

"The idea of the butterfly effect is that one small action can have lots of repercussions to the point it has a significant effect. For example, if a butterfly flaps its wings, then eventually, through a series of events, it causes a hurricane. Like, say you couldn't drive to the rugby tomorrow because your car won't start—"

"I'd get some lucky bugger to drive me."

"But say that didn't work. Maybe all your friends had food poisoning." Gavin opened his mouth to butt in again. "Gavin, say that happened, and instead of you playing, Theo got to play instead."

"Theo is a kicker, so he can't take my position."

"I don't care what position he plays. Please listen!"

"Fine," he replied. "But you're making my head hurt.

You always used to do that when we were sleeping together."

The scent of his bitter aftershave made her nostrils burn. "Weren't we dating, not sleeping together?" Gavin shrugged again. "Never mind. Back to what I was saying. Theo gets to play and scores a winning kick. The England coach sees the game and takes him to the Rugby World Cup. While there, he gets a massive sponsorship deal and becomes a big celebrity. As a result, he meets his true love, a beautiful American who wouldn't have met him when he was a minor Bulls player. They get married and have a baby. No one would have predicted this happening due to your car not starting."

"But Theo is nowhere near as good as me, and that ugly fucker wouldn't attract a gorgeous anything, and my car is a Ferrari. It wouldn't ever have a problem. Your theory is bullshit."

"Maybe I'm not explaining it well."

"Babe, it doesn't matter. Some people are clever and shit, but some are the lucky ones, like us." Even if Josh didn't have her heart, she'd never sleep with Gavin or anyone like him again. There would be no tenderness or finesse. There wouldn't be any foreplay or respect for her body. "I've got a natural rugby skill that makes me a god among men, and you have a fine ass that gives guys lots of fantasies. We don't need words or smarts to show how fucking awesome we are." As they arrived, he thumbed in the direction of the bar, bringing their conversation to a halt. "Anyway, this is me."

"Have a nice night," Evie replied as a woman bounded out of the bar and into Gavin's arms.

"Oh my God, I saw you at the cinema earlier when I was with my niece," the fair-headed woman said to Evie over Gavin's shoulder. "She said you're a ballerina."

"No, she's not. She's a glam—"

"I teach ballet," Evie replied, cutting Gavin off. "Your niece is one of my students. She's exceptional."

"It's made a massive difference to her confidence. So you're really not a ballerina full-time? She couldn't stop talking about how incredible you are. Do you perform?"

Evie swiftly curtailed Gavin's guffaw with a glare. "No, not anymore. I did as a teenager, but things happen." Things like your family disowning you after a man spreads lies about you. His behaviour had caused her to hate ballet for years, but teaching the classes was her way of embracing Evie rather than hiding her behind the barrier of Bianca.

"Thank you for everything you've done for Tilly. Your classes have changed her life."

A glow filled Evie's belly. If she could help one child the way no one helped her when she was a dancer, it would be worth it.

"Are we going inside or what?" Gavin grumbled. "I'm thirsty."

"I'll go get the drinks in. It was nice to meet you properly, Evie the ballerina," Tilly's auntie called out as she pushed through the doors.

"She deserves better than you. I'll never know why these stunning women give you the time of day," Evie said before turning and heading off.

As she continued down the street, Gavin yelled, "You could join us. I've always wanted a threesome with you."

"Bye, Gavin. Try not to be a twat," she shouted back as she deliberated her route to the care home. The staff had said she didn't need to come, but sitting with her grandma

STALLING IN LOVE

was the only thing that made sense tonight.

Chapter Four

"I've got to go, Tasha," Josh begged, trying to extract himself from her claws and escape her doorstep attack. *I'm one step away from being dragged into her lair.*

"But, Kong, you haven't come into my pad for a coffee. You'll need it for your stamina," she pouted and twirled her blonde hair around her finger.

He grunted at his nickname. It had been given to him by the team because of his massive body and hairy everything. Crowds chanted it on a Saturday in celebration or humiliation. It was more humiliation these days. According to Twitter, the furry unkempt beard hiding at least half his face and his clumsy play meant he was an ape. During one of their late-night conversations, he suggested to Evie that he shave it. Her response had made it impossible to sleep due to his unrelenting erection. Apparently, without a beard, the women riding him in the future would have nothing to hold on to.

"Fuck," he mumbled. Why was Evie back in his head?

"You read my mind," Tasha giggled before grabbing the strings of his hoody to drag him closer. Tasha couldn't be all bad—she worked at the charity—but she wasn't the woman for him. There was only one woman he wanted, and she'd made her feelings obvious when she walked off with Gavin. "Are we fucking then, Kong?"

"Please don't call me that." His frustration with Evie wasn't the only thing biting at his confidence. The name Kong left him feeling freakish and undesirable even as Tasha's hands slid closer to his waistband.

"I'll scream out whatever name you wish when you make me come."

"While that is a kind offer, I need my sleep for training," he replied as her hands reached his crotch. He jolted back, dodging the plant pots surrounding her doorstep. On the face of it, Tasha and Evie weren't that different. Both carried confidence wavering on domineering, which was a massive turn-on. But Evie was introspective and fascinating. She always had a fact or theory to share with him or a story that would make him smile. Those evenings they'd spent practising his drills on the training fields were some of his favourites from the last year. He never knew why she joined him, but he valued her friendship even as she heckled him while jumping up and down. Her demands were relentless, but they made him a better athlete, as did the smiles or celebration hugs she rewarded him with at the end. Evie laughed off how sweaty he made her and would never fail to throw some coarse words at him too. But he needed someone safe that he wouldn't hurt. Sex and love didn't come into it.

"Earth to Josh!" Tasha screamed. The diamanté on her nails caught the moonlight and nearly blinded him. "Hurry up and get in my bed. It's getting cold."

"Aren't you tired too?" he asked, desperately searching for a reason to escape. How did the other rugby guys deal with this attention? He'd spent enough evenings standing on the edge of the dancefloor alone as fans seduced players beneath colourful lights. That's how he'd met Evie when she was her alter ego, Bianca. She'd been swinging on a pole in a club before jumping onto his teammate's lap.

Tasha grabbed at Josh, but he was quicker than her. He held her hands to keep her still. Her hands were softer than Evie's, but her fingers weren't as long. Where Evie's nails were well bitten, Tasha's were like talons.

"Oh, are you going to tie me up? Make me your dirty bitch?" Josh dropped her hands quickly. He didn't know if he was into that, but Evie was the only person he wanted to experiment with. Josh threw his head back. The last ten weeks spent trying to get over Evie were wasted. He needed to go to the one place that reminded him why he couldn't be with her.

"You're not going to tuck me in?" The bottom lip protruding from her mouth was unnerving. Was she about to cry?

Josh attempted the polite brush-off. "Tasha, I'm not the man for you. There is someone, I'm sure of it, and they will give you all the sex you want. But I'm not up to the job. So I'm saying goodnight because I need rest."

Her eyes lit up. "Tomorrow night instead then? I'll be the girl your mum warned you about." Josh chuckled. What about the ones his dad had warned him about? "You like that idea, don't you, you sexy beast."

Maybe he should set her up with one of his teammates. That wasn't going to solve his problem tonight though. It was time to employ his rugby skills. "What's that?" he asked, pointing into the open doorway she wanted to drag him through.

The fake diversion worked. As Tasha turned, he took his opportunity. He skimmed the pots as he jumped over them before sprinting down the uneven stone path.

"Come back. I want you inside me. Your cock wants

me, Kong. It was like a baseball bat in the cinema," she shouted loud enough to annoy the neighbours.

The fantasy of Evie straddling his lap, his erection trying to press itself against her as she ground into him, caused him to stumble as he pushed open the gate. He righted himself quickly, familiar with the adrenaline that hit when pursued, although he usually had a ball in his hand when rivals came for him. "It's been lovely. Your charity appreciates your donation," he shouted as a rush carried him down the street. "Let's never do it again."

Finally, when he was sure Tasha wasn't chasing him, Josh slowed his pace and meandered towards town and the home he shared with a couple of his teammates.

As usual, his thoughts drifted to Evie. Lust and longing ripped through his chest. Tonight, she resembled a rock chick with her flippy grey skirt, tight black jumper, and leopard print ankle boots. While she was never far from his thoughts, it was a slap across his face when he'd seen her at the cinema. His blood had run cold before flaming through his limbs.

He slumped against a lamppost and sucked air into his lungs. Slowly he counted to ten. He ached to discover every part of her before taking her to bed and possessing her. Could he make her scream until she lost her voice? He pulled his hand down his face. He wasn't experienced enough for any woman, let alone her.

There were days when they were together when his dark moods threatened to drown him, but although she'd never asked the reason for them, she'd repeatedly drawn him back into the light with her charm. There was something unexpectedly endearing about her.

Why am I here again? It was the same place he always ended up after nights out. At least, it had been until he'd become a hermit ten weeks ago. He no longer accepted invitations to the pub or team socials in town. If not for the charity, he wouldn't have been out tonight. Now he needed to visit the reason for the list and apologise again for who he used to be.

His hands grabbed at the vertical wooden slats. The lack of adrenaline and the shame coursing through him left him weary. Tears of sadness or exhaustion brimmed in his eyes as he jumped over the collapsing wooden fence, not caring about the smears of moss covering his jeans. It creaked under the strain of his body, but it would hold because it had for the last ten years. Nothing had changed, and it never would because of his actions.

Josh stumbled, nearly crushing the flowers flourishing from the beds. The smell of lilies and roses filled the air as green trees loomed above him. The weathered gravestones welcomed his return as the blackness of the night surrounded him. There was no sound. He was alone, aside from the presence of the dead, but it didn't scare him. This place was like a second home, a refuge from the world. Even blindfolded, he would find his way through the maze of graves without face-planting in the dirt. It was as if a beacon of light called out from the murky depths and filled his soul. Finally, he reached the one grave he was here for and sighed a long slow breath.

"Hey, I've been thinking about you. I've missed you. Sorry I haven't been by in a while." Josh paused. He didn't expect a response from the lump of stone, but he waited anyway. When nothing came, he sank. The wetness from the damp ground seeped through his jeans to his knees.

Even in the depths of the darkness, the words shone brightly from the slate grey gravestone.

Safe Now

He should have kept Lulu safe. He was the reason she was here.

"I saw Evie again," he whispered, although he hadn't needed to say her name. Evie had been all he'd talked about for most of the last year as he sat at the edge of Lulu's grave. "I wasn't expecting to. She was beautiful but maybe exhausted too. I hope she's okay. Lulu, whenever Evie is in front of me, I get all these emotions I haven't the capacity or skill to deal with. Pain, anger, awe, and guilt."

His bear-like paw rubbed at his beard. "I get so horny too. I shouldn't be saying this to you, but I don't have anyone else. How do I get her out of my head?" A cooling breeze tickled the nape of his neck as if the ghost of Lulu taunted him.

"The thing is, I don't mean anything to her. I'm another guy who she hides the real her from. She has secrets. At best, I was a stopgap for her. Evie can have any guy because she's stunning and funny and always goes after what she wants. If she truly wanted me, we would be together, but instead, I'm a fool who entertains her when she's bored while she does goodness-knows-what with someone else. But I want her. I want all of her: mind, body, and a spirit I can't fucking handle."

His head fell, and he held it between his hands. "I shouldn't want anything to do with her, should I? When we nearly kissed earlier, the reasons we shouldn't be together were in bright letters in the back of my head. Evie doesn't fit the list, and the list keeps people safe. You'd have stayed safe if I'd had it before we got together. Besides, can you imagine what my dad would say if he met her? He'd crucify me. She is the most confident person I know, too confident sometimes." He chuckled. "I'm in awe of her, although she reckons I can't stand her. That's if she thinks about me at all. Dad would ridicule her for her past. Even if she didn't have one, he'd hate how empowered she is. She'd run rings around him. You know how he gets when women do that. Lulu, I crave her. Every second I'm away from her, I wish I were with her, but when I am, I mess it up like I did tonight. I'm fucked up. Maybe this is my punishment for what I did to you. Karma has come for me."

The air flooding the depths of his lungs carried across the breeze when he finally released it in an agonising sigh. "I'll never forgive myself for what I did to you."

Chapter Five

The church clock chimed the early hour. The darkness crowded Josh as he took in the greys and whites of the gravestones surrounding Lulu's last resting place. He knew all the names of those buried around him as if they were his old friends. He shouldn't be here. The team was playing a home game against the Hawks in the morning, and according to the press, the London side was on form and baying for blood.

"I've got to go, but I promise I'll visit sooner next time." Easing himself to his feet, he tried to ignore the turmoil that ravaged his internal organs. The stomach cramps that had dogged him for months returned with Evie's entrance back into his life.

It didn't take long to exit the graveyard the way he'd arrived, although he managed to dodge all the flowerbeds this time. But as he cleared the fence and trudged across the road, he fixated on dragging himself out of the despair that overwhelmed his heart after seeing Evie. A blaring horn pulled him out of his overthinking, and he froze as if stuck to the tarmac as a car hurtled toward him.

A painful screech of metal heralded the vehicle coming to a sudden stop. The hulking four-by-four finally sat silent, a hair's breadth from Josh's frozen form. The scent of burnt rubber filled the air.

He always knew Evie would be the death of him. His leg quivered during his attempt at humour, and he braced himself against the bonnet to stop collapsing under the strain of the near-miss.

The door to the vehicle opened, and an Irish accent bellowed out at him. "What the fuck, Josh? Was your date with Tasha so bad that getting hit by a car was a better alternative?"

The driver appeared from the shadows. His body was as lean as Josh remembered, and a sigh of relief escaped his lips. Josh attempted to keep the emotion from his voice as he cleared his throat before speaking. "Aidan, buddy, it's been too long. Maybe you should have spent that time learning to drive."

Aidan Flynn was Evie's ex-boyfriend and a former teammate who'd retired from rugby nearly a year ago to pursue his other passion. Within months of leaving the brutal sport and, with the support of his beautiful wife Sophia, he'd opened an art gallery of his and others' work. Aidan and Sophia's relationship had been a perfect example of a problematic beginning, due to Aidan's battle with a possible long-term health condition and Sophia's struggles with trust.

There was a noticeable shake to both of their bodies from the near-miss as they embraced like long-lost friends. Life may have dealt them a host of unexpected events, but they were best friends and ready to support each other in times of crisis.

"Hold on." Josh pulled away, eyeballing Aidan. "How did you know I was out with Tasha tonight?"

"There are photos of you two together all over social media." Aidan must have seen it on Sophia's accounts.

Sophia worked with Tasha and Jack. "It's like you have an electronic shrine on her accounts. Did she leave her nail marks on your back when you gave her your special King Dong treatment?"

"You're such a prick," Josh replied without malice.

"It's not my prick we're talking about. Were you reliving your glory moments as you stumbled across the road?" Aidan added with a wink.

Josh shuddered, but the darkness around him soaked it up. Car accidents ripped at his heart and always would because of Lulu. "Sod off, Aidan. Nothing happened. I politely left her on her doorstep and thanked her for a lovely evening."

"And she let you get away?" Aidan's incredulity shouted loud enough for those in the graves to hear. Aidan had experienced Tasha's grabbing hands at the art event where he'd met Sophia and during a rugby photoshoot at the charity. According to Sophia, Tasha proudly stated multiple times that she wanted to be remembered by all who met her.

"I had to run for my life before she trapped me in her basement and made me her sex toy," he joked. "Anyway, what are you doing out this late? Don't tell me you left Sophia alone with baby Patrick while you partied?"

"Not a chance. Those days are long gone, thank God. Sophia demanded ice cream tonight, and who am I to argue?"

"You're kidding me? The great Aidan Flynn, the man who was a bigger player on Friday night in town than he was on the pitch on Saturday, is now at his wife's beck and call? I'm shocked, I really am," Josh teased, throwing his hands high.

Aidan chuckled. "What can I say in my defence? I adore her, and I would do anything for her. Besides, ice cream makes her horny as hell, so I get fudge brownie by the gallon when she asks for something sweet." The twinkle in his blue eyes was no surprise. On several occasions, Josh nearly caught them having sex in Aidan's car. "Besides, I'd much rather spend my Friday nights cuddling her than trawling the clubs for a rugby groupie. That's how I met Evie, or Bianca as she called herself then, remember?"

Josh rolled his eyes. He remembered everything from Evie and Aidan's tumultuous past and "Bianca's" reputation in the local clubs. "Subtle reference to Evie there," he replied sarcastically. Josh's stomach spasmed at the memory of Evie and Gavin walking away from the cinema.

"I remember how you two were at the art gallery opening last year," Aidan continued, oblivious to Josh's mood. "Loads of people commented that you were the new couple of the moment. I'd presumed you'd be fucking by now."

Josh glowered. It was late, and Aidan was pushing. Josh's head throbbed. "Why?" he snapped.

Aidan bristled. "Because the chemistry between you two reminded me of when I first met Sophia. You smiled and laughed so much at the gallery opening. But it's not just that. I've never seen Evie like she was with you, and I've never seen her look at anyone like she looked at you."

"Not even when you 'dated' her?" The memory that Aidan spent intimate moments with Evie left a sour taste in Josh's mouth. They were hateful to be around. If they weren't arguing, they were hellbent on destroying each other's lives. The unexplained sale of the sex tape that had violated his best friend was another reminder that he didn't know her and couldn't trust her motives with anyone, including him. It was Aidan's place to forgive her, not

Josh's, and he'd seemed to have moved on, so Josh followed his lead, but the question of why was still unanswered.

"No, not then. Evie was feral and self-destructive with me, and I was as bad, maybe worse some days, but you've got the real Evie when she's with you."

"It doesn't matter how you believe she looks at me. I'm another guy. I need someone sensible and a girl-next-door type. Evie is alpha, and I need someone to let me—whatever, it doesn't matter." Josh had a longer list of attributes, but Aidan had scoffed when Josh had shared the list before.

"Josh, you're one of the best guys in the world. You will do anything for anyone, but you're messed up regarding women. You want all these things that aren't real. Didn't you say your future girlfriend has to 'refrain from swearing and not be out of place at a garden party'? Mate, that isn't you. I've seen you spit your drink out in laughter when Evie swears, and your housemates said that you're happiest after arguing with her. Why won't you tell me what happened in your past? Because the Josh I've known for years cares about all people and never judges. What made you write that list for a woman that wouldn't make you happy?"

Josh grunted with a surly stare. "Hold on, didn't you used to want a woman who was 'a bit easy and filthy as fuck'?"

"And I was a dickhead too. The moment I met Sophia, I wanted her. Lists didn't matter. I see the same thing between you and Evie. Evie is feisty, with a mouth like a roadie and a love of trouble. I'm pretty sure that's one of the reasons you like her, and you also like her because she is a good person. You two are very similar."

Josh willed the conversation to end, but Aidan was unrelenting.

"I stand by that statement. And if your issue is due to her Bianca days, then get over it. Everyone has a past. I may not know what you were up to before you trained with the Giants, but I'm sure you got up to stuff. There's got to be something that made you write that list. It doesn't fit with who you are," Aidan said with a pointed stare before chuckling. "Did you kill someone once?"

Josh hid his shudders with a grunt.

"One day, you'll lose Evie for good and kick yourself for it."

"Maybe I already have. She went home with Gavin tonight." Josh shoved his hands in his pockets and kicked a stone lying in the middle of the road.

"Gavin? Seriously?" A long slow breath left Aidan's mouth. "I'm sorry, mate."

"It doesn't bother me." Josh replied. *It's not like I can give her what she wants, and she's probably aware of that.* He faked a yawn. "Anyway, I've got the game to rest up for."

"Okay, good luck," Aidan replied as Josh started to amble away. "Oh, by the way, we're getting Patrick blessed next weekend. Pop by and bring Evie with you. I'll send you an invitation."

"I'll be there. It will be nice to see Sophia. I always preferred her to you," he shouted with a cheeky wink, although he was already too far for Aidan to see it.

He'd find the woman that fitted his list or stay single forever. He'd lasted this long alone.

Chapter Six

"The usual," Evie heard for the tenth time that shift as another grizzly bearded rugby fan made his demands. Evie gazed around the worn wooden pub. Her sheer animal print blouse, which she often wore during her shifts because it hid the split lager stains, clashed with the seventies geometric-style carpet. And her pleather leggings made her stand out more than the cobalt bra she wore under her blouse. When she was Bianca, she wouldn't have been seen dead in the cold and dingy pub. The smell of urine and stale beer added to an already grubby atmosphere; even a lick of paint wouldn't improve it. The place needed burning to the ground, yet she had an incomprehensible fondness for it. A hint of a smile tickled her lips as her second favourite customer waited.

"Captain, I have no idea what you believe the usual is, but I'd suggest rum with a side of scurvy. Do you want it before or after you sing a sea shanty?"

The white beard waggled as he processed her cheek. In truth, he was a welcome distraction from the rugby match beyond her eye line. Gavin and Josh were playing, and she didn't need reminders of her mistakes.

"Oi, Sandra, where did you get this smart arse?" he shouted at the pub owner while jiggling a thumb in Evie's direction. "She's on her period."

"Give her your bloody drinks order, Bob. And don't pretend it's the first time you've seen her. She's been working here for months," the withered barmaid hollered, her bosoms heaving with every breath. The heavy smoking habit wasn't doing her any favours, and her platinum beehive hair was starting to wilt from the day's exertion.

"Bob, I like to call it 'On the blob'. And based on your attitude, I'm guessing it's your time of the month too. Need to borrow a tampon? I'd be delighted to tell you where you can stick it," Evie replied with a raised middle finger.

"Don't you know the customer is always right?" His white eyebrows danced as he chided her.

"Always a right dick, from where I'm standing." She blew him a kiss and added a wink to send her point home.

"Evie," Sandra called out in warning. There was a shout of frustration from the right of the pub, where rugby fans crowded around the television. Evie ignored the temptation that clawed at her. She'd only gain a headache if she gawked at Josh as he played rugby.

Bob jumped to Evie's defence. "Leave the girl alone, Sandra." His sour beer breath hit her from across the bar. "She livens the place up, although she can't remember what I drink."

"I love you too, Bob," she replied, tipping the pint glass and pulling on the tap. His favourite lager slowly filled the glass. Hops hit the back of her throat. "I know what you drink, but I can't resist teasing you, you grumpy bastard, even if you like a lager that smells of rotten fruit."

"I wouldn't have our interactions any other way," he replied, giving her a wink before gawking at her breasts. "I love everything about you, from your smart mouth to that arse that bounces around this place."

"There's nothing bouncy about this pleather-covered arse, old man. Firm and toned from exercising every day." Evie wasn't lying. These days she ate well, exercised religiously, and barely drank. Old acquaintances would die of shock if they saw her now. "Now sod off with your pint and get back to the game, or you'll have a coronary from not having had alcohol pass your lips for two minutes."

"Yeah, yeah," he replied, supping the top of his pint and getting the foam caught in his beard.

"How do you get away with it?" Jack asked from his wobbly stool at the bar.

"It helps that I have tits they can't take their eyes off," she joked. "But they're a nice bunch of guys, just a bit grumpy. So I give as good as I get."

"I can see that." He gripped the worn wooden bar with his left hand as his stool threatened to tip him onto the floor. "You're a great addition to my local."

"Because you're not the only person under ninety here anymore?" Evie replied, giving Jack lip as he resumed sipping his cider. "You're out of place though. Isn't your type more likely to be wearing dungarees and sipping cocktails while dancing to Queen in a brightly lit bar?"

"Surely you're not stereotyping gay guys?" he asked with a raised eyebrow.

"No, I'm bloody not! I'm talking about marketing managers who have secretly longed to perform in a Broadway musical. You miss being the lead in all those school plays."

A guffaw escaped his lips. "I shouldn't have told you about my dreams. Everyone has something to get them through the day, and musicals are my thing. But don't tell anyone, especially not the guys here who wouldn't know their Roxie Heart from their Jean Valjean. And don't forget I know your dreams too. I wish you'd let me see you dance."

Evie ignored the reference to her love of ballet. Maybe one day she'd stop associating dance performances with the most painful time in her life, but it was unlikely. The excitable ten-year-old inside her tried to remind her that all she wanted to do was dance. Since leaving her childhood home, Evie quieted her with sobs and a hardened heart.

"Besides," Jack continued taking the hint from her silence, "I don't drink here to talk musicals, but because Dad and I would come here regularly when he was alive. The punters might be a bunch of old farts, but they're surprisingly open-hearted." Evie sipped from her pint of water before marvelling at the wisened clientele over the top of the glass. Jack had a point. "They let you work here, after all."

"I'm not going to give you free drinks as a thank you every time I'm on shift, Jack."

"It was worth a try." He shrugged with a smile.

The shouts from the assembled fans caught their attention. The Bulls played their hearts out on screen, and everyone gave their full support except when they were lamenting their form.

"They shouldn't have signed The Destroyer. I bet that arsehole couldn't control his own balls, let alone a rugby-shaped one," Bob grumbled to the guy beside him, who wobbled on his feet. Alcohol fumes radiated around the pair. "Shame Aidan retired. That man was a legend."

Jack returned to Evie's face, but she looked anywhere but at him. "How were Gavin's balls and his control last night? I swear he's been hobbling all match."

Evie topped up her nearly full glass, but Jack wouldn't back down. Instead, he stared until she answered. "I wouldn't know. I left him at a bar with his hook-up, who was clearly too good for him. The guy's a twat, but he's not my twat."

Jack raised his eyebrows.

Evie hit back. "Did you think I'd go home with him after everything?"

"All I'm saying is that the Evie of the past got with anything, according to the papers. Which was fine and your choice. I'm not slut shaming, before you start on me, but…" Evie's scowl didn't falter. Would she ever get away from the fucking reporters' lies? Jack continued quickly, "You liked Gavin, maybe loved him and would have done anything for him once upon a time. And you love sex too."

Everything Jack said was true. Avoiding his subtext, she focused on the rugby match on screen. Players in swashes of crimson danced past evergreen-clothed bodies. One of the smaller players threw the ball, and a member of the Bulls team jumped in the air with the prowess and strength of a winged horse. Suddenly, the ball flashed across the screen as it travelled from one set of hands to another before teetering temporarily. Then, as a Hawks player ran for it, a crimson uniformed player chucked it again. The sport was like a beautiful ballet, perfectly choreographed and yet performed by those who would never fit a stage, let alone a tutu. Bodies in red and green fell like tumbling trees, one on top of the other, before springing back up and starting again.

Every push was aimed towards the line and a try that would bring victory. Although there was beauty to the action, it was carnage. Violence and aggression were masquerading as perfectly controlled pieces. The camera focused on Gavin for a second before crossing to Josh. He panted like a tired dog. Sweat dripped down his face, collecting in his beard, while his hair clumped haphazardly on his head. And yet she still wanted him.

I'm fucked up. She was transfixed when he bent and stretched on the field during a pause in the action. Thighs she'd straddled the previous night displayed his strength and prowess. Illicit ideas controlled her, and she imagined him demanding she wait naked and bent over for him. His bare, sweaty body ground against her in her fantasy while his muscly forearms pinned her to him. The gruff voice that had the power to make her wet would call out her name before whispering his adoration for everything she was. He'd growl his dirty intentions in her ear, and all she'd be able to do was purr for him. *I need to get laid.* But only Josh, or her imagined version of him, made her thirsty. She hadn't had a hint of horniness for anyone else.

"Am I wrong? Didn't you used to like him like that?"

"Who?" Her fantasies of Josh's naked body faded, but as she pressed her glass against her cheeks, the cooling touch proved her face was aflame. It matched the heat between her thighs.

Jack followed her gaze to the television screen, but the camera panned to the crowd. She held a sigh of relief.

"Gavin, remember?" Jack asked, waving his hands to get Evie's attention. "The guy who used to destroy your lady garden when he wasn't destroying other women."

She coughed to cover up relief that Josh was still her secret. "Yes, Gavin used to destroy my pussy regularly. Come on, Jack, you can say pussy," she teased.

Jack glared. "Stop trying to change the subject."

"Fine, yes. I liked him. I cared deeply about him, but I

was a twat to believe he felt the same. I wanted to be loved. Anyway." She moved on quickly, hiding her vulnerability. "You know that the only way I'd get near his balls now would be to kick them. He's a prick."

They laughed loudly and were gifted a silencing stare from Bob.

"I was wondering," Jack started cautiously.

"Yes? Spit it out."

"The way you sometimes talk about your old life…" Jack bumbled.

"Yeah?" she asked snarkily. The years before she'd moved to the town remained buried, and she had no intention of sharing them.

"Do you miss glamour modelling? Do you have any regrets?" he finished at speed.

Evie looked at the rotten ceiling as if it offered clarity, but the peeling paint shared nothing but despair. Instead, she took a deep breath. "I miss the money, but the modelling wasn't all it was cracked up to be. I was desperately unhappy. I was selling stories for Gavin's career to have enough money to survive and for other reasons that we're not going to discuss. For some women, it's a fantastic career that gives them what they need, but I didn't do it for the right reasons. I'm ashamed of some of the things I did. I'm not ashamed of modelling, and I have some great shots of my body that will make me smile for many years, but I hurt some people and caused problems for others."

Jack opened his mouth, but Evie cut him off. "But I'm the only one who gets to be ashamed of those days. And I will never regret the incredible people I met and that I lived a life some dream of." Evie considered the butterfly effect theory. The hypothesis filled her headspace when she wasn't imagining a naked Josh. Without glamour modelling, she wouldn't have met Aidan and Josh.

But that didn't take away the damage from her past. There was a man she refused to talk about from before her modelling days, and he loomed over her life like a dark cloud when you hung out the washing before work. But if people knew, they'd hate her and not believe her. She couldn't be rejected by those she loved again.

"Who is *he*?" Jack asked, pointing out the attractive blond player relentlessly pursuing the ball like a tiger cub on a mission.

"That's Max. He moved to the first team from the under-twenty-ones at the start of the season. He spent his twenty-first birthday party last year with Josh, as he was scared of what the rest of the team might do to him." Of course, Josh had protected him. "I bet Max has a lot of pressure to deal with because he's the coach's son. I'll introduce you if you ask me nicely. He moved in with Josh about six months ago."

Jack's gaze didn't leave the screen. "But you and Josh aren't friends anymore. Although you're desperate for him to touch your lady garden." So Jack did know.

"You mean I want him to fuck my pussy until I can't walk," she snapped back, intent on making Jack blush.

"You said it," he replied quickly, catching her out.

"That's not what I meant. Besides, Josh wants someone without a history. I have a past, and I don't care if I offend people or swear or say the word pussy. I found a list of traits that detailed what he wants in a future partner hidden in his bedroom drawer. I was trying to find a charger. Anyway, it's like he wants the anti-Evie." Bitterness threaded through her words.

"Evie, sweetheart, what he wants doesn't exist." Jack

held out his hand, but Evie was rarely tactile with friends.

"I get the impression it did once." Her mouth turned into a frown even as she tried to fight it. No one should have power over her emotions.

"It didn't, not even then," Jack replied ominously.

"Didn't you two go to school together? What was he like?"

"What you'd expect." Before Evie clarified Jack's meaning, he changed the subject. "I've been invited to the blessing of Aidan and Sophia's baby next week. Unfortunately, I can't attend the ceremony because of a work thing, but maybe the party after. Do you want to come as my plus-one? Josh might be there," he teased in a sing-song voice.

"Probably not," she replied with a sigh.

"Whatever, babe, you're coming. Now tell me more about Max, and I'd like the usual, please." Jack waggled his empty glass in her direction.

Chapter Seven

"You were at the grave again, Josh." How did his dad know?

"What are you talking about?" Josh asked. He was supposed to focus on stretches, not his dad's berating. He knew the mantras. *A good player stretches every night before bed and every morning when they wake, no matter what.* It was one of the many rules his dad had instilled in him when he was a teenager. It was already nine in the morning, and he hadn't completed them because Evie-related fantasies had distracted him, and now he was being chewed out on the phone.

"Is that tone, Joshua? It sounds like it, but you wouldn't use tone with me."

Josh paused as he glimpsed himself in the mirror. With his baggy vest and baggier shorts, it was as if he was trying to hide every part of himself. A typical day then.

"Sorry, Dad." Josh held back a sigh of annoyance. His dad wanted the best for him. He always had, whether it was pushing him to excel at rugby or move on in life. In one radio interview, the guy asked him what he'd be doing if he wasn't a rugby player, and he genuinely didn't know. It had been so instilled in him by his dad that it was his path in life that he'd never considered what else he wanted. But did he want to play rugby, or did he do it to make his dad happy?

That question had been in a box for years for good reason.

"It's fine." But his dad's grunt suggested otherwise. "Your mum is worried about you though. You hate to stress her out, especially as her health isn't great. She was on the verge of tears tonight when she told me that you should be moving on with your life and not visiting Lulu's grave."

Guilt filled Josh's intestines like a sickness that clung to every unfilled space. He slid down the door of his room and cradled his head. It was as if he was the eight-year-old boy who'd accidentally kicked a football through the greenhouse window and lost his pocket money for a year.

"I'm fine," his mum called out in the background.

"Please don't undermine me, darling." There was an authority behind that comment that made Josh uneasy. His father rarely saw women as equals. The need to defend his mum added to Josh's growing guilt, but when he'd tried before, it ended with a nastier argument and his mum telling him there was nothing that needed defending. But the last time she'd said she was happy, it was with tighter lips and tenser shoulders. He should protect her more, but he didn't want to upset her. Acid burnt his stomach, and his dad wasn't letting up. "Why were you at the grave? Her parents mentioned it at the pub last night, so don't deny it. You must have dropped a cinema ticket or something. You're the only person other than them that visits."

Josh squinted as if that would bring a quicker excuse. Because he needed someone to talk to that wouldn't tell him he was a screw-up. It's what his dad would call him if he knew Josh fantasised endlessly about a beautiful, feisty vixen who held his heart in her hands. Submissive women had been the only women suitable for his dad. "I was passing."

"I don't believe you. Guilt took you there, boy. You

did what you did to Lulu, but it's the past now, and you need to move on to someone better," his dad demanded. "What about Jane, the neighbour's daughter? She's a nice woman and three years younger than you…"

Jane was precisely that: nice. On the face of it, they seemed compatible. But he didn't want a twenty-five-year-old woman who spent her evenings eating cabbage dinners, followed by two plain digestives and a cup of tea in bed, wrapped in a floor-length flannel nightdress, by eight-thirty pm. There was someone out there for Jane, but it wasn't him. Instead, he wanted a woman to push him, who made his heart pound with anger and exhilaration and turned arousal into a battle of wills until they both surrendered to the pleasure controlling them.

He wanted Evie.

His dad rambled, leaving little seeds of judgement to ensure the guilt would last longer than the phone call. "Why don't you listen to your dad? I always know best, and I'm concerned you'll mess up your rugby career if you carry on like this." Of course rugby was the priority. Once more, Josh wondered if he loved his career enough, but the thought was fleeting as his dad continued his lecture. "You need a good, proper woman."

"There is someone, actually," he blurted out before slapping a hand to his forehead.

"Oh?" That one word carried a snap of wrath. His dad prided himself on being aware of everything in Josh's life.

"It's no one. I met this woman through a friend, but we're not together." He fumbled for words as he backtracked. "We're friends."

"If you say so, boy. Make sure this stranger fits the list. We don't want any more accidents, do we?"

"Of course not." Josh was suitably reprimanded. Evie wasn't sensible, and he'd watched her break the rules numerous times. Once she'd broken into the local Lido and skinny-dipped while Josh kept a weary eye on the entrance in case of security guards. There was the night she declared she could fit eighteen marshmallows in her mouth, and he'd had to give her the Heimlich manoeuvre. The memory that stuck out was the morning they were trapped in a field with a bull. They walked to a pub for a roast dinner, but instead of running, she sang AC/DC tunes at the bull until the farmer came and threatened them off his land. They'd run like gazelles before jumping a high wooden fence. Evie filled his memories with laughter that threatened the guilt his dad piled on. "I've got to go, Dad. Aidan and Sophia are having baby Patrick blessed today, and I can't be late."

"Okay, have fun. I'll tell your mum you don't have time for her."

"No, wait," he called out, but his dad hung up. Josh typed a quick text to his mum apologizing, but his thumbs struggled as his anxiety grated.

Josh attempted his final regimented stretches, but it was impossible with the tension squeezing his limbs. He stepped towards the shower and imagined her. Evie was the one person who'd ease the anguish. How was that possible when she was part of the problem? But it didn't stop the erection pressing against his boxers. Getting himself off in the shower as he fantasised her bum grinding against him might relieve the exasperation from the call and set him up for the day. Why did someone so wrong for him fill him with unwavering happiness while simultaneously destroying him? And would it ever end?

Chapter Eight

"**I** can't believe they're having the blessing in the art gallery," Jack whispered conspiratorially to Evie.

The gallery was a simple white space in the middle of town. On an average weekday, the walls were adorned with paintings from different collections, and sculptures were positioned artistically around the room. When Evie visited the previous month, she'd spent hours mesmerised at how the artwork caught her attention or forced her closer, depending on where she was in the room. Alone in the space, she'd fought for the meaning behind the different pieces. One painting in particular of a ballet dancer as flames burnt around her brought memories of her past. There was also a portrait of Josh painted by Aidan. She'd tried to ignore the piece, but she'd found herself on the brink of caressing the purple of his cheek where he'd been in a recent pitch altercation when Aidan had walked through the door.

Evie took in the expanse of the gallery. Drawings of baby Patrick covered every wall, and colourful balloons and banners proclaiming the celebration of his blessing filled the white space. Aidan and Sophia's adoration for their firstborn made Evie's heart swell, but an unsettling itch of her skin quickly followed it.

She hadn't been to a family party in years. What was it

like to be loved by your family unconditionally? She stretched her arms over her head to study the guests without Jack noticing. Josh's hulking form should've been impossible to miss at the busy celebration. If anyone could distract her from the pain of her past, it was him.

"The last time I was here for a big event, I was with Josh," she whispered. "I miss being friends with him and how he laughs at my awful jokes. Hell, I even miss the overgrown, tangled mess of a beard he was protective of whenever someone mentioned a trim." She covered her mouth, regretting the confession.

"Still not heard from him?" Jack asked before smoothing down his crisp shirt and joining her in gazing around the room.

"No, and if I'm lucky, he won't be here, and it won't be like the worst winter in the arctic between us again." If you didn't count the heat between her thighs when he'd touched her at the cinema.

"Evie, whatever happens, be assured that you're gorgeous. I never believed I'd get you in a flowery dress."

"This dress is a bit lady-at-a-garden-party for me." It was a pink floral cotton monstrosity, but she didn't want to hurt Jack. The thin straps gripped her shoulders. They were working overtime attempting to hide her bosom from the salivating gazes at the pub shift earlier in the day. The dress was fitted on her top half and rested on her hips before flaring out to her knees.

"Makes your boobs massive though." Jack had a point. They were like pink circus poodles demanding attention. "Well, fuck me, isn't that Max, that rugby player you talked about last week?"

Evie tried to spot the new fixture in Jack's fantasies, but she surreptitiously investigated every nook and cranny of the gallery to locate her fantasy.

"He's at four o'clock," he hissed with excitement. "No, that's your four o'clock. My four o'clock!"

"Chill out, or you'll sweat your skinny chinos off. They're fabulous on you, by the way."

Finally, her gaze locked on Max. His golden hair shone like an angel's halo. "He's unbearably cute. You've picked your new dream boyfriend well."

Her stomach smacked the floor as she locked eyes with Max's companion. Josh licked his lips as he stared back at her. Evie squeezed her eyes closed to rid herself of the filth threatening her composure, and by the time she opened them again, Josh was talking to Max. She used the opportunity to check him out properly. Smart grey trousers gripped his legs. They avoided being obscenely tight, but it didn't take much for her to fantasise about the bulge she'd felt against her. It was practically teasing her sex in the way it pulsed. The white shirt he'd neatly tucked into his trousers claimed ownership of his torso, which was what she wanted to do. It possessed him as if it was a second skin. Who'd dressed him? Josh only had hoodies, jeans, and sportswear in his wardrobe.

That was when she glimpsed his chest. He'd undone the top couple of buttons of his shirt. She hummed with need as she spied the smattering of dark chest hair beneath his open collar.

"Maybe you should introduce yourself," she stuttered. "I'm going to say hello to Sophia and Aidan and give them the present."

"You're not coming with me? I need a wingwoman," Jack begged. "And you can brush those boobs against Josh. Then he'll demand to jump into your bed, and voilà, you will be in control again. All thanks to me."

"His excitement isn't the issue. And you'll be fine." Evie shoved him in the direction of Josh as Max strode toward the drinks. She ignored her lousy timing and sidled toward Aidan and Sophia.

She used to be the most confident person in every room. She'd never shied away from a guy she was attracted to before. What went wrong? Maybe it's because she didn't care then. She'd treated everyone like shit and drank enough alcohol to be oblivious to the rejection. Her dating history was a who's who of the local shitbags. They were vacuous, insensitive bastards with permanent hard-ons. They fulfilled her temporary needs initially, and if they didn't, she'd manipulate them until they did. Because of the man from when she was eighteen, she'd needed men to desire her. What turned her stomach was that none of them stopped to ask about her or care for her. But Josh wasn't like that. He wanted to learn the things she'd been too scared to tell him. How could she get a guy like Josh while hiding who she was? Evie couldn't manipulate him into being with her, especially when she didn't fit his ideal of a perfect woman.

Misery followed her like a shadow as she reached Aidan and Sophia.

*****

"I'm surprised to see you, Jack." Josh fumbled his words as he reeled from Evie's presence. Fuck, her tits were unbelievable in that dress. The thin straps would have been easy to push from her shoulders, and the thin cotton material would have offered him no resistance had she gifted herself to him. Instead, his craving would have controlled every action as he claimed her body with his lips.

"Sophia offered an invite to her nearest and dearest. Tasha didn't receive an invite, which I'm sure will disappoint you." At Jack's cheekiness, Josh chuckled, but his gaze remained pinned to the way Evie's summer dress cinched at her waist. He itched to lift the material and—

"Weren't you standing with someone a moment ago?" Jack invaded his musings.

"Yeah, Max. He's gone to get some drinks. He'll be back soon."

"Cool." Silence descended. Was Evie annoyed that he was here? There was always something missing from his friendship with Evie. She never let her barriers down fully. Not that he did either. Jack's small talk continued. "How's things?"

"I went to the grave last week." The words left his tongue before he could stop them. "I hadn't visited in a while."

"Why did you go?" Jack always listened, even though he didn't understand Josh's reasoning. Jack was Lulu's best friend when they were teenagers. The friendship had faltered a little when she started dating Josh, but Jack remained there for her until her death.

"I missed her." Silence surrounded the pair. Waves of joy blessed the guests as they celebrated the start of a new life that hadn't been tainted or destroyed, yet silence surrounded the duo again as they revisited their memories of Lulu. "I wish I could do everything again, but do it right this time."

"You didn't do anything wrong."

"I killed her. I destroyed her life. If I hadn't rowed with her and wound her up before she drove away, she would be alive now. Instead, I'll be alone for the rest of my life, and it's what I deserve."

"You didn't kill anyone, and you don't have to be alone. That is your choice and not your burden. There are plenty of women out there who care about you and deserve a chance."

"But—"

"Stop living in the past and open your bloody eyes," Jack growled between gritted teeth.

"Do you mean Evie?"

Max suddenly reappeared. "Sorry, I didn't mean to butt in. I was worried your beer would get warm," he joked. Soft grey eyes stared at the now quiet pair.

"It's okay," Jack replied eventually.

"I'm Jack." Josh heard the introductions happen around him. "You must be Max."

"Sorry, where are my manners?" As he attempted proper introductions, a gasp caught his attention. Gavin bulldozed his way through the crowd. Josh fumbled for words. "What's he doing here?"

"Shit," Max whispered, reflecting Josh's mood. "Aidan's lucky to be alive after the illegal tackle that guy did to him last year."

The crowd of guests turned collectively to Gavin's entrance. The inane giggles of the woman hanging onto his arm captured the attention of anyone who wasn't already gawking at the unwelcome pair. "He knows how to make an entrance," Jack replied sardonically.

Gavin marched to Aidan as the woman bobbed next to him. With her towering spike heels and skirt that held her thighs together like superglue, she struggled to keep up with him. Even from a distance, she reminded him of Evie's alter ego, Bianca, albeit a younger version.

"What's he saying? And who's that woman?" Max

whispered.

"She's a glamour model," Jack replied.

"But he's dating Evie," Josh uttered.

Gavin and his date joined Evie, Aidan, and Sophia. Gavin rambled close to Aidan's face. Evie's shifting stance suggested discomfort, but everything else remained a mystery.

"No, that ship sailed a long time ago," Jack replied before giving Josh and Max an abridged version of what had happened after the cinema.

But Jack's perspective on the situation was cut short by Gavin's increasing volume as he bellowed across the room, "This is Candarall. She's my new girlfriend."

The grimace on Evie's face fascinated and saddened Josh. A polite smile quickly replaced it as she chatted with Candarall.

"I think she had a run-in with her once. I read something in the papers a couple of years ago before Evie stopped modelling," Jack whispered.

Josh stared at Evie's lips, but her words remained a mystery. She was hard enough to understand when she was by his side and silent. Her body language gave him nothing concrete from this distance. Then, unexpectedly, she strode across the gallery towards the doors that led to the garden.

"Shit, I'd best go," Jack said.

"No, you stay and talk to Max. I need to have a chat with her anyway. Hopefully, my presence will keep Gavin and his new girlfriend away if he tries to follow her and cause more problems." Josh stalked after her before Jack convinced him otherwise.

Chapter Nine

An ornate abstract structure held Evie's gaze. A mixture of wing-like shapes fought with a curved frame and lumps of white stone that rose from the bottom plinth. As the sun reflected off the sculpture, making her tumultuous thoughts spiral, Evie swore loudly.

The feet crunching on the gravel behind her cut short the rest of her expletives. It had to be Jack wanting to support her while also demanding gossip. He was the ideal best friend and a massive pain in the arse.

"I don't want to chat or be rescued," she announced without turning. Jack would presume she was distressed about seeing Candarall, as if her life was simple enough to be about one thing.

The heat from the body behind her permeated the ramblings of her mind. That wasn't Jack. Josh's rough hand cupped her naked shoulder. She knew his touch better than her own. Her sigh climbed up her body before slipping from her lips.

The silence was unbearable. Was Josh hesitating or planning his escape? Suddenly his finger brushed her skin as he made circles against the nape of her neck, and Evie sunk her teeth into the flesh of her thumb to stop her moans from escaping.

Josh eased her hair to the side and placed tentative kisses against her shoulder. His natural musky scent teased her as it filled her lungs, and lust dragged at her stomach at his light caress. Even if she hadn't been able to smell his natural scent, she'd have known it was him. No one made her feel like he did. Josh possessed her with a finger.

She bit her thumb harder. His kisses travelled from the nape of her neck. His lips briefly brushed her shoulders before he continued to the parts of her back that her dress didn't reach.

His hand slipped to her waist, and he pulled her against him. Evie breathed her consent when his telltale hardness pressed against her.

Josh squeezed her hips as she ground her bum against him. He growled her name as she found a rhythm that made him harder. His fingers dug into her. The art that had confused her was forgotten as Josh bunched the material of her cotton dress. Rough skin from his other hand brushed against her thigh. The temptation to make him beg for her was impossible to resist, and her arm snaked behind her body, enabling her to stroke him where he throbbed against his now skin-tight trousers.

"I came out to comfort you," he whispered, his breath tickling her skin. Goosebumps rose on her naked arms.

"You're doing an outstanding job of it," she purred.

He stumbled over his words. "You're beautiful, Evie. I can't get enough of you. But I came out here as a shoulder for you to cry on because of Gavin and his girlfriend."

Immediately Evie stiffened. She stepped away and forced distance between them. The knitted brow and downturned mouth that greeted her when she glared at him didn't stop her resolve. "Why the hell would I be upset because of them?"

"Because Jack said you have history with her, and we know about you and Gavin. We saw you storm out."

"I didn't storm out. I came outside because the situation was too awkward, and it wasn't like I could join Jack. He was with you!"

Josh threw his hands in the air. "And what's wrong with me?"

Her limbs twitched at the adrenaline gushing through them. She was as angry with herself as she was with Josh. Why did she continue to want a man who gave her mixed signals? Josh must have sensed she was close to fleeing because he reached for her hand.

"Don't," she grunted as arousal surged between her thighs.

"Let me apologise. Please, Evie," he begged, but he didn't reach for her hand again.

"What are you apologising for?"

"I don't know. But I won't let you storm away in anger." The anguish in his voice caused her to giggle. The little noises soon became belly-shaking laughs as concern creased the skin around his eyes.

Evie's life had been littered with bastards, and although Josh wound her up, she would testify to anyone that wanted to listen that Josh wasn't an arsehole. He confused and exhausted her and made her want to scream, but he wasn't like Gavin. He had a heart, even if he didn't always understand how to use it and misread situations frequently.

"Come and sit down," she requested, grabbing his hand and directing him to a bench that looked upon a steel fountain. It was another abstract piece, and it joined others dotted around the garden to form an outdoor art exhibit.

Some sculptures communicated beauty with classic curves and delicate aspects, while others were mishmashes of styles and materials that suggested a conflict between ideas and conception. Max's dad, Charlie Owen, who coached the Bulls, had created the steel fountain. Charlie was known for his charm, dedication, and ability to rule the team with an iron rod. But he hadn't been known for gifts in creating things of beauty until Aidan had discovered it and incorporated his pieces into the gallery. If players on his team attempted to tease him, he made them run extra laps. He may have been artistic, but he was also bloody-minded. All the lads called him Bossman out of fear and respect.

Water trickled musically from the fountain. The sculpture's sounds filled the uncomfortable silence that Josh created between them. They used to talk about everything months ago, even discussing masturbation schedules, but now small talk was impossible.

The silence burrowed into her brain like a worm laying its eggs until she couldn't take it anymore. "What's going on, Josh?"

"What the hell is that sculpture meant to be? Is it a cat licking its bum or a tree trying to wave down a passing motorist? I don't get art, especially not Bossman's stuff." His brow furrowed, and his mouth twisted to one side.

This time she stifled her giggles. Josh's confusion turned his generally grizzly appearance to adorable. "I meant, what's going on with you? Although I get your point about the sculpture. I can't work it out either." *Like I can't work you out.*

"Last week, when we were outside the cinema, and you went off with Gavin—"

"Nothing happened," she cut in. "I walked with him to

a bar."

"I know. Jack told me." Josh took her hand gently in his. The mixed signals were exhausting. Evie sat deathly still on the uncomfortable wooden slats of the bench and waited. "You wouldn't tell me if something was hurting or upsetting you, even if it was digging a hole in your brain, would you?"

Her laugh was unconvincing.

"Is there anything you want to talk to me about, Evie?"

Even a crumb of his care was too much. Too many men had let her down, and Josh would be another. That's if his motives weren't as destructive as some of the guys from her past. Peter's face flashed in front of her. Would she ever be free of the man who had manipulated her emotions for his own gains? Josh would reject her again if he learnt the truth.

"No, but thank you for being here and your willingness to listen," she replied stiffly, struggling not to yank her hand back and protect her heart.

"For you, always." Josh's head dipped closer to hers, and his fingers traced the wide pink flowers on her dress. "You look lovely today. Your dress is very pretty."

"Thank you." A blush threatened to redden her cheeks.

"It doesn't suit you though."

"What?" Evie attempted to yank her hand away, but he was lightning quick and soothed her skin with his thumb.

"I've said the wrong thing—sorry. All I meant was that it's not an Evie dress. You're not soft flowers and baby pinks. You're beautiful in it, but you're stunning in everything."

Her cheeks reddened against her will. Josh was right though, because it wasn't an Evie dress. No one called her beautiful. She was sexy or fuckable to other men, but no one called her beautiful.

She'd barely opened her mouth when a message beep from Josh's pocket grabbed his attention.

"You and my parents are the only ones who message me," he mumbled as he fished in his pocket. He strained and twisted because he refused to let go of her and instead insisted on using the hand farthest from the phone. She'd never had a friendship like the one she'd had with Josh. Aside from Jack and Josh, she hadn't had a genuine friend for years.

He looked up from his phone to stare at her uncertainly. "Do you want to come to mine for fun and games?".

Chapter Ten

He held Evie close as they reached his place an hour later. It would be carnage in the house, and Josh didn't want the moment to end. The time on the bench and arguing and laughing had reminded him of the old days. Somehow, they'd held hands the entire time on the long route to his house, and although Josh struggled not to ask questions about what she'd been up to since that moment in his bedroom ten weeks earlier, he enjoyed being with her. He'd missed her so much. They used to hold hands all the time when sitting on the sofa or going for walks. He shouldn't have let go of Evie but instead let go of the past, stood up to his dad, and sorted out his brain. But the thought of doing any of that scared him even now.

The townhouse was a mess, as usual. Three rugby players in their twenties living in a small house meant filthy surfaces, not plush designer cushions. A half-hearted sigh left his mouth. He shouldn't be living with the guys, but the idea of living alone freaked him out.

"It's board game night," Josh explained to Evie when they stepped into the living room. "Sunday nights, the day after a match, usually involves chilling before we start again with practice on Monday."

"Oh, right. That's what you meant by fun and games at

your place."

"What were you thinking?" He shared a smile that turned his mouth up slightly at one edge. Evie narrowed her eyes and stuck her tongue out at him.

"You're hard as nails, but you're trying not to blush, Evie," he teased. His belly flopped with happiness. He loved making her cheeks red, and she hated his effect on her, which made him love it more.

"Oh, fuck off," she replied with an eye roll, reminding him of Evie two years earlier. She was hard work when she was her alter ego, Bianca. However, he was usually too busy judging her and protecting Aidan, who was a nightmare too. Bianca flirted with rich sports stars in the clubs and drank liquor like it was heading for prohibition. But it wasn't until she'd allegedly tried to get pregnant by Aidan and lied that she was on the pill that Josh's distaste for her escalated. After Aidan, she'd bled dry the men that hung around her like dogs. And he, like some self-appointed perfect guy, judged her instead of reflecting on his behaviour and past. She was a complex onion, and every time she shared something, he cared about her more and wanted to understand her better. Yet she held back. Would that ever change?

"I wasn't thinking anything, and I'm not trying to stop any blushes," Evie replied. Her reddening cheeks said otherwise. Evie used to lie quicker than downing a gin with one gulp. In the Bianca days, he'd presumed she had no conscience, but now he could admit he'd been too busy judging her to see her strength and vulnerability. "Besides, you've been rosy red the entire walk here." She gave him a wink.

He chuckled, but his laughter hid the fantasies of the

games he longed to play. He wanted this powerful woman begging him for pleasure as he teased her. Her breasts were rarely far from his mind. Before Evie, he'd been the most committed player on the team, and yet in the last two months, his coach, Charlie, had punished him for daydreaming during practice by making him run extra drills. How would Evie taste, and what would it take to make her come on his tongue? Would it be easy to bait her lust, or would she make him work for it and have him shouting for release?

"You're considering naughty games too," she teased in his ear. "You'd best tell your cock it's got no business being hard. It's board games night."

She briefly stroked his swelling cock to enforce her point. That momentary touch tempted him to act on his desires. But instead of carrying her upstairs so she could straddle his face while he licked her into submission, he froze as his fears cut into his consciousness.

Evie yanked her hand away. "Sorry, I shouldn't have done that. We're friends, and that's all."

Before he could correct her or explain himself, Max called out, "Are you guys playing truth or dare with us?"

"Seriously?" Evie shouted back, leaving Josh to follow her into the living room.

He huffed as he entered the room and found Max and Lucas, his two housemates, and five other players from the Bulls team. They sat in a circle around an empty glass beer bottle. It wobbled as if recently spun.

"How long did I leave you alone? Long enough for you all to turn into teenagers?" he asked the group, who stared sheepishly back at him. "Aren't we playing tactical board games tonight?"

"We got bored of the brain stuff, so we moved on to

the drinking games," Lucas slurred. He hadn't been with the team for more than nine months, joining them from the Giants. Perfect blond hair often caught the eyes of the ladies, especially as it combined with a natural brown tan that made every sun seeker jealous. His old reputation as Lothario hadn't followed him to his new team yet. The rumour was that he'd slept with his coach's wife. Lucas hadn't denied it, and whenever questioned, he'd wink, then shrug and laugh so arrogantly that Josh considered slapping the grin off his face. "Are you gonna play truth or dare or what?"

"I'm getting too old for this house." But he was protective of the two guys, who barely fended for themselves. They didn't know where the iron lived even though they asked before every night out and, inevitably, Josh would iron their going-out shirts for them.

"Join us, Grandad," Max joked. "We won't make you do anything too bad. Lucas has already streaked round the garden, and Matt has downed a shot of chilli sauce."

Josh shook his head, but Evie took a space on the floor next to Max. She gave a winsome smile as she patted the empty space beside her. "Come on, grumpy pants. Join us."

Jealousy nibbled at his belly when Evie's leg pressed against Max's. Maybe he could use the game to ask Evie questions he'd been too scared to broach before. He threw his hands in the air and grumbled under his breath as he eased himself down, but the grins around him suggested that they didn't care about his reluctance. Evie's dress hid her legs from him, but her breasts fighting for freedom from the weak straps were the perfect distraction. His blood rushed away from his brain.

"Truth or dare, Josh?" Evie asked with a satisfied

smile, pointing at the bottle that landed on him.

*****

The game had been uneventful for Evie so far. Learning Josh had never had sex in a park wasn't the revelation she hoped for, although the one highlight of the game was Josh's Adam's apple while he downed two jaeger bombs in twenty seconds. She bit her lip hard when he wiped the liquid off his lips while staring at her.

"Truth or dare?" Max shouted before giggling.

"It shouldn't keep landing on me. It's a bloody fix!" Josh argued.

"Do any of us seem bright or sober enough to fix the bottle? Truth or dare? And stop stalling, or we'll make you do something shitty," Lucas slurred, pointing at Josh, his eyes half open. These guys were lightweights for rugby players.

"Fine. Truth," Josh grumbled, slapping Lucas's finger away.

"Have you ever seen Evie naked?"

The heat from where her hand rested on his thigh filled the neediest zones of her body.

"Evie's blushing," Max shouted. "He definitely has. I bet you've had sex or got close to it."

"Of course not. We're only friends." Josh replied. Evie eased her hand from its comfortable position on his thigh before returning it to her lap as if scolded. "And I haven't seen her naked either. What a waste of a question, guys."

"I don't mean in real life. Have you seen photos from her glamour modelling?" Max added.

"That's not a Josh thing to do," Evie replied, waiting for Josh to back her up, but instead, he swallowed uncomfortably. His Adam's apple bobbed in time with the strained noises emanating from his mouth. But guys made a point of telling her they'd seen her naked like it was a power thing. Josh never treated her like those men did.

"It's not fair on Evie for me to answer that."

Her eyes flicked to his face and then his dick, where his erection strained at his trousers. No one else had noticed, but Evie stared even as she tried not to. Was he remembering the ones he'd seen and getting hard for her? Fucking hell. She squirmed against the wetness in her knickers.

"It's dare time then." Lucas grinned like a Cheshire cat before dipping his head to Max's as they colluded on Josh's fate. Whatever they decided wasn't going to be pretty. Another player, Banjo, loudly bemoaned his itchy cock and balls that he'd been forced to shave due to an earlier dare as the lads mumbled and winked at Josh.

An evil glint hit Lucas's eyes as Max piped up. "We dare you to show us your tattoo."

"What tattoo?" he replied too quickly.

"We know you've got one. We saw it near your groin when you forgot your towel the other day."

Evie's ears perked. "You've got a tattoo?" she whispered, but Josh gave Max a hard stare.

"Josh, mate, you already rejected answering the truth. So this is your only option unless you want to return to the truth question," Max replied giddily as Lucas clapped his hands and laughed.

"Fine, I'll do the dare." As one, the group stared at Josh until, slowly, their gaze gravitated lower. "But I'm only showing one of you."

Josh grabbed Evie's hand. "Come on, Evie, we're

going to the bathroom, and I'm locking the door. I'm not going to give these fuckers a chance to put it on TikTok."

And he pulled her up and dragged her to the bathroom as she giggled with glee.

Stay calm, she repeated as she took in an awkward Josh. He stood against the white ceramic bath, his fingers creating a drumbeat against his thighs as he refused to meet her eye. The combined horrors of sweat and cheap aftershave radiated around them, but it did nothing to dispel her excitement. Expectation gripped her belly.

"Come on then. Let's see what you've got. Drop your trousers," Evie commanded. She glanced in the mirror above the sink and saw the smile of a wild cat baying for feed plastered across her face.

"Can't you say you've seen it?" he moaned.

"Shove those sexy, tight trousers down and show me your groin, big boy." A chuckle threatened to pop from her throat, but she held it in. Being in control of Josh made her want to dance.

"You're loving this too much. You don't need to see it," he murmured to the floor, refusing to return Evie's stare.

"Josh, baby, you've seen me naked, apparently. So it's the least I deserve."

His eyes flicked up, meeting hers, before he sighed loudly in frustration.

"Still no denial then," she added. However, it appeared that showing her his tattoo was the lesser of two evils, because Josh immediately unsnapped his belt, unbuttoned the trousers, and slid the zip. The pulsation between her legs was a familiar response when Josh was around, and Evie mentally gripped it, scared that she might never feel it again.

He watched her as he undressed. It was as if the white walls suddenly shrank with each passing second of heat. Her unfathomably dry mouth made it difficult to swallow. It felt like her tongue had swollen in preparation to please his hidden cock. Perspiration slipped along her neck and down her chest as Josh sunk his thumbs beneath the waistband of his skin-tight black boxers.

"They're kind of obscene in how tight they are, but I had to wear them," he commented, noticing her fixed gaze on his groin. "My trousers wouldn't fit anything else underneath them."

"You could have gone commando," she whispered. Josh's hands eased the boxers down. It was easy to imagine the same fingers pulling her panties down in the exact controlled style.

Every move was a tease, as if he was giving her a well-rehearsed show, yet with his knitted brow and mouth pulled to one side, he was completely unaware of his effect on her.

"Is that how you dressed today, Evie? Commando?" Maybe he wasn't completely unaware.

The gruff noise expelled from his lungs had her moistening her lips in expectation.

"I'm glad you picked me to see it," she said breathlessly, remembering that she was there to see the tattoo and not the cock she'd fantasised about.

Josh's hands cupped his dick, refusing to give her a glimpse of the prize that had pushed against her a week earlier.

"Well, show me then," she requested between eager breaths deep enough to make her chest rise and fall.

"You can see it from there."

Evie stepped closer. "No, I can't," she whispered.

Each prowling step reflected the lust that climbed through her body. She bent down slowly. Her face was inches from Josh's crotch as she knelt before him. One of his hands fisted his shirt, causing him to inadvertently reveal a hint of his perfect abs, while the other covered his cock. She ran her tongue across her lips and leaned closer.

Chapter Eleven

Air puffed out her cheeks before escaping from her mouth as Evie gazed at the tiny tattoo between his stomach and hip. It was a perfectly drawn crimson butterfly.

Compelled as much by curiosity as the temptation to touch him, Evie traced the butterfly's wings with the tip of her finger. His inking was transfixing. Josh's body jerked beneath her digit, accompanied by a pained grunt that made her hum in need.

"Please don't, Evie. It's bad enough that your head and lips are in that position, but if you keep touching me like that, I won't be able to keep my dignity for much longer. It's straining to meet you, if you get my meaning. And it's not helping that I can see down your dress either."

Once upon a time, the comment would have made her shrug, but not now and certainly not with Josh. His heated gaze and his naked skin beneath her finger had wetness collecting in her knickers more than before. Evie reached for his hand while she drew her tongue slowly across her lips.

Instinctively her hand brushed his, the temptation to reveal his erection to her mouth taking hold. "I want—" But suddenly the bathroom door handle rattled.

"Oi, hurry up. We're getting bored out here," the guys

chimed collectively from behind the door.

Evie stood slowly, under a daze of lust, while Josh quickly pulled his boxers and trousers up, fastening them in haste.

"Please don't say anything about the butterfly," he whispered gruffly before he opened the door to a waiting audience.

*****

It took ten minutes to avoid verbal diversions before they returned to the game. Josh held his breath every time the boys asked Evie a question, but she remained tight-lipped against their interrogation. Whenever she uttered that she had seen a tattoo and revealed nothing more, he inched closer, wanting to hold her close.

Her scent had changed as she left the bathroom, teasing him while they returned to their positions in the circle. As much as she enamoured him, he was scared. *She'd stared at me like I meant something to her.*

Giggles from where she sat with Max made his neck itch. The intoxicated rugby player touched her bare arms, making her laugh. She was allowed friends, and that's all Josh and Evie were anyway, yet his face burnt as Evie and Max laughed in his direction again. The fear that she might have told Max the details about the tattoo brought bile to his throat. She reminded him of Bianca, and Josh edged away from her to create a barrier, protecting his heart from humiliation. If Evie had asked, he would have told her that the tattoo was from his past. If he said the tattoo reminded him of Lulu, it would open up a part of him that she'd hate. Lulu adored butterflies. In his darkest moments, Josh questioned whether he'd got it as punishment for her death or to honour her.

"You've made his cheeks red," Max whispered loud enough for Josh to hear. "Were his bum cheeks the same colour?"

His emotions threaded together, and he closed his eyes to gain control over them. A voice like his dad's reared up in his head. *You're weak and a screw-up.* Josh shook his head, but the unsettled feeling remained.

The spinning bottle landed on Evie.

"Truth or dare?" he asked as his dad's voice continued to insult him.

"Truth," Evie replied with a knotted brow.

He'd had questions on the tip of his tongue all evening, but now they were impossible to reach. He fumbled for something, but his rapid heart rate increased his brain fog, making the questions as impossible to see as clouds on a black night. Then, finally, Max's earlier question to Lucas filled his head. "How many people have you slept with?"

Her reply was quick. "Eleven."

Max whispered in her ear, and she giggled. His brow furrowed as he tried to decipher if he was the reason for their laughter.

"He doesn't believe me." Josh shook his head, but Evie carried on, leaving him no space to explain the reason for his confusion. "I'm not ashamed of my past. I see it a bit like the butterfly effect. Everything that has happened in my life has been for a reason. My choices, different events, and a bit of luck have decided the course of my life. I loved one of those guys, or at least I thought so at the time, and I cared for all of them."

There was so much she wasn't telling him, and as the brain fog cleared, he remembered one of the questions he'd wanted to ask: had she ever been in love? How could he get her alone to ask and to explain that he wasn't judging her?

Banjo called out, "Right, let's get on with the game, shall we?"

Before he offered an alternative, the bottle landed on Josh.

"How many women have you slept with?" Evie asked, eyeballing him before anyone else opened their mouths.

Silence gripped the group once more.

"I'm not answering that," he said, remembering Lulu again. She'd been his first and only.

"You're going to bail on a question again?" Banjo teased.

"I'll do a dare." Every question would lead to more, and there was so much that he couldn't share.

"Okay, fine," Evie responded, a timely reminder of her compassion. Maybe he'd allow himself a moment of vulnerability and share something with her. All these secrets were exhausting, and the impact of hiding them was getting worse. He dug his nails into the flesh of his palms. "Someone give him a dare."

"I dare you to kiss Evie," Max replied quickly.

"That's not fair on Evie," Josh snapped.

Evie shrugged. "I'll do it. I've got nothing to be scared of."

The group rounded on him noisily as Lucas added, "You kiss Evie, or you have to tell us how many women you've slept with. It's that simple."

"Fine," Josh replied with a loud huff. "But not in front of you guys. We're not at a school disco."

Before anyone argued, he jumped up and pulled Evie towards the bathroom for the second time that night.

As Josh stood in front of Evie in the bathroom that never got cold, a familiar fear crept upon him. What if he embarrassed himself? It had been years since he'd kissed someone. The arousal flooding his system wouldn't help either.

"We don't have to do this if you don't want to," she whispered, shifting awkwardly from one foot to the other.

"Don't you want to?" he replied but not with the relief that he had a way out. He wanted to kiss her, but what if he fumbled it? His dad had told him that men should be strong in every situation, although thankfully, they'd never talked about sex or any form of intimacy. But no one was as strong as Evie, and she was a beautiful force to be reckoned with.

"Yes, of course I want to, you wanker. But you seem to be struggling." He dropped his head, but then she added, "And you've always been too chicken."

Josh stepped closer and tentatively stroked her cheek with his knuckles. The way she leaned into him gave him little sparks of assurance, but he trembled as he cupped her face with both hands. Would she bolt, or would he?

Stop fucking thinking.

"We don't have to do this if you don't want to," she whispered, her bow-like lips encouraging him closer like a siren drawing him to certain death.

"Shush," he replied, staring into her eyes. She worried her lip with her front teeth. There was too much fear of the unknown, of the unexpected, between them. His confidence had flown away like balloons slipping out of little hands.

Josh dipped his head, and he kissed her gently on the lips. Fire returned to his body at a blazing pace, and he repeated the kisses harder with each touch of his lips against hers. She parted her lips and welcomed his tongue before thrusting her hands into his hair and pulling him closer and harder against her. Grabbing her bum, he tried to gain control. She whimpered against his lips.

She rubbed against him, trying to align their bodies. Josh met her actions and gripped her tighter. He pulled her against him as his confidence soared. She whimpered again as his erection ground against her. How was it this good with clothes on? He fisted her dress, dragging its hem higher. She moaned her agreement into him, and he reached a hand between her thighs. His thumb brushed her knickers. The thin gauze was drenched in her wetness. One of her hands held him there as if showing him how she liked to be pleasured as she made beautiful, delirious moans. He pushed her hair to the side and kissed her neck, but his hand never left her pussy, which she now ground against him. Her breathing was getting heavier and her begging louder.

Suddenly a beep from between her breasts stopped them both.

"What the hell?" Josh pulled away as she reached down the front of her dress and pulled her phone from her cleavage.

"It's where I keep it when I have no pockets," she explained, glimpsing the screen before answering.

Was he that bad that she'd stopped to answer her phone? He shook his head as he attempted to regain his bearings.

"Yep, it's Evie." She turned away, blocking any intrusion from his prying ears. The other person's words were a mystery. "Okay, I'll be there soon."

Evie glanced in his direction.

"You're going?"

Her face was blank as if she was unaffected by him. "Yeah, but I'll message you later."

"Don't you—" But she'd already left the bathroom. Was Josh a warm-up for who she really wanted? The slamming front door echoed around the house and acted like the wake-up call he needed. He needed to listen to his dad and find someone else.

Josh confronted the confused faces when he returned to the living room. "We're going out drinking, so get your stuff, lads. Fuck training tomorrow. I'm in the mood to get wasted." *And fuck everyone else too.*

Chapter Twelve

Josh wobbled down the street, straining at his phone and talking to the night that surrounded him. "Where's her shitting number?"

The alcohol dulled his senses as he stumbled alone past houses and side streets. He'd spent the entire night drinking more units than he could count and thinking about settling down with Evie. But she didn't want him, and even if she did, she wouldn't want to settle down in a house with a white picket fence and dogs or cats running around.

"I'd get her a fucking sheep if asked for one," he shouted to the pigeon cooing next to him before laughing loudly and resuming his poking of the phone screen to get her number up.

He'd got to T and saw Gavin's number under the label TWAT. But, of course, he'd been at the club too.

"Pigeon, I fucking hate that guy."

At the club, Gavin had mocked him like he always did. Josh usually ignored Gavin's taunts, but the alcohol put him in the mood for fighting, and he let Gavin have it. His team helped him out of the club before the bouncers kicked him out.

"I nearly made her come tonight," Josh said as he attempted to swagger past the pigeon but tripped over his feet. He righted himself and leaned against a wall to avoid face-planting on the pavement. The trip didn't dull the number of pints and shots still filling his system. "I'm calling the woman who was soaking for me earlier."

"Yes!" he hollered, finally getting the phone to connect. But, unfortunately, it went straight to the voicemail.

"Evie, you're not answering. Why aren't you answering?" he slurred. "Guess which prick I saw tonight at The Red Club. Gavin was with some random woman, not the glamour model who's nowhere near as beautiful or sexy as you, FYI. I'm rambling, and I need to get to the point. What was it again? Oh yeah, I got into a fight tonight for you. Gavin was being a dick, but I sorted him. I punched him in that fat, ugly face of his. I defended your honour because you're my fair maiden. Yeah, I like that, fair maiden. The thing is, I need you for lots of reasons."

Josh sighed and sat on the concrete.

"I can't stop thinking about you. I really like you, you're amazing, and when you smile, I feel like I've conquered a fucking mountain, and I get horny about you too. And I want to see your needy face again. I've been hard since you moaned and ground yourself against me in the bathroom. That wasn't a dare thing, was it? I saw a picture of your boobs once. I want those boobs in my mouth. It doesn't matter what size your boobs are because I have a big mouth. Does that turn you on, or do I sound like a teenage boy? I get a bit like that around you because—by the way, I'm drunk. You might not have worked that out. I've hidden it well so far. Anyway, I don't think only about tasting your tits but other parts of you too, and I want to fuck you. I fuck you a lot in my daydreams. I want to do you cowgirl, doggy—"

The voicemail cut him off. He stumbled to his feet and wobbled down the empty street.

"Shit." Josh tried to call her back but couldn't hit the right buttons. "I've loads more that I want to say. I didn't get to the part about Lulu, my feelings, or the fucking perfect noises Evie made earlier. Or did I?" he shouted to no one.

Suddenly he found himself at the rickety fence of the graveyard. Josh flung himself over the splintering wood and landed on his wrist, but the momentary pain was as quickly forgotten as the unfinished phone call, and he meandered to his familiar spot.

"Here again," he said, flopping onto the wet grass. "Why do I always end up back here with you?"

Josh lay on his bed, the paper lampshade above him swaying as a breeze flowed from his top window.

What a fucking night. That morning he'd woken in the graveyard to a vicar prodding him with a dirty black boot. With one look at his watch, Josh jumped up and bolted for the rugby grounds, vomiting in a stranger's garden as his hangover split his head in two. And then it got worse.

You messed up because you're a fuck-up. Again, his conscience took on his dad's voice. He swiped his hand in the air as if to knock it away, making himself wince. Fucking wrist. He was banned from practice, possibly on the bench for the next game, and chewed out by his coach— the morning from hell. He should be warning his dad, but instead, he left his phone where he'd thrown it before dropping into his bed.

The one crumb of joy that morning had been the ugly bruise on Gavin's even uglier face. He'd glowered at Josh as his coach dragged him into his office. As Coach ranted about his injury and smacking Gavin, a massive group of lads from the team had pushed into the office, denying that Josh hit Gavin on the night out. Lucas shouted that Gavin must have smacked himself in the face in the name of self-improvement. Josh swore his coach struggled not to laugh, but it didn't matter. Josh had fucked up, and if his wrist didn't heal and he didn't play the match, there would be repercussions from his dad.

The team doctor gave him a whisper of hope, and he'd said Josh was able to drive and should be okay by the end of the week. But what if it was the mistake of his career?

Josh tapped his left hand absentmindedly on his bare stomach. Before Evie, he was hypercontrolled in every aspect of life. But the raging sickness in his stomach reminded him that he'd made his own choices last night. Coach still hadn't renewed his contract for the next season, and only two games remained in the current season. "So why did I fuck up so bad?" he ranted to the air.

Evie hadn't rushed away to hook up with Gavin, so what secrets was she hiding? And why wouldn't she trust him?

It was as if the crimson butterfly tattoo beneath his shorts poked him in the side. It was a branding from history and a reminder of unrepeatable mistakes and his secrets. But the night before he'd shown Evie some of the real him, she'd rejected him. Josh turned over and screamed into the pillow. He'd worked hard to push all his needs and hopes down. It wasn't just sexual stuff. He wanted to have fun, mess around, and make mistakes, but he'd chosen this self-controlled lifestyle to protect those around him—until Evie. She brought out the real him, and that was dangerous.

His cock twitched. It was the last thing he needed when he should be calling his dad or finding a way to fix the mess he'd made, but it was fruitless. Evie had this undeniable effect on him, and the hangover horn wasn't helping either. The sickness in his stomach turned to fire when he recalled the whimpers she'd made as he rubbed her clit through her knickers. The taste of orange juice that lingered on her tongue had sweetened the kiss. How can such a filthy tongue taste of sunshine?

Josh's left hand reached underneath the waistband of his shorts, and the crappy morning faded away as Evie became his focus. Every other concern quietened as he palmed his erection with long, hard strokes. The pre-cum was enough to lubricate it and make it shudder beneath his quickening touches. His whole body thrust in anticipation of the next rub. He treated the length of his shaft to wet skin-on-skin contact, but the image of his cock sliding between Evie's breasts forced his climax closer. Each stroke of his palm mirrored his fantasy, and he grunted softly as a new pressure replaced his hangover. His hand moved increasingly quicker along his cock. He shook, his breath ragged, the roar of thunder inside him—

The shrill ring of the doorbell nearly knocked him out of bed. Stars danced in his eyes as he focused on his room's plain walls. The piercing sound dragged him back to the reality that stretched out before him. He should leave it. But Max and Lucas were at the practice he was sent home from. What if his dad had found out about his wrist? There would be hell to pay if he didn't answer the door to him. Josh shuffled to the door as his hangover blistered his senses.

He ripped the door open, bracing himself for one of his

dad's power trips. But Evie was standing on his doorstep. Her eyes blazed with anger, and her hand fisted near his body as if preparing to beat the door down. *Why is she so fucking hot when she's angry?* Her pink lips shone in the sunlight, and tendrils of strawberry blonde hair slipped out of her bun as she glowered.

"Josh, what the fuc—" Suddenly, she froze.

*****

Evie gritted her teeth. She was here to shout at Josh, not salivate over his body. Her anger had been brewing since she'd heard the start of the message he'd left her. If her phone battery weren't dying, she'd have listened to the rest, but she needed to keep some battery in case of emergency calls from the care home. They were several times a day now.

Why did Josh defend her yet continue to hurt her by rejecting her? His changing emotions were exhausting.

But standing at his door, her wrath snapped to lust. It rushed through her veins like she'd injected herself with it. The heat surged between her legs. He may have dark circles under his eyes and a flummoxed expression, but it did nothing to replace the memory of his fingers against her clit. Saliva filled her mouth at his solid, defined muscles that testified to his diligence in the gym. The thick dark hair that covered his chest begged for her. It made demands of her fingers, tempting her to run them through it.

"What a greeting," he replied, forcing her to look at his face. At his darkened stare and the way he puffed air from his cheeks, she bit at her lip and crossed her legs, but nothing could obliterate her Josh-induced arousal. "But talk quieter. My head is killing me."

Her brow furrowed. "Why aren't you at practice? I went there to find you," she shouted back.

Evie glanced at the bandage wrapped around his wrist, but before she launched into a tirade of questions, his eyes dipped, and his gaze travelled the length of her body. "The same dress as yesterday, eh? A bit late in the afternoon for the walk of shame."

"I haven't had the time to change," she snapped. "Stop accusing me of shagging around. I'm not Bianca anymore, not that I was shagging around then either, and there isn't an issue with that anyway! Besides, I'm not the one practically naked and answering the fucking door."

"I'm sorry, Evie. You're not Bianca anymore, and as you say, there aren't issues with someone shagging around. I'm in a shit mood today, and I should get over my hangover alone."

"Don't be such a melodramatic shithead. I need to come in and charge my phone. I haven't been home since yesterday." She sensed his hesitation, but she'd come all this way and needed to check her messages. "Please, Josh."

He opened the door wider and let her slip in. She resisted brushing up against him, but his breath caressed her neck as she passed him. She held back a moan as he led her to his room.

"Where have you been all night and all morning?" he asked tentatively.

"I've been busy looking for you to yell your arse out for getting into a fight in my name. I don't need you to do that. I can take care of myself, and stop judging me on my past or the past you've made up. You're such a judgemental prick sometimes. Whatever you believe about me is wrong, and more importantly, it hurts when you talk about me like

I'm worthless."

Josh stopped in the doorway to his room, bringing her to an abrupt halt as she smacked into his naked back. He turned to face her. His dark eyes had softened. "I'm truly sorry, Evie." His hands reached for hers, and she allowed him to hold her. Josh's thumbs stroked the inside of her wrists. He took deep breaths as he fixed her with his stare. Josh slowly shook his head and closed his eyes before speaking again. "I'm sorry for how I spoke to you last night too. You're not worthless. You're strong and beautiful and deserve only good things."

The expression of care on his face rippled her insides. Only a handful of people seemed to care for her, and the number was diminishing quickly.

"I don't know why I say these things or keep trying to hurt you, but the problem is me. I guess it's linked to the tattoo and other things." She wanted more, but when his soft gaze rested on her face and his fingers brushed her wrist's pulse points, she trembled against him.

"You're cold?" Josh asked with concern laced through his voice. "Let me grab you a jumper."

She wanted to cry out, bring him back, and stop their moment from ending. But even with the memory of his hand between her thighs, she couldn't make the first move. The reminder that he'd rejected her outside the cinema was still too fresh.

Her confidence increased as he chucked on a T-shirt. She'd remember his naked chest later, but getting herself off to him wasn't the problem. There was too much going on, and vulnerability wasn't an option. The words "tell him how you feel" burned in her chest, demanding she confront their situation, but Evie couldn't turn them into action. The last months took their toll; fear worked at her every day, binding itself to her brain before shutting down her mouth and body and making action impossible. She was becoming a shell of herself. She opened her mouth to tell him, but fear snapped it shut. What if she couldn't find the courage to share her pain with anyone?

Chapter Thirteen

Josh smiled as Evie ripped apart the late lunch he prepared for her.

She moaned in satisfaction while shoving the bacon roll dripping with melted salted butter into her mouth. The view was mesmerising, but a niggle of worry about when she'd last eaten remained. The dark circles under her eyes were nothing new, but every moment they spent time together, she appeared more tired than the last. He sipped his coffee, his worry distracted by how good she looked in his jumper. A glow filled his belly as she furtively sniffed the collar. It was way too big for her, but when she rested her lips against the cuff that hung over her wrist, he knew he'd never ask for it back.

"So why are you home?" she asked as she chewed with all the class of teenage rugby fans. For once, he didn't overthink his need for perfection or repeat the list in his head. Instead, he revelled in her.

"Promise you won't laugh or shout at me." Evie's shrug was enough to pull the words from his mouth. "I got wasted last night and turned up to practice late, hungover, and with a dodgy wrist from falling while drunk. It might heal in time for the weekend, but Coach ranted that he'll bench me for bad behaviour."

"Fuck, Josh. You're usually the most dedicated player." Her words surprised him. Evie didn't reprimand him or shame him. It wasn't in her nature, but he wasn't used to sharing his mistakes without consequences. The way she licked the remaining ketchup from her fingers in earnest with unashamed hunger added to the tentative smile on his face.

"But," she continued, her forehead creased like it always did when she was deep in thought, "it does explain the message."

"What message?" A prickle of a distant memory inched beneath his skin.

"The message you left me last night. Don't you remember?" she replied before gulping her coffee.

Before he could process what she meant, Evie crossed to her phone. Evie played his message, and Josh jumped when his drunken words sliced the quietness of the kitchen. The actions of the previous night came storming to his consciousness. That must be how she knew about his fight with Gavin. That was why she was livid when she'd arrived.

In a panic, he tried to reach for the phone. Flashbacks swooped through his memories like they were being carried by demonstrative witches on broomsticks, dropping at the forefront of his mind and spurring him to action. He stalked across the kitchen, but his hangover dulled his normally tightly honed hazard awareness skills. Evie's wedge shoes caught the edge of his foot, and he slammed into the hard oak door. But it didn't stop him from lumbering to the phone. The words "tits" and "doggy" echoed around the kitchen like humiliating laughter before he hit the delete button. But his secret was out.

Josh's eyes flicked anxiously to Evie's face. The masochist in him was desperate for her reaction.

"Why didn't you tell me these things?" she broached.

The memory of the message raised the heat in his cheeks. If he hadn't made it evident before, the answering machine must have revealed his inexperience. He couldn't be weak. Hadn't his dad drummed into him that no one laughed at a real man?

"Because what's the point? If you wanted to be with me, then it would have happened. I know you, Evie, remember? I saw what you used to be like when you wanted a guy. Nothing stood in your way. So I must be a game to you, someone to annoy before the next guy like Aidan comes along."

Her face dropped. Were her eyes watering? But then her mouth twisted into a sneer. "Wow, you've put all your insecurities on me. Maybe you didn't tell me because I don't fit your fucking list. I found it a couple of months ago before you kicked me out of your bedroom and stopped speaking to me. It wasn't a joke, was it? You want the anti-Evie, so you push me away and then blame me?"

"You're right. I have a list because I don't want to hurt anyone or get hurt." His face burnt as he finally exclaimed why he'd run from her. "Sometimes, I think I get you, but I remember the old you. You used to tell people that Aidan held some significance, yet you sold your sex tape to the highest bidder. You sold stories about him to the paper. I don't want to be another victim of yours."

"Victim? Are you fucking kidding me?"

He was taking out his embarrassment from the recording on her, but it freed his genuine beliefs. Unable to debate them with reason, they spewed forth like a shaken bottle of fizzy beer when the cap was popped. "You could have damaged his career. You nearly destroyed him. And it almost ruined things with Sophia. So what's to stop you from destroying me?" *I'm scared.* But he couldn't admit that to her.

"You fucking arsehole. After all the time we spent together over the last year, I thought that you knew who I was and that I wasn't capable of that anymore. I have a past and made hideous decisions because of what has gone on in my life." Josh attempted to jump in and defend himself, but he couldn't stop her vitriol. "But you never bothered to ask questions about why I did things. Instead, you judged me and made assumptions about things you know nothing about," she roared. "I would have explained, not that you deserve it. So you fantasise about fucking my body but can't stand the person I am? How does that make you any different to Gavin?"

"I'm nothing like Gavin!" he spluttered as she rounded on him.

Evie poked him in the chest as she ranted. "You wish you weren't. You criticise me because you've decided I'm only after sex, yet that's all you want from me? You judgemental bastard, I believed we were friends, but even Gavin doesn't hurt me like you. Be careful of that high horse of yours. I hope when you fall off, you break your fucking face. And you can shove your list up your arse. If you're not careful, you'll end up alone, but maybe that's what you want because you're too scared of living like you want to."

Everything she said hit like a cricket ball against his chest. Pain flooded through his system. There was truth in her words, and the version of him she revealed made him hate himself more than he already did. "I don't—"

"You don't get to speak to me anymore. You say you know me, but you're fucking wrong." Rage spilt out as she swiped her shoes from the floor. When she ripped the phone from him, the searing heat from her hands scorched his skin. Recoiling from her grab, she teetered for a moment but quickly righted herself, pushing away his attempt to steady her.

"Then tell me your secrets, Evie. What is going on with you?"

But she was gone.

"Evie, wait," he called out, terror lacing through his words, but the door slammed, nearly rocketing off its hinges.

Chapter Fourteen

"Not that I care," Evie shouted to the sky, lambasting Josh's lack of contact since their fight several days earlier.

A teenage girl passed her while saying into her phone, "I just saw this old woman shouting to no one. This place is well weird."

Does she mean me? Fucking teenagers had no idea about life. That was a lie as much as her shout to the sky. As a teenager, Evie was forced to leave her home and run to the only relative who cared because a man called her a liar and got away with it. One minute, Josh had been her best friend, yet days earlier he'd turned on her and said what he thought. With everything going on, she needed the catch-up and meal Jack had promised her. She continued down the road to the restaurant in town.

And how dare Josh say she wanted another Aidan or that he'd be one of her victims. If she wanted some rich stud, she wouldn't be mooning over a yeti who lived in a house share with two rugby boys. He hadn't said anything untrue, and she hadn't taken the time to explain the sex tape and the reasons behind it. But why hadn't he asked her instead of letting those feelings fester? She recalled the many times Josh had picked her up or been her respite when life got too much. He held her hand and told her funny stories when she found herself shaking and on his doorstep because of her sick nan, and he never made her explain why she wasn't her usual self. Josh and Jack were her only friends, and yet neither of them knew about her past or all the reasons why nan was the only family member she had left.

Evie had jumped from topic to topic like this for days. Luckily, she hadn't lost her job with the number of orders she'd got wrong and the glasses she'd smashed. Of course, it helped that all the men at the pub adored her for listening to their problems.

Even with everything he'd said, she still wanted Josh. He was always intrigued by what little-known fact or theory she'd share at every opportunity. In those moments when her past came back to haunt her, she rushed to Josh, and he'd found a song on his personally created Evie playlist that instantly lifted her mood. He'd listen when she shared ideas to improve his rugby, and they'd supported each other's fitness goals. She wouldn't have given up smoking if not for him. Her doctor had told her that whatever changes she'd made in the last twelve months, she should continue them because her heart was healthier than he'd known it to be. The rollercoaster of emotions and irrepressible attraction they'd never spoken about had been their downfall.

"And what about that drunk phone message?" she mumbled to the sky before pushing the door into the restaurant. It was like Josh didn't understand how to talk to women.

She'd had messages like that from others before, but they were never as funny, adorable, or as hot. She'd only seen Josh drunk once due to his disciplined lifestyle, but the voicemail reminded her of that time. It was all the best bits about Josh but times a hundred. It was as if alcohol gave him freedom. Why couldn't he find that freedom sober? Maybe it was time to give him up as an error of judgement and move on. He was the one she imagined when she fell asleep, pretending to cuddle up to him. It was also his head between her legs, nipping at her thighs and sucking her clit, that she fantasised about when making herself come. Yet he made her feel like an object when before it hadn't been like that. Was there a way back?

Tonight, she'd rant about it with Jack and then move on. No more shit. She was done.

Candles flickered across the dimly lit restaurant, their light dancing across the faces of couples, hinting at their expressions but never giving away their true intentions. The Italian restaurant was a mixture of intimate round tables and leather booths. Scents of pasta sauce and garlic rose into the atmosphere, filling the lungs and teasing the stomach. Evie growled in anticipation.

When did she last eat? Food was easy to forget when life was a series of complications and gut-wrenching decisions. It was weird that she focused so much on Josh and his caveman behaviour when her nan, whom she loved more than any other, would soon be gone from her life. Maybe she was focused on him because it was easier to deal with something she could fight than something she had no control over.

"Can I help you?" the impeccably dressed maître d' with a dark twitching moustache and a disinterested gaze asked.

"Yes, I'm here for dinner."

The place radiated expense. Evie knew from her past as arm candy that the prices were beyond the contents of her purse. Some guys who'd tried to woo her brought her here, showering her with gifts and expensive champagne. It was usually an attempt to get her into bed. To say they'd fucked a glamour model meant a jump up the Lothario league, but other men had been misguided or lonely. They believed she'd teach them things or give them a chance to feel like a "real" man. She usually listened to them talk about their problems before returning to her nan for the latest cosy detective drama on television.

One couple in the restaurant caught her eye. The steak on his plate made her mouth water. Was his date eating spaghetti lobster? She crossed her fingers that Jack was paying. She needed to earn thousands for the care home, but returning to glamour modelling was an option she didn't want to consider. It was a lucrative job if you tolerated the seedy photographers that bribed you with promises of what they'd do for your career, but she'd hated that time. The modelling came at a price. You had to offer something in return.

Gavin seemed like a loveable prospect when she was modelling because of his money, career, and willingness to protect her if she asked him to. But she wanted to embrace her passions. She had a secret notebook at home where she wrote down her designs for a dance school. She added notes about what dances she'd perform on stage, including the positions and ideas on set and costume. But it was just a dream. Even if she had the money, her past had destroyed her love and courage for performing. Instead, she taught a ballet class to children once a week before rushing home to design her perfect dance school. Dreams couldn't become a reality for people like her.

"Do you have a table booked? As you can see," he said, glancing at her tired, pale pink T-shirt, skinny jeans, and flat shoes with disdain, "we're inundated with clientele."

She used to turn heads when she walked into that restaurant with heels that made her tower over pricks like the guy glowering in front of her and designer dresses that drew all eyes to her long legs, tight arse, and perfect breasts.

As if he'd heard her internal rant, the maître d' leered at her breasts, which peeked out of the V of her T-shirt. The stare turned her stomach. The old her would have sashayed in wearing her trademark skimpy leopard print dress and told him to fuck off, but nothing more than a squeak came out of her mouth. She sighed her sadness, cleared her throat, and mumbled, "I have a table booked. My friend probably booked it under his name. Jack Forrester."

Without more than a courteous "Follow me," the man whipped up a menu and led her to one of the quieter booths.

But Jack wasn't in the booth. Instead, the one guy she wanted to avoid forever wriggled in the red leather seat. Josh checked his watch before his gaze flicked around the restaurant. Suddenly his eyes locked on hers. He froze immediately.

"Fucking set-up," she whispered under her breath.

*****

Josh pulled the collar of his shirt away from his neck. A drop of sweat travelled slowly down his back.

The maître d' glowered at Evie until she sat reluctantly at the table. The maître d' had pissed him off before Evie arrived. Josh bit his tongue until it hurt when the moustached guy made him feel like he was infiltrating some secret society. That wasn't new for Josh. With his unkempt appearance and lousy dress sense, he rarely fit in, but no one was allowed to treat Evie like that. Josh wrestled with the temptation to fight her battles. Her stiff back and pursed lips were probably due to him rather than any restaurant employee. He needed to say sorry a million times before he could demand better behaviour from others.

After taking her drinks order and giving another eye roll that made Josh's hand itch, the maître d' left them alone.

"I've got a good mind to rip that moustache off and shove it down his throat," he grunted. "The way he's sneering at you is seriously pissing me off. You're better than anyone here, including me," he finished softly.

"He's doing his job." She wrinkled her lips in a smile. "And apparently, his job includes being a judgemental wanker."

Josh laughed, but then silence between them returned. He huffed and puffed as he fisted his serviette and worded his apology. If Jack had told him this was a set-up, Josh wouldn't have come, because facing Evie was scarier than his coach and his dad combined. He'd hurt her and couldn't reverse time to undo it. He caught his reflection in the silver cutlery, unsurprised that he was glowering. Suddenly he found Evie staring at him with a raised eyebrow. "Spit it out then, Josh, or you're going to run out of breath to huff."

He smiled half-heartedly. "You always rightly call me out. I'm sorry, Evie." He rushed the words that he'd stewed on for the last three days. "What I said to you was cruel and indefensible."

"But you meant it," she stated, proving that she met all conversation head-on, including apologies.

"I guess. Kind of." Josh's shoulders slumped in defeat.

"You're not a bitch, and you were right when you said I was judging you. I guess I'm scared because sometimes all I remember is the old Evie. She's there. I'm scared of what you might do to me and how you might humiliate me. You can be ruthless."

"True, but I only do it when I need to, and I don't try to sound callous. I don't do it to you unless you're being a dickhead, which you were on an almighty scale on Monday."

Josh nodded. He'd let shame control his words, although he stood by his fears.

"I had my reasons for the things I did in the past," Evie continued. "I did despicable things for fucked up reasons, but I made the decisions with the knowledge I had. We all have a past, and I'm not a perfect angel that brings joy and sweetness wherever I go. Bianca is a part of me. Sometimes I'm jealous of how confident I was in those days and how I wish I were her again, just for ten minutes. I would have thrown my drink over the maître d' by now if I was Bianca. But the me you get is the real me in the here and now. I have secrets, but when you're not being a dickhead, I like you and trust you. I didn't tell anyone about the butterfly or ask you about it."

"I know, and I should have been grateful about that." Josh took a deep breath and tugged on his beard. He softly asked, "Will I ever learn your secrets?"

"Will I ever learn yours?" she countered.

The question should have terrified him, but she combined it with a smile that eased some of his adrenaline. "The butterfly tattoo? I got it because of an ex-girlfriend." He shoved his hands under the table to hide their tremble.

Evie stared at him. Her face was blank, and her thoughts indecipherable. "And you've been too scared to tell me?"

Josh nodded. His shaking fingers tapped the bottom of the table, drawing her attention. He pushed his hands under his thighs, but the adrenaline filled his limbs. Evie's eyes softened, and she eased her head to the side. She took a breath.

"Have you decided what you're eating?" The maître d' appeared at their table without warning. He pursed his lips as he looked at the pair of them. "Your friend Jack is putting it on his account, so don't worry if you're wondering how you will afford it."

Josh sunk in his chair even as his dad's voice told him what a real man would do.

"We've decided this place doesn't fit our vibe," Evie snapped.

"Excuse me. Doesn't fit your vibe?" His eyebrows nearly touched his dodgy hairline.

Evie jumped up and grabbed Josh's wrist as his hand was impossible to reach.

"It's a bit stuffy, and the staff are a bit judgy. You know?"

"The fair is in town. Maybe you'd be better suited there," he sneered as his eyes crawled down Evie's body. Although Josh wore a checked shirt with his jeans, his beard was untamed and his whole manner untidy, yet it was Evie he seemed to have a real problem with.

Josh stood and met the maître d' head-on. "If you look at her like that one more time, I'll smack your face so hard that your mum won't recognise you," Josh whispered between gritted teeth. "No one judges Evangeline. She's a fucking goddess."

The maître d' shrugged, making his placating words as

false as his French accent. "I'm sorry, sir, madam." He nodded in Evie's direction. "I didn't mean to offend."

"Yes, you fucking did," Evie replied. This time she slipped her hand in Josh's good one and pulled him away from the table. "Come on, Josh. I hear the fair is in town. Maybe we'll find some real people there. This place is too fake," she added as she dragged him from the restaurant.

Chapter Fifteen

They sat on a bench, wolfing down hot dogs. The scent of sweet candy floss mingled with sausage grease and filled Josh's lungs. Teenagers screamed from the rides, and a beaming woman jumped in Josh's eye line as she cheered her partner on at the coconut shy. Josh chuckled to himself.

"What's got you laughing?" Evie asked as she chewed her dinner.

"I should thank the maître d'. He was right. This place suits me a lot more. You fit in anywhere, but places like that aren't for me—although it was nice for Jack to pay for us to go," he added quickly.

"Jack set us up, so he doesn't get kind words until I've had a go at him. And the maître d' was a wanker, so he's not getting our thanks either. I don't fit in anywhere, not anymore."

Josh opened his mouth, but Evie cut him off. "I've changed since I was Bianca. I'm not as confident or as cocky. A lot of it was alcohol, but also, I was hurting from stuff that happened in my past."

She tossed her rubbish in the nearby bin and turned to Josh. "What you said on Monday and things you've said before really hurt me. I thought you knew me, yet you made me feel like nothing. I thought you cared about me. I know you're scared, but I can't hurt you, not just because I'm not that person anymore, but because I care about you."

Josh looked down. The shame was unbearable, but Evie lifted his chin and stared into his eyes. "Don't you dare say things like that to me again, Josh. That was your last strike. From now on, you ask me questions and tell me your fears, or this friendship won't work."

She rubbed ketchup off the side of his mouth with her finger. "And thank you for telling me about the reason for your butterfly. I will ask more questions when you're ready, but not tonight."

"I'm so sorry for Monday and before, I really am. I have this voice in my head that tells me that I'm a fuck up and that I'm not enough." He held back that the voice was his dad's. "It's no excuse that I was hungover or thinking about being benched. I care about you more than I've cared about anyone for years, and I'm scared of hurting you." She opened her mouth, but he cut in, "And I hurt you anyway. I promise to keep talking and sharing and not to do that again. Always call me out for my shit, because as much as I try not to, I might slip up again."

"And the list? Why does it read like the anti-Evie? Do you genuinely want someone who is sensible and the girl-next-girl type? Because if you do, Josh, then I know what is between us is only a friendship."

Josh's head lowered again. He took a deep breath and fisted his hands to hide the tremble that came with baring his soul. "Sometimes I want a woman who fits the list. It goes back to hurting people, but when I look at you, I only want you. It's like there's a battle inside me. It's no secret that I fancy you, but you're so much more to me. You're my best friend." His heart beat rapidly, and his fists shook. Sadness filled his heart. "The last ten weeks without you were some of the worst I've had in years, but when I'm with you, I can't—I can't—"

Evie edged closer. "Why do we always end up on benches?" She cut his anguish with her caring presence.

Josh smiled and held her hands, relieved that she'd reprieved his anxiety. "Fuck knows. But I want to say sorry for pushing you away outside the cinema too. I've let fear rule me for so long that I don't know how to stop it."

Evie grinned. "Then let me help you."

Heat climbed up his neck as he looked at the V of her T-shirt.

"Not like that, you filthy fucker." Josh laughed. "I meant, let's do something you're scared of. And not that I'm encouraging drinking, but you have no training to get to, and you don't need to be super disciplined. Besides, there's a good new beer that we serve in the pub, and I think you'll love it."

"But the last time I drank—"

"You left me a message that made me smile," she said quickly. She rushed to a nearby seller and was back in moments. She handed the beer to Josh.

"The Beast from Within," he read the label out loud.

Evie shrugged and smiled. "It reminded me of someone."

Josh chuckled before downing it in three gulps.

"I want you for more than sex, by the way," he spluttered.

Evie's brow knitted together, and she stared at him over the rim of her coke bottle.

"What you said on Monday," he qualified. "I don't always show it properly, but I care about you more than nearly anyone in my life."

"Sweetie, if you only wanted me for sex, we'd have

fucked like rabbits by now." She winked, disarming him instantly. She made him laugh and turned him on with one phrase. Why weren't those things on his list? She finished her coke and disposed of both bottles. "Right. What scares you, other than me?"

He stared at the ride that flung people around on swings that looked like they wouldn't pass a safety test.

"Then that ride it is. And if you get through it, I'll win you a teddy bear and buy you ice cream," she said, pulling him to his feet.

"Shouldn't I win you a teddy?" he asked as he tried to delay their walk to the ride.

"Sweetcheeks, you need to rest that wrist, and besides, if you do it, I'll only be looking at your sexy bum," she teased. "And I want you staring at mine."

She stood in front of him and looked at him over her shoulder before grabbing his hand. The temporary distraction worked. As he stood in the queue for the ride, imagining her bum in those jeans bent over the booth of the coconut shy, he conceded there was no getting away from the ride or Evie. His heart soared with fear-filled excitement.

*****

The funfair had been what Evie needed. It felt like their friendship from months ago before lust got in the way. It was a relief to get unspoken issues out into the open. The argument days earlier had been cruel for both of them, but it was what they'd needed to move forward. Although if not for Jack's sneaky tricks, they wouldn't have dealt with the aftermath. They were both so stubborn. But with their friendship rekindled, the sexual tension sizzled.

Occasionally she'd test Josh by patting his arse or stroking his arms while talking to him. It was an act of trust but accompanied by a tantalising tease—the flirting of two people testing where they were with each other. Josh's eyes locked with hers, and although he wore a hint of a smile, she couldn't guarantee what he thought.

"I owe you a teddy. Sorry, I didn't win you one," Evie said as Josh grabbed her hand. He brought it to his lips and brushed her knuckles with his lips. Light filled her belly.

"You got me through that terrifying swings ride. You gave me an evening of fun and made me laugh, especially when you shouted at the manager of the coconut shy for cheating, even though it was obvious you can't throw." Evie shrugged with a cheeky grin. "But more importantly than all of that, you forgave me. You don't owe me anything."

"That's where you're wrong," she replied, pulling him closer. Teasing him was irresistible. He swallowed loudly. His Adam's apple bobbled. Evie licked her lips as his eyes locked with hers. "I owe you something sweet that melts on your tongue."

Josh's brow furrowed. Suddenly he smiled broadly, threw his head back, and laughed. "Ice cream. You owe me ice cream for the ride."

"And I thought you were just a pretty face. I can't get anything past you," Evie replied with a wink before dragging him to the ice cream vendor.

Although she'd only drunk soft drinks that night, Bianca-style confidence filled her. Surely Josh's presence wasn't more empowering than alcohol? He'd matched her cokes with local beers that gave his cheeks an adorable glow.

Evie reached for a little plastic spoonful of ice cream and popped it between her lips. Using her mouth to its full effect, she sucked the spoon dry. Every last drop of the creamy fluid-like substance slipped down her throat, coating it with a chill. Her heavy-lidded eyes fixed on Josh, and she purposely toyed with the end of the spoon as it rested between her lips. Her trust that he wouldn't hurt her grew with her confidence. She turned and licked the utensil to remind him of her capabilities, and occasionally her tongue peeked out, flicking around the inanimate object before she sucked hard once more.

Josh wetted his lips and slowly swallowed as he moved from foot to foot, his eyes never leaving her mouth. His whole body trembled as she clenched her thighs and sucked once more.

"Don't you want any ice cream?" she purred with fresh empowerment.

With his finger, he pushed his collar to the side. He reminded Evie of a horny cartoon cat. Pixelated hearts would probably jump out of his eyes if she continued teasing.

"I'm happy watching you," he joked, but his voice strained.

Her amusement was her downfall. The next spoonful didn't make it between her lips. Instead, the ice cream slipped off the plastic. It dove to the V of her T-shirt and landed on the curve of her breasts. Josh's eyes pinned on her chest with the same combined awe and desire he'd given when he rubbed her clit.

The heat from her skin melted the ice cream quickly. Sticky, wet dribbles of ice cream dripped lower.

"You okay?" she asked tentatively. The hunger emblazoned on Josh's face was new, and her belly flopped with lust as her hormones woke from their slumber.

"We need to get you home. Clean you up," he grunted.

"But—"

"Please, Evie. Let me take you home." His pained desire paused as his eyes softened and his cheeks heated. She smiled and nodded. A tickle of excitement criss-crossed over her shoulders. He couldn't be drunk, but he had to be at least tipsy. Sober Josh wouldn't act like this.

Evie's gaze never left his face. "I'll get us a taxi," she replied with a heat that blistered her body.

CHAPTER SIXTEEN

What if he changed his mind? "I don't have to stay," Evie said uncertainly when they were in the taxi, but Josh silenced her with a touch. His finger trailed down her chest before dipping between her breasts. An intimacy that had been missing from their moment in the bathroom on Sunday night accompanied the touch.

Evie sat, wide-eyed, as he raised his digit. Melted ice cream covered the tip. He fixed her with his dark stare as his finger disappeared into his mouth. Slowly he sucked every last drop off, causing her core to burn in anticipation of what might be next.

"You taste better than I imagined," he hummed, licking his lips.

Her words died in her throat. This side of Josh was unexpected, and she didn't know how to counter it.

He rubbed the loose strands of her strawberry blonde hair between his fingers, and Evie ground herself in the worn leather seat beside him. It was as if he was caressing her scalp. A tingle passed through her limbs, and goose pimples covered her naked arms.

"You don't wear your hair down these days," he said as he toyed with a strand of her hair, just enough to cause an unexpected sensation of pleasurable pain.

"Not enough time to style it," she whispered.

"I like when you have it up too," he said with a voice so deep it reached between her legs. "It means I can do this." His lips brushed her neck, and she gasped in pleasure.

"We're here," the taxi driver called out, ceasing their moment.

Josh wobbled as he got out of the taxi. She didn't want to go home, but what if they needed to spend more time on their friendship, or what if Josh—

"Come on, Evie," he called into the taxi.

"You're drunk and should go straight to bed."

"I'm tipsy at best. Trust me. Now get in here if you want to." His smile was devilish, and it filled her with filthy fantasies.

"But I thought—"

"I've got to clean you up, remember? I can't have you all sticky when you've not made it to my bed."

She caught a choked chuckle from the taxi driver.

"Okay," she consented with a giddy smile. Josh grabbed her hand and swept her out of the taxi and to his door.

Within moments she was in the hallway with Josh behind her.

The slam of the door made her jump.

"Everyone is out; we have the place to ourselves," he said, mistaking her quiet for confusion. "Now, come with me."

She was good at sex, yet the promise of something with Josh left her knees trembling like she was a teenager on her first date. Evie stumbled when Josh took her hand and guided her up the stairs to his room. The fear of what this meant for them was undeniable. She'd wanted this for so long. What if it was awful or he'd had better?

Closing the bedroom door behind her, she turned to find Josh statue still and tracking her movements. His erection through his clothes made her mouth water.

I'm his midnight feast.

"I've wanted to kiss you properly for months. What we did in the bathroom was incredible, but I want to do it properly when it's not a dare and when there's no idiot men on the other side of the door listening," he stated. Evie's breath hitched. There was no reluctance in his voice. It was nothing like the Josh she'd witnessed before.

There was a tenable charge to the room, and her confidence surged.

"So why haven't you, Josh?" she teased, dropping her bag and rolling her shoulders to draw attention to her cleavage.

"Timing," he growled. "So you want me too, then, do you?"

His look of intent was one aspect of his control. The normally faltering Josh was coaxing fear from her body with a seductive tease. But her friend was in that aroused body too. The speed with which his Adam's apple bobbed and the subconscious scratching of his wrist revealed his nerves. It was a surprising turn-on. He wasn't casually making demands or bored until she took control. He wanted her, and it mattered. She wasn't another generic fuckable body. His eyes dropped to her breasts, and he licked his lips. Her pussy clenched.

"I'd hate you to think I'm using you to fulfil a need or that I don't respect you, because I do, but shit, Evie. I want to know what it's like to kiss your breasts, your nipples rubbing against my tongue as you push them against me. I want to worship every part of you." His truth hit her hard.

She couldn't recall any guy speaking to her like that and meaning it.

His eyes bored a hole into her body as she took the hem of her T-shirt and slowly drew it up.

Josh's body shook as he stepped closer. His gaze licked her naked skin as if scorching flames devoured her form. Her mouth was bone dry, and as she flung her T-shirt to the side, she repeatedly swallowed to stop her tongue from sticking to the roof of her mouth. But his next move was agonisingly slow. Evie bucked her hips as if willing him to act. He shook his head and reached for her hands, pinning them above her head with one hand while his fingers stroked her wrist.

"This is how I wanted to kiss you before." His palm cupped her face, the care behind his caress like purifying baptismal water.

With his thumb, he delicately traced her lips, and it was like he was gradually joining Evie to him. It was simple and yet intimate. Each stroke was attentive and filled with adoration. Her heart seemed to stop at his worship of her. Opening her lips slightly, she took a moment to graze the pad of his thumb with her teeth.

The juddering erection pushing against her wasn't enough. She wanted more.

"Evie," he warned with a grunt more masculine than she expected, the lust between them more potent than she'd experienced. The pained grin on his face was magnificent.

For a moment, they stood, transfixed, studying each other's faces.

Josh's head dipped, and he leant his body against hers. Then he reached around to her neck and eased her closer, bringing her lips to his. His peck was firm but brief. She whimpered at the barest of contact and received a chuckle that rumbled against every inch of her form.

"Not enough?" he whispered against her lips. His closeness teased her body, and she rolled her hips against him before stopping him.

She breathed him in. "No," she barely said before he pulled her against him again and kissed her with a fiery passion.

Blood instantly rushed between her thighs. His tongue nudged her lips open, and he feasted on her. Their tongues were fighting yet indulging in a mutual appreciation of each other. The months of teasing and unspoken needs culminated in a kiss that gave release while demanding more. His hands dug into her hair, and she pulled him hard against her, barely resisting the desire to rip at his shirt. Her heart thundered as it swelled with delight.

Suddenly her knees bowed as the backs hit the edge of the bed. She fell against the softness of the duvet and languished in the view of Josh's hairy chest as he undid his shirt. A thrill hit her belly as he made her fantasies a reality. He paused at the shiny buckle of his belt, his face a silent question.

She nodded with a toothy grin and was rewarded with a trembling Josh ripping at his belt. He yanked it through the loops before depositing it unceremoniously on the floor. He pulled his jeans down and off too.

His thick erection peeked out of the front of his boxers. "Fucking hell," she whimpered, and she reached for the edge of his waistband.

But he stood back. Her earlier fear threatened her excitement until he added, "I want you to. I've never wanted anything more, but I won't last long if you so much as touch me. And I have to last a long time for you. You deserve to be pleasured until you can't take another second." She hummed in adoration as he eased down the cups of her bra and thumbed her nipples. "I've fantasised about you naked for longer than you know."

She quickly shirked off her jeans. His eyebrows raised in surprise, but he didn't say anything. Instead, he was transfixed by her legs. His gaze travelled from her lace thong to her delicate dancer's ankles. She whipped off her bra while he was distracted.

"Fuck," he murmured as his eyes fixed on her chest and he removed his boxers. His dick bobbed in appreciation, and he absentmindedly palmed his cock. She thrust her pelvis into the duvet at the glorious sight of pre-cum beading the tip of his cock.

"Your breasts are beautiful," he grunted before diving onto the bed. Her gasps turned to moans when his lips wrapped around her nipple. Then, in a frenzy, he pleasured her. One moment, his tongue was lathering her flesh, and the next, he was biting the tip of the nipple. Her sex thrust against his body as he leaned over her and combined gratification and pain to tease her mercilessly. Josh's caresses rewrote the memories of hurt caused by guys from her past. His touch was as healing as it was agonising, and she immersed herself in every flick of his tongue.

A moan of exhilaration made him suddenly raise his head. "I did that?" he asked.

She nodded vigorously, and his mouth transformed into a grin, making her smile as widely.

His lips brushed down her body as he watched her. He gripped her knickers between her fingers and dragged them down her legs before tossing them across the room.

"Evie, your pussy is fucking everything." His mouth

hovered above her pussy. His breath caressed her clit, and she fought not to thrust her hips to meet his lips. "I wonder if you moan when I do this."

He pressed his hand into her stomach as he licked her, his tongue flat against her pussy. Evie cried out as he sucked at her clit. Her hands grasped his head and stroked his hair as he tasted her. His beard brushed her thighs, tickling them and adding to the sensations that threatened to overwhelm her. His tongue dipped inside her, and she writhed on the bed against his touch.

He lifted one leg over his shoulder, and his tongue went deeper. Evie's chest rose and fell as she screamed and gasped for breath. She hadn't had anyone go down her in so long, but it hadn't been this good. His teeth brushed her clit, and she dug her nails into his scalp. He looked up at her with a grin that made her heart ache. Her wetness covered his beard. Timing had been against them too many times, and she desperately wanted more.

"Josh. I want you inside me. I need it."

"Fuck, Evie, I want it more than I can explain, but I haven't got anything. You know, anything safe."

She pointed to her handbag, which she'd dropped by the bedroom door. Josh jumped off the bed and brought it to her. Evie fished through it as her whole body shook and her pussy ached. "It's my lucky Josh condom."

Josh's chuckle was strained as her fingers closed in on the foil wrapper, and she held it aloft.

"Would you put it on for me?"

Josh grunted and stared. No one had looked at her in awe before, but Josh's thick erection distracted her from revelling in the moment.

She ran a finger up his cock.

"Evie," he grunted between gritted teeth.

"Sorry." But she gave him a devilish smile and slowly slid the condom down his rigid member. She lay back and opened her legs wide, inviting him closer. Josh kneeled in front of her. "Fuck me," she panted as he lined up his cock.

He was gentle at first, but he began to thrust as she moaned her encouragement.

She pulled his hand to her clit, and he eagerly took note. Zips of electricity hit her belly as he rubbed her clit like she'd taught him days earlier.

"Yes," she hissed.

Each time she coached him, he followed without question.

His cock pushed into her, faster and harder each time. She moved her feet to his bum cheeks to pull him deeper. Each time he slammed into her, she pulled him against her. Her throat was hoarse from shouting out his name. Occasionally he'd slow while his mouth worshipped her breasts before he resumed pounding her. Sparks of unyielding arousal overwhelmed every nerve ending in her shaking body.

"I want to come. I'm close, but I want you to come first."

"Rub my clit and bite my nipple as you fuck me," she instructed. Josh's eyebrows lifted in surprise, but he followed her request, and soon, the telltale storm of tightening muscles and frantic bursts of tension made her back arch. Her mind went blank as she screamed with joy. Endorphins saturated her limbs as everything clenched was released, and her orgasm roared like a hurricane.

Wave after wave of ecstasy continued to shake her already quaking body as Josh bellowed her name and came inside her. Her orgasm was like nothing else. Josh collapsed beside her but continued to stroke her skin, aiding her in coming down from her climax. Evie's body continued to pulse and throb as he stared at her in awe.

"I need to tell you things," Josh whispered once her breathing had calmed. "I promised."

But she shook her head and whispered, "Tomorrow, okay? We need sleep."

He nodded and gave her a sweet smile as she released him from the condom. Josh chucked it in the bin before returning to the bed and kissing her forehead. Then, wrapping both of them in the duvet, Evie snuggled up against him and drifted into a deep and necessary sleep.

Chapter Seventeen

Bright sunshine blinded her, and Evie winced as she opened her eyes. Everything ached. Where was she?

Framed rugby posters hung on the walls, joined by one of Aidan's paintings. She was wrapped in a navy-blue bedspread with red spots. Josh's room. It reminded her of a student returning home from university to find his parents had decorated in his absence. She reached out a hand to ask if he was Peter Pan. Her fingers brushed against his pillow.

Fear bubbled below the surface.

Evie slipped on one of his T-shirts. Although she was sore in places she hadn't used for a while, his musky scent left her craving more from him. But why had he left her alone? Sex rarely made her vulnerable. Often it was a simple act that didn't need romanticising, but this was different. It wasn't that Josh was the first guy she'd slept with in a couple of years. It had meant something.

Evie searched for him and eventually found Josh in the kitchen. He perched on a stool at the kitchen counter, his back to her. His muscles rippled as he stretched his arm in the air and moved his head from side to side. Did he have to be so fucking irresistible? Tentatively she pecked him on the cheek. "Morning, sexy," she murmured.

Josh jerked away and stared at her over his shoulder. It

was as if she'd put a Taser to his groin, not kissed him.

"I've got to go," he grunted into a phone she hadn't seen clutched in his hand. He walked to the other side of the counter, and a berating voice, audible from his earpiece, followed him.

The words were a mystery, but Josh's anxiety, evident from his wary face and eyes that darted around the room, seeped through her.

"Okay," he replied to the mystery male. The countertop became a barrier between them, and Evie had no intention of crossing it.

Was this the regret-filled rejection she'd tried not to anticipate?

Josh dropped the phone onto the counter. He dipped his head and stood as still as a statue.

*****

Josh used the countertop as his ballast, hoping it would keep him steady against the emotions threatening to overwhelm him.

"I was surprised you weren't still in bed," Evie said.

"Yeah, I had a call," Josh replied, refusing to look at her. The night before had been incredible. That morning, his heart soared as he lay in bed, staring at her sleeping, smiling at her cute snores that she'd deny if he told her she made them. How did he get so lucky to wake up next to his best friend?

And then his dad had phoned, and his world crashed. His night with Evie was everything. Finally, he could embrace the real him that wasn't scared of every choice. It wasn't just that he'd made her moan and scream for him, although that meant more than she'd know. It was that he felt genuine joy in her presence.

"I'm surprised how hungry I am after everything we ate last night." He barely heard what Evie said as the call from his dad poked through all joy he'd felt in the last twelve hours.

He fisted his hands as his dad's words from their phone call filled his head. How was their conversation already seared into his memory? Josh had barely managed a hello before his dad launched into his lecture. "You'd better tell me what you did, or you won't cope with the amount of trouble I will bring on you. The deal was no secrets between us. I can't protect you like I did before if I don't know what you did. So what did you do to your wrist that got you dropped from Saturday's game? They won't sign you for next season now. You've fucked up again."

"It's nothing," Josh had attempted to explain. "I can still drive, but Coach wants me to rest it. I was climbing over a fence and lost my footing."

"Were you drunk?" How had he known? "We've talked about your reckless and selfish behaviour before. Is this about Lulu?"

And that was when Evie kissed him and called him sexy loud enough for his dad to hear.

"I've got to go," Josh had said, his face burning in humiliation.

"Who is that? This conversation isn't over. You've been lying to me a lot recently. I won't share this conversation with your mum, as it will make her ill. However, I will be in touch soon."

"Okay."

"And say hello to your new friend. It sounds like

you've got another woman to destroy your life. There's something wrong with you, boy. Goodbye."

The phone had gone dead.

"Earth to Josh," Evie shouted, waving a palm in front of his face. "Are you going to cook something or—"

He reared back. He needed space to plan how he was going to manage his dad. Should he call him straight back, visit the house, or leave him to cool off? He hadn't disobeyed his dad since before Lulu's death.

"What is going on?" Evie demanded her hands on her hips.

Josh blinked and stared at Evie. His stomach bubbled, and acid climbed up his throat. He walked to the sink, but she followed him and tapped his shoulder until he turned to face her. "Why do you always have to be like that? Why can't you give me space? There's always an argument on your lips. Some women are soft, quiet, and submissive." What was he saying? He needed to calm down. He would have made her breakfast and taken it to her in bed, but his dad had riled him. What if she'd heard how his dad had spoken to him? Would she think he wasn't man enough for her?

"You want me to be submissive?" she ranted with a twisted mouth. "Yes, Josh, no, Josh. How would you like your toast, oh Supreme Being? Maybe I should suck your cock and open my legs while I scream about your sexual prowess and praise your mighty truncheon. You are my king, and I will bow in servitude as you shove your cock wherever you like."

"Are you saying I'm crap in bed?"

Her eyebrows nearly reached her scalp when she spat, "You got crap in bed from what I said?"

He wanted to crumble in a corner and let the world go

on without him. There were too many expectations. Evie stared at him like he was a specimen in a jar. He'd woken with a smile. He wanted to give her breakfast and hold her as they planned their day. But now his frustration was out of control. What should he say?

"You're different this morning. You were sweet and caring last night. Don't get me wrong; you were incredible too. But I'm waiting for you to reject me like you normally do," she said, her voice softer than before. Her gaze was unrelenting.

Josh's shoulders slumped in defeat.

"Who was on the phone? My Josh is confident, a brave man with a beautiful heart. But your body language said the opposite. Who does that to you?"

"None of your business," he replied, unnerved by the ease with which she saw through his façade. Shame instantly covered him when she turned away. Evie didn't cry in front of others, maybe not at all, but it was evident from her hunched shoulders she was upset. He'd fucked up again. She wanted his truth. He stepped closer. "I'm sor—"

"Fine, you keep your secrets. I'm going. I'm not standing here while you use me as your emotional punching bag before you inevitably reject me again." Evie strode out of the kitchen.

Josh ran after her, but she was fast when angry, and he reached her as she stormed through the bedroom door.

"Speak to me, please," he asked frantically, but she didn't turn or acknowledge his request. Her back was an impenetrable wall. "Evie, I need to talk to you." But it was as futile as trying to tie shoelaces while wearing oven gloves.

Suddenly he spied her T-shirt behind his plastic

bedroom chair. She must have tossed it in the corner the night before. Josh scooped it up and held it tightly to his chest as she continued her search for her clothes. He needed to explain the call.

"I can't find my top," she mumbled absentmindedly, purposely turning away from him as she thrust her arms into her bra and hooked it. She tossed things around the room. Suddenly her green eyes narrowed when she saw what he clutched. "Give it back."

"Not until you talk to me."

"I'm not talking to someone who speaks to me like you do. I'll walk out of here without it."

"I'm sorry, Evie." His reward was a roll of her eyes. "What have I got to do to get you to stay and talk to me?"

"There's nothing you can do." At the loud vibration of her phone on his nightstand, Josh turned. With him temporarily distracted, Evie whipped the T-shirt out of his hands before reaching for the phone.

"There's something I need to tell you," he said, but she was too busy answering the call to hear his mumbling. Second best to a piece of plastic.

He deflated when she said, "Okay, I'll be there as soon as I can." Evie rushed around the room, reaching for clothes and strewn items until she tossed her bag over her shoulder and headed out his bedroom door.

"Please tell me what's going on. I'm sorry about earlier. I want to tell you some stuff, maybe not now, but later today." Desperation filled his voice. It was time for honesty.

She turned and stared as if she'd already forgotten Josh was there. Her face was deathly pale, and her legs tremored. Josh stepped closer. How did he deal with this version of her? "I don't know how long I will be. I've got to go."

"Then let me come," he asked, defeated.

"Fine." She surprised him, but he kept his face neutral. "You can drive me. It will be quicker by car. I'll meet you outside. Can you lend me a jumper? Because we could be a while."

Without waiting for an answer, she left the room. Was this another ruse, and she'd be gone before he got outside? He grabbed his essentials, including his favourite jumper. It was from the only Six Nations match he'd played in and represented one of the proudest moments in his life. He didn't let anyone touch it, let alone borrow it. He'd told his dad he'd lost it so he couldn't demand it for himself.

"Thank you," she said as he locked up. He wasn't sure if her thanks or that she was still there surprised him more.

He reached for her hand as they got in the car. She didn't pull away as she told him to drive to the other side of town.

What the hell was going on?

Chapter Eighteen

Josh kept his mouth shut and focused on the road.

Evie gave minimal directions and revealed nothing about the destination, but he didn't challenge her. Her stoic face conveyed nothing. Was the chill in the car because of their altercation or related to the destination? As he turned into something resembling a care home car park situated on the outskirts of town, his shock was evident, but she didn't notice or chose not to say anything. It was as if she'd turned to stone. She was drowning. How could he rescue her?

They walked a stark white corridor before turning and walking down another equally soulless space. It was like a dream or a nightmare. The intense heat from the care home barely registered as Evie's sorrow came off her in waves. Who were they there to see, and was this who had been calling her all these times? The home was possessed by intense sadness, as if the souls in the rooms were waiting for something awful. Evie faltered as they neared the end of the corridor. Why hadn't she mentioned something before now? Had she carried this level of sadness for months? Maybe she'd have trusted him if he was a better friend.

They came to a sudden halt outside a bedroom.

"Will you wait here?" she asked with a voice icy enough to fight the furnace of the sweltering space.

Without waiting for an answer, she ducked into the bedroom. Her hunched shoulders and slow gait suggested she headed to a battle she couldn't win.

Through the gap in the heavy door, Josh made out a person lying in a bed that reminded him of a hospital. The smell was similar too. A hint of burning sulphur hit the air and left him questioning his senses. He continued to stare through the small gap, moving his head from side to side to see more. The bed covers were ivory white, but the person in the bed was a mystery. Not that he'd recognise them anyway. He didn't know anyone from her life other than Jack. She was his best friend, but he didn't even know if she had a family. The bedroom carried the same air of hopelessness that he'd seen on Evie's face when her phone rang.

There was a nurse in the room too. She gave Evie a sad smile. Darkness held the room and its occupants captive. Josh stared in confusion and terror.

"I can't believe Mrs. Draper won't be with us much longer." Josh jumped at the soft voice behind him. He turned to find a woman in a blue nurse's tunic. "Poor Evie has been such a tower of strength, but I'm glad she won't be alone, not today." She seemed a bit cliché ridden, but maybe she'd help him understand what was happening. Of course, Mrs. Draper had to be Evie's relative because they had the same surname.

"I'm here for her if she'll let me be."

"I can't believe Evie's gran has only been here eighteen months. It feels a lot longer," the nurse said with a gentle smile. Her thick-rimmed glasses and tight grey perm reminded him of an owl. The image distracted him temporarily but not long enough to stop him from realising that they'd become friends a little over eighteen months ago. It was also when Evie had appeared to change from Bianca. She'd eventually quit smoking, partied less, and didn't spend her spare time drunk. "The last couple of months have been the worst."

"Because Evie has been busy?" Josh towered over his new companion, but they didn't appear intimidated as some people did at his height. It was another thing he hated about himself.

"No, because Enid, Mrs. Draper, has been dying from a tumour. Evie's here every day, and she's been working all the hours to pay for the care. It's expensive, but Evie wanted the best support. She's never grumbled or complained though, but bless her. All the nurses have talked about how exhausted she is whenever she visits. Enid's death will hit her hard."

"And you're sure Enid is going to die today?" It sounded too false and cold to say this woman's name in the context of death when he hadn't known her. Why hadn't he asked Evie about her family before now? She hadn't asked about his, although she might have glimpsed his dad at the grounds when she attended Aidan's practices years before. Maybe neither of them wanted to bring up topics that would ruin the safe space they'd created with each other.

"Yes, I'm afraid so. We've been waiting for the last fortnight, but it won't make it any less painful. Evie has often rushed in, wondering if it would be that day, but we're certain we'll say goodbye to Enid within the next twelve hours."

That explained the phone calls, the times she'd run out, and why she'd worn the dress from Patrick's blessing overnight. And he'd accused her of doing the walk of shame. He'd made it about him when she was suffering. *I was a bastard to her.* But this wasn't the time to wallow in his shame or throw himself at her feet in apology. He needed to be there for her in whatever way she needed.

"I'm Josh, by the way," he stuttered, unsure whether to shake the nurse's hand or smile.

She pulled him in for a hug, and he hung there as she replied, "I'm Jane."

"Hi, Jane," he said with an awkward nod before she pointed out some chairs, and they sat.

They stayed together in silence for hours or minutes, eyes fixed on a stiff and uncompromising bedroom door. Finally, the nurse that had sat with Enid when Evie arrived came out. When he explained that Enid had slipped into a coma and that there would be mere hours left, Josh verbalised the obvious question.

"Shouldn't someone call the rest of the family?"

"Evie's the only family Enid has. No one else has visited. So she's been alone in all of this, until today, until you." Jane gazed quizzically. Did she realise she'd shared confidential information, thinking he was closer to Evie? Surely Evie had more in her life than just him.

"You should sit with her. Evie will need you," Jane instructed.

"Evie never lets me help her," Josh protested. "If she wanted me, then she'd ask."

The wise owl's eyes pinned him. "Evie brought you with her. From what I've learnt over the last year and a half from Enid, Evie has her reasons for closing off from people. Right now, more than ever, she needs someone by her side. By bringing you along, she's chosen you to be that person."

Josh stood, unconvinced, his fears rising in his chest. But he'd made her bring him along, and she only let him because she needed a driver.

He opened his mouth, but at the glare from Jane, he pinned it shut. He couldn't go in there. Evie didn't want him with her, or she would have said it because she always said what she thought. He attempted to stand, but his legs turned to lead, fixing him in the chair when he should be comforting his best friend and the woman he adored. He reached for his phone. Jack would know what to do better than him.

The bright red exit sign beckoned him. Maybe it was time to give Evie what she'd desired before and leave her alone for good.

Chapter Nineteen

Evie stroked her nan's hand gently, unable to look away from the faltering movements of Enid's chest as she breathed. Her other hand hung limply by her side as if, limb by limb, she was sinking. She arrived in time to say goodbye, but it hadn't been long before Enid slipped into a coma. Evie watched and waited. The skin on Enid's hand was thin, and Evie made out the tiny blue veins threading from her wrist to her fingers. The hands that had always been ready for a fight were like tissue paper. The battle was nearly over. Evie promised Enid that she wouldn't die alone.

Evie swept a finger underneath her eyes, but she had no tears. Her dad had told her that cold people like her didn't cry. Evie would be alone soon, and it was exactly what she deserved for hurting others. Her nan had been the life and soul of every social event, but now she was barely a shadow of herself.

"I love you, Nana," she whispered. "And I'm scared of being alone."

But as Evie stared unblinking at the only person who had loved her unconditionally for who she was, she accepted that she had no one.

Still, the tears refused to fall, but it was as if her heart wept. Memories of their time together replayed on a loop, clumping to form leaden pain inside her stomach. Enid had suffered but especially over the last two months. Cancer had eaten away at her stomach before possessing the rest of her body like an unnatural sickness. At least it had never got her brain.

A sob rose in Evie's throat. It was the first day in eight years since moving to be with her that Evie hadn't heard her nan laugh.

Don't cry, don't let it out. The grief would consume Evie if she did, and she needed to function. No one would help her, and she needed to fight to survive.

I'm all alone now.

A strong hand slipped into her shivering one. Josh sat motionless beside her. He gave her a gentle smile, but his eyes wavered uncertainly.

Together, they sat in silence and waited. Josh's presence made things a bit easier. The pain ripping at her heart was more acute than she'd believed possible, but her loneliness subsided for now.

They stayed like that for several hours, not saying anything. Josh moved to offer her refreshment. She didn't argue or fight when he encouraged her to drink or nibble on biscuits. Their hands never parted, even when she got up to kiss her nan softly on the cheek after the nurse told her she was gone.

"I'll never forget you. I love you. Thank you for always loving me, no matter what," Evie whispered as heartache threatened to force her crumbling in a corner.

The rest of the time passed in a whirlwind. There were discussions with the nurses at the care home, but it was like Evie was a ghost, and instantly she forgot the conversation if she had heard it in the first place.

Lying in Josh's bed, the duvet wrapped around her, and her head resting against his chest, she recalled how he'd helped her upstairs. He'd gently undressed her like a sick child before tucking her up and joining her. The care was more than she'd experienced from a man before. It was more than she could cope with, and finally, she cried. They were like heavy raindrops, splattering the burning asphalt after an intense heatwave. Her protector was gone. Her nana was the only person who had always been on her side and loved her beyond reason. Everyone left or pushed her away, and Josh would be next.

"Sorry," she whispered between sobs so intense that it was as if her heart was suffocating under slabs of concrete that strangers strode over obliviously.

"It's okay, Evie, I've got you." He kissed the top of her head.

The hands usually used to destroy others when he played on the rugby field held her gently as she wept.

Eventually, exhaustion ravaged her body and mind, and her tears slowed. But her pain would always be there. Her nan had talked about friends and family who'd died. She'd described a theory of grief she'd read by someone called Tonkin where grief was a jar with a ball in it. The ball was your grief, and the jar was your life. She'd explained one night over tea and toast when Evie had returned in the early hours after partying with local influences or footballers; it was impossible to remember because there'd been so many nights out. Nan said that the ball didn't get bigger or smaller but that the jar grew. Grief was always there, but life changed, and you filled it with new things until one day, your grief wasn't the most significant thing in your life.

The room was dark, the blinds drawn, which made it tricky to decipher whether it was night or day. But nothing mattered anymore.

While lying in the darkness, it was as if her heart was barely held together by masking tape. Her contemplations risked her sniffles turning into sobs again until Josh said the unexpected. "Tell me about your nan, please. I want to learn more about her."

She'd had no idea that it was what she needed until he'd asked. Her stories poured forth, and soon they laughed about the day a flying beach umbrella hit her nan or when she'd threatened a burly bullying youth with the back of her hand if he carried on "being a cheeky whatsit." Nan had said to him, "Young man, you're not too big to put over my knee."

"He was too big though. He made you look average height!"

As soon as she'd finished one story, another fell from her lips. Her favourite was when three pensioners called at the house to take her nan out on Valentine's Day. "So she made all three go out simultaneously on a quadruple date with her. It was quite a spectacle, especially when they demanded to share a rickshaw. The best part was at the end of the night when they all attempted to be the last guy to kiss her goodnight. Ultimately, we had to call the police to stop them from waving their sticks at each other. The policeman who broke it up became her new boyfriend. She was a charmer, my nana, but only when she wanted to be. The policeman had been my favourite, but the relationship didn't last long."

"How come?"

"Nan loved being single. She dumped him the day he bought her roses and declared his love for her. She used to tell me, 'The moment you accept their roses and love is the moment you agree to put up with their faults and their massive bag of shit forever. You might as well give up on your sanity and independence. Never again for me.' What a woman she was."

The hours of laughter were interspersed with tears. Eventually, Evie couldn't talk or cry anymore. The emotions attempting to own her body left her exhausted.

"Thank you," she offered Josh before kissing him sweetly and snuggling up. Quickly she fell under the spell of sleep, his warm body keeping her safe.

Evie stared at Josh's fluttering eyelashes. What was he dreaming about? Tears prickled in her eyes, but she wiped them away with the back of her hands. If only she could rid herself of grief as quickly. There was a hint of joy resting in her heart too. She'd been close to shattering or getting so drunk she'd have made painful mistakes last night, but Josh was there for her, and his care had stopped her from breaking.

She stretched her arms under the duvet to cuddle him. She gasped, but he barely stirred. He was rock hard.

"Maybe I should say thank you in the only way I can," she murmured as she slid down the bed and started to lick his cock. Josh moaned in his sleep, inadvertently spurring her on. She engulfed his erection with loud slurps and was rewarded when his fingers clutched at her hair. It took a quick glimpse to see his eyes were closed. Was he sleeping through this?

Evie worked his cock with her hands and mouth, gripping the base while taking him deep against her tongue. She fought the grief that rose in her like a spectre. Desperation controlled her moves as she tried to forget everything else and focus on Josh, whose gentle thrusts sped up. She pulled away.

"Josh, slow down," Evie whispered through his sleepy fog.

Suddenly he froze before pulling her up towards him. He opened and closed his eyes several times, and she pushed him away.

"I have to do this. It's all I'm good for," Evie pleaded.

But instead of arguing or letting her go, Josh pulled her into his arms. Tears prickled Evie's eyes, and she shook violently against him. Last night was the first time she'd allowed him to see her vulnerability, and she regretted it now that slithers of light appeared from the gaps in the curtains. Fear ripped through her, but she willed herself to quiet the voices that threatened to stab holes in the dam she used to keep her grief at bay. She couldn't bear his rejection. The way he'd comforted her as she'd sobbed her heart out was beyond anything she'd had in a long time, and now he was doing it again.

"You don't have to give me a blow job, Evie," he said as he held her close.

"Wasn't it good?" Pleasing men was all she was good for. Memories of Gavin's insults stabbed another hole in the dam. Grief was spilling through.

"No, not at all." Josh eased her head away from his chest to look at her. He implored her understanding. "Fucking hell, you're as amazing at that as you are at everything else."

She released the deep breath she hadn't realised she'd held. "Then why did you make me stop?" She hated the weak voice that replaced her normally confident one.

"Because you don't need to do this. I'm not going to take advantage of your grief."

Her head dropped in shame. "I want to do something I can do. I hate feeling useless and pathetic. This might stop the pain temporarily. You were hard when I woke up, and I wanted to make you happy in the only way I could."

It was impossible to gather her thoughts, but Josh's quick kiss surprised her, as did his following words. "You make me happy in many ways, and when you're around, I don't see anyone else. I can't get enough of any part of you, and you're exceptional with my dick, but that's not all you're good for. You're loving, caring, and awesome in too many ways for me to remember right now, especially with the blood rushing from my brain. But I want you to do whatever you need right now. Grief hits people in unexpected ways, and it rarely makes sense."

Josh's kind words stabbed at the dam, too, but Evie fought to keep a tight hold on the pain. "I needed taking care of last night, and you did more than I asked for." Her voice was so quiet.

He nodded, but his eyes narrowed suspiciously. "Yes," he replied, drawing out the word.

"And sometimes I get angry when you try and protect me, and I don't want you to."

"I'm sorry I do that. It's been drummed into me that women need protecting."

"Well, I don't. I need someone to hold my hand." Evie paused. "I thought if I got you off, I could stop feeling for ten minutes."

"What makes you think I'd last more than two?" he teased with a grin that made her breathe a sigh of relief. His humour broke the tension. She gripped his head between her hands and kissed him hard on the mouth.

"I don't know what I want now. So you're not going to reject me for changing my mind?" Her vulnerability was spilling out.

Instead of words, Josh made his promises with kisses. He stroked his fingers through her hair. Evie wrapped her legs around Josh, and they made out as the house started to get noisy with blundering rugby players. Doors banged, and Max and Lucas shouted to each other about kit and breakfast. But Evie and Josh continued to kiss and hold each other. She'd give him a blow job, and it would be the best he'd had, but for now, being safely in his arms and revelling in his kisses was all she wanted.

Chapter Twenty

Evie's belly ached in a way that left her satisfied. With a famous Josh fry-up inside her and the tingles from the closeness they'd shared, she was ready to face the next battle. He'd managed to do the unthinkable and given her overwhelmed brain a temporary distraction, but the last remnants of calm would be gone soon.

"I need to pick up some stuff from my place. I need a change of clothes and a shower with something other than Lynx. You guys have every type known to man. I should go to the care home too," she said, running her plans aloud.

"Will you let me drive you?"

"Yes, of course," Evie said with a smile.

"Cool," he replied, but the grin he attempted to hide as he took the plates to the sink made a little glow fill her heart. Things in her life wouldn't be good for a long time, but his little smile gave her hope for the future.

Evie kept the conversation going as the car headed to her place, but there was no need to fill the silence like before. Occasionally Josh's hand brushed her thigh as he changed gear. It didn't matter if it was deliberate or accidental. She gave him a quick peck on the cheek. His smile was contagious, yet guilt tickled the back of her neck. Should she be smiling? Her nan had just died. But her nana would have told her off first for believing that. Enid had been dying for months and had forced Evie to find joy. She'd be elated to learn that it was Josh causing the precious moments of happiness.

But there was so much to do, and most of it would involve googling what to do when someone dies. Evie hadn't organised a family gathering before, let alone a funeral. And there would be the inevitable confrontation with her parents. Would they come or ignore her nana as they had her for years?

"I can't believe Nan died eight years to the day that I moved here, the twentieth of April," Evie whispered absentmindedly.

"That means today is the twenty-first of April?" Josh's hands snapped back to the wheel, gripping it tightly in panic. "Shit, shit, shit. I lost track of the dates."

His whole demeanour transformed, instantly turning him into a tightly coiled spring. "Is it okay if we take a quick detour?"

"Sure," she replied. Josh swung the car around at such a speed that she gripped the dashboard to stop her careering into him. The atmosphere suddenly had an edge. "Thank fuck I kept the present in the car."

Josh floored the accelerator and launched the car down the road before turning so sharply that Evie fell against him.

"Where are we going?" No response. Her Josh had changed, and it unnerved her.

Suddenly he hit the brakes. Evie's body jumped forward before the seat belt yanked her against the seat.

"Sorry," he mumbled without expression. "I'm not sure

how long I'll be. I guess you can come in if you want." He didn't wait for her reply. Instead, he flung open his door before slamming it and running around to the boot.

Evie eased herself from the car. Before she asked any questions he probably wouldn't answer, he headed down a pristine driveway with something shiny in his hands. She ran to keep up with him. Perfect flowers in bright pinks and yellows directed them towards the red-brick semi-detached house, edging a path that shone like someone had jet-washed it that morning. Not a pebble was out of place. The lace curtains in every window were poker straight and sparkled brightly in the sun blinding Evie. It was like something out of a catalogue for *Stepford Wives* homes.

I'm out of place already. She'd found a change of clothes in her bag, but her ragged denim skirt and T-shirt were for an emergency for a reason, and she needed something fresh. The best addition to the outfit was Josh's Six Nations hoody. It kept her warm and brought her comfort when she wore it. She shoved her hands into the middle pocket and took a sniff. She didn't care that she smelt like a teenage boy on the pull because it was like Josh's arms were around her.

"Whose house is this?" She panted as she tried to keep up. Her health was better than ever, but there wasn't an exercise regime in existence that enabled her to keep up with a professional rugby player on a mission.

"Oh, sorry," he replied, finally slowing his strides. He turned, and Evie held in her surprise at his wild eyes and taut lips. "This is where my parents live."

She pulled the elastic from around her wrist and used it to force her shaggy hair into a bun. "I'm about to meet your parents?" she squeaked.

"I guess. Sorry, you can wait in the car if you want," he replied nonchalantly. "I had to come by. It's my mum's birthday."

"Maybe that would be b—" she replied as they stood on the welcome mat that read "WIPE YOUR FEET! Thanks in advance. " But before she finished her reply or commented on the passive-aggressive doormat, the front door swung open.

"Ah, Joshua. I wondered when we'd hear from you," announced a man who resembled an older, shorter version of Josh. He was attractive, with blue eyes and slightly greying hair, but there was something about him that Evie didn't like. Maybe it was because she'd never met a guy's parents before, and she and Josh hadn't yet defined their relationship.

Suddenly the stranger's stare rested on her. His stern face changed to a brighter one, but with the added charm, there was a fakery around the edges that unnerved her. She'd bet he was the one who'd picked the doormat.

"And we're lucky enough to have you bring a lady to visit. Why didn't you warn us?"

Again the tone was bright but chastising too. She'd spent enough time with guys like this to be able to work the bad ones out. It was men like Josh she'd had no experience with. No wonder he was the biggest mind fuck she'd encountered.

The man reached out his hand for her to shake. "It's nice to meet you…"

"Evie," she supplied.

"Ah, Evie. What a beautiful name. Is it short for Evangeline, a lovely French name?"

"Ummm, yes."

"Ah, I love everything about France, except their rugby

team, of course." He chuckled, making her want to join in, although she'd have preferred to walk away. "I'm Robin, Josh's much more attractive dad." She nearly gagged. "It's great to meet you. Sadly, Josh has never mentioned you, but we look forward to hearing something. Surely, she's too beautiful to be your girlfriend, Josh. And what a nice jumper she's wearing. I'm sure you used to have a jumper like that before you told me you lost it."

"Your son is an amazing man," she uttered, but Josh's dad spoke over her, directly to Josh.

"Give your mum her present. She's been worrying about you as we waited for your visit. And don't forget to give our *surprise* guest a drink. We have wine if you don't consider it too early."

"I'm not drinking at the moment."

"You're not a teetotal type, are you? A woman like you should be having fun, especially if you're spending time with Josh. The unfortunate lad drives most people to drink." He tucked her arm in his and dragged her to the living room. "Josh gets his best bits from me, but then that's obvious."

"Ummm, right," she mumbled.

He laughed loudly. "Clever girl. Now tell me all about you."

Charm dripped from every pore. Robin listened to what she shared like she was the most crucial person in the world, but Evie refused to drop her guard. Her skin itched like she hadn't washed it in years. Robin was attentive and asked questions and gave opinions to appear likeable. Jokes fell effortlessly from his mouth, and he tested where he stood with casual touches to her arm when he offered her compliments. She sensed that if she said she didn't like it, he'd suggest he was the same with friends. Josh was nothing like him. They'd had a conversation early into their friendship where Evie had explained she wanted him to hug her or hold her hand if he wanted to. The few moments he instigated contact, Josh often paused, waiting for her consent.

Robin tried to be her confidant and asked thoughtful questions under the guise of being her new best friend, but he was angling for weaknesses. "I bet you don't realise how beautiful you are." Once, she would have admitted that she didn't. She'd worried about what people thought about her and presumed they believed she was stupid. He was like Peter, the guy from her past who learnt her secrets and used them to manipulate her. She'd fallen for everything he offered. The butterfly effect that led to her current life started with Peter.

Evie bade her time with Robin. She dodged his questions politely and used the opportunity to ask him questions, but his games were relentless. "Josh is a great player but can be a difficult adult. Some days I worry that he'll never be happy because of how he treats people and the things he says behind their backs. Like the things he's suggested about you…" Frustration and lies poured from him. He'd already admitted at the front door that he'd never heard about her. "You were with him yesterday morning, he told me. I had no idea he was sleeping with more than one woman. But it's not up to me to share these things. I'm looking out for you."

Smiling sweetly, she continued ignoring how his hand "accidentally" brushed her knee, although it made her skin crawl. It was as if Peter was sitting next to her again. Peter had destroyed her relationship with her family and instigated her fear of rejection. Bile hit the back of her throat at her memories of him.

Robin patted the seat next to him when they'd first sat, leaving her pinned next to him on the smaller-than-two-seater sofa. Like the driveway, the room was immaculate. *The Daily Mail* newspaper was folded neatly and sat on fanned-out magazines about various sports, including rugby. Evie inspected the floor for crumbs, lint, or anything that suggested the house was lived in, but the room was flawless. The cushions were plumped to perfection, and no one had left a mug or a watermark anywhere. Instead of making it a home, the room was sterile. As much as she hoped it was because Josh's mum was house-proud, a niggle told her it was due to the sinister man by her side. Every sentence was conniving. The speed with which he'd attempted to manipulate Evie, a stranger he'd never expected at his house, convinced her that his behaviour was ingrained. The guy was a grade-A piece of shit. He leaned closer. She shoved her hands in the pocket of the hoody and tried to recall Josh's arms around her. "So what went wrong with Josh? For example, what caused his recent drunken episode?" he asked.

The question caught her off guard, but immediately she rushed to Josh's defence. "I don't know. I wasn't with him. But I'm sure he had his reasons."

The mood of the room changed. "No reason is good enough to stop him playing. I shall be a laughing stock if he doesn't play on Saturday."

Evie waited for five ticks of the ugly carriage clock on the grey stone fireplace. How had someone as caring as Josh grown up in a soulless place? "I'm sure he'll be fine. The wrist is nearly healed."

Robin's eyes narrowed, and she prepared herself for

another snide comment. "I know my son, and he doesn't do things like this. While you're a beautiful and enchanting woman, you're not a qualified doctor, although I'm sure whatever it is you do, you're an expert at it. I believe I recognise you but can't remember from where?" He winked and slyly squeezed her upper thigh. She was under no illusion that he knew her from her glamour modelling. The bastard was trying to shame her.

Evie carefully removed his hand from her leg. She trembled as she remembered Peter's hand on her thigh.

Robin grinned. "Strong women have always been Josh's downfall, especially those with bodies like yours. I hope you're not another destroying—"

"Dad," Josh jumped in. How long had he been there? They faced away from the door; he wouldn't have seen his dad's hand on her leg. "Leave Evie alone. She's an incredible woman. My life is better because she's in it. Neither Evie nor her body are any of your bloody business."

The anger in the room rose like an electric storm snapping at the atmosphere.

Father against son, and she was caught in the middle.

"Evie, I'm sure my wife would love to meet you. And there's birthday cake in the kitchen. Please have some; you need to put meat on those bones. I need to speak to my son in private."

She'd been politely told to fuck off, and she didn't like it. "But—"

"It's okay," Josh said softly as he walked over to her. He looked towards the door as if he was willing her away.

Although Josh defended her, his shoulders slumped in defeat. She and Josh were coated in Robin's toxicity already.

Evie defiantly kissed Josh on the lips before walking

out of the room and felt a flush of satisfaction when he kissed her back just as hard. Josh closed the door behind her, and immediately she stood against it, attempting to listen to what was said. But Rose, Josh's mum, suddenly beckoned her to the kitchen table. The room was as emotionless as the rest of the house, although Evie recognised aspects of Josh in his mum. There was a nervousness to her. She'd accidentally bang cupboards and stare at the door, expecting what Evie presumed would be a reprimand, but her smile and gentleness were a copy and paste of Josh's. She'd made the best cup of tea Evie had ever drunk, and although the slice of Victoria sponge was like heaven, a bitter taste refused to leave Evie's mouth even with every sweet crumb blessing it. She shouldn't have left Josh alone with his dad's poison. The need to rescue and care for him was so strong it was like physical pain. Josh made a lot more sense now.

Evie and Josh walked up the stone steps to her flat. The mood had soured since the visit to his parent's house. Evie had been the only one to speak on the journey to her nana's place. She'd commented a couple of times on how lovely his mum had been, but his responses had primarily been nonsensical grunts. Something had happened between Josh and his dad, but he refused to give away anything. Rose gave her a piece of cake to take away, and Evie asked for the recipe, not that she had any intention of baking, but that was what you did when you met the parents of the guy you wanted to be with, right?

Robin had said polite goodbyes, attempting to

convince Evie that he was the good guy with her best interests at heart, but they'd left pretty swiftly. That suited Evie. Robin was a twat, and she couldn't bear another second with him or of seeing what he did to Josh.

"This building smells of… I don't want to think what," Josh grumbled.

"I've got used to it. I guess I don't smell it anymore. Besides, it's a public area. What can I do about it?" She wasn't going to fight him.

"I can't believe you live here. The security is awful."

His eyes were on her back as she jiggled the key in the lock with the special knack her nan had taught her years ago. Memories of that day caused a bubble of anxiety to rise in her throat. She tried to shove the monster back into its cage as she had done daily over the past eight years. "It's fine. I can handle myself," she said as much to herself as him.

"The neighbourhood is dodgy too. I swear I saw someone shooting up heroin in an alley."

He was trying to get to her. He'd been to this flat plenty of times and not had a problem. Was this his dad talking or the real him? "As if you'd know what that looks like. You've hardly grown up around anything less than middle-class perfection. Besides, I can't afford anything else, and I'm not here much anyway."

He bristled at her response. "You're out a lot…"

"Was that a question or a statement?" she finally bit.

"Doesn't matter," he replied, walking around the room, picking personal things up before returning them with a sour face.

"I've had a lot on, you know, with my nan dying."

Josh froze. Her attempt to throw him a dig and shame him into silence had hit its target. Josh fell onto the sofa and took deep breaths. "I'm sorry. I'm acting like a shit."

"Yes, you are," Evie replied but tidied the room in an attempt to give him space. She busied herself as she asked her next question. "What did your dad say to you?"

"It doesn't matter."

"Josh," she said as she knelt before him and lifted his chin. "You can tell me."

Josh fisted his hands even as he looked at her. "I know I can, but I don't want to talk about him. I don't want to let him into this thing between us. He's part of why I've taken so long to get this far."

Evie opened his fists and held his hands gently, but she didn't push him further.

Josh looked around the room. The flat was a bit messy compared to his, and a bomb site compared to his parents' house.

"Will you come and live with me? I'm worried about your safety now that you're alone here," he asked with a softened stare.

"You share with a bunch of rugby players, and based on Sunday night, it would be carnage. We've barely stopped arguing. One step at a time. Besides, I need to pay for the funeral, and I can't afford rent at yours."

"You wouldn't be paying rent. And if leaving here is about money, I can give it to you. I've got money."

Evie dropped his hands. "I don't want to be your charity," she said, unwilling to admit that living in the flat was about being close to her nana. Memories of her nana were everywhere. The custard splodge that never went away, although they'd both scrubbed it until the carpet frayed. The laughter from the postman seeing Enid naked when she'd reached for a parcel and her dressing gown opened.

There was also the night they'd smoked cigars on the anniversary of Evie moving in.

Nan told her never to be sad about how her family had treated her and that the most significant thing she could do was be the genuine version of herself. Evie was finally getting there. This was the home where she'd experienced love despite her mistakes. Her love was so powerful that it had leaked through the walls. Neighbours had been joyous because of her nana. They called it The Enid Effect.

"But don't you have a family to help pay for the funeral?" He was trying, and she wanted to reach for his comfort. Maybe she should let him in.

She glanced at the clock struggling to stay on its rusty hook. "Shit, I'm late."

There was so much to tell him, but this wasn't the right time. Evie grabbed her spare clothes and her sports bag.

"For what?" He followed her like a wary dog. "Can I drive you?"

"I've got to go to work, Josh. I'll explain it all later, I promise." If she let him help her, there would be more questions, and this wasn't the time. She needed to keep her job, especially now.

He stood in the corridor as she yanked the door shut. Evie dashed away and left Josh and his unanswered questions at the top of the stairs.

Chapter Twenty-One

The growl of Josh's stomach echoed around the car. What just happened? He stared listlessly at his phone, attempting a message. He wanted her to be safe, but she couldn't even trust him to share something about her family. This sort of thing would keep coming up. Within a couple of taps of his phone, he'd arranged lunch with Jack. Maybe he could help him make sense of Evie.

An hour later, over a protein-filled lunch of chicken and quinoa salad, Jack and Josh exhausted most of the issues that harangued their lives. Jack explained that he'd had an on-and-off relationship with Dante, the maître d' who'd been so rude to Evie. It was officially off since Jack had caught him sleeping with several colleagues and strangers from apps. Dante justified his cheating because it was Jack's fault for not defining exclusivity.

"And I fell for that explanation the first couple of times. But last month, I caught him with a waiter when I picked him up from work for our anniversary meal. That's it. I'm done now." He sighed. "No more dating for me. I'm going on an elective relationship drought."

"The guy is a wanker. He was a dick to Evie, and you deserve way better than him," Josh grumbled, rushing through his chicken. He'd focused his life on protein and carb loading. But what if he wanted more than perfect living and an obsession with training? He'd never considered other options before, but there was a lot he'd removed from his life since Lulu's death.

"Exactly. But that's enough about Dante the dickhead. So what's going on with you? Don't get me wrong, I enjoy reminiscing about school days and chatting about our lives, but I suspect there's more to our catch-up this time."

The café was near their old school. It tended to be quiet enough that they wouldn't get overheard gossiping. It was primarily mums in sportswear chatting over a salad and a cup of coffee. Occasionally there'd be a single person on a laptop hiding away in the corner or a pensioner making eyes at a woman with a blue rinse and a twinkle.

"What makes you say that? We catch up regularly," Josh replied on the defensive.

"Not like this. You plan everything. You're the least spontaneous person I've met, Josh. I bet you did your stretches by 10:45 last night and then repeated them this morning at seven before a heavy egg breakfast."

Josh blushed as he remembered his morning routine that day. It involved no stretches unless he included the flex of his back when he bent Evie over the kitchen counter once his housemates had left. He'd happily start every day with those stretches.

Jack dropped his cutlery to his plate with a clang. "Oh, Josh, what does that facial expression mean? You're going bright red."

"It's nothing—well, not nothing. I was with Evie this morning, and it was nice." Jack raised his eyebrow. Josh sighed loudly. "Fine. It wasn't just nice. Being with Evie has been amazing, although she's going through a lot with her nana dying."

"She messaged me. I'm glad you were there for her."

One of the mums in the café stared at Josh. She gave him a wink, and he grumbled as he chased the last bit of chicken with his fork. Why would a strange woman wink at him?

"Yeah, me too. I hate that she's been alone. She won't let people in. But we're good together, except when we're fighting, although sometimes I wonder if we both enjoy winding each other up. How messed up is that?"

"I don't need the details of your sex life," Jack replied with a smirk that caused the heat to travel up Josh's neck like a blanket. "So what is up? Because something is."

"Today, I had to pop home for Mum's birthday, and Evie came. She met Dad." His words and the unspoken meaning hung in the air. Jack knew all about Josh's dad.

"I've got so many questions that I don't know where to start. But can I say that this is the longest we've ever spoken without you mentioning Lulu? That's significant, mate." *I spoke about Lulu that much?* "So tell me, how did Evie cope with him?"

"She was okay. Mum liked her, but then who wouldn't? Dad said Evie is like Lulu and suggested my career is going to shit because of her."

"Evie is nothing like Lulu. I expect your dad was pissed off because he couldn't manipulate Evie. And your rugby career hasn't gone to shit. He was trying to dent your confidence like he always does."

Robin had poked a finger in Josh's face as he'd drummed into him that Evie was a ball of fire, and unless Josh forced her to submit to his wants, she'd burn him to death. And then he'd hugged him and explained that he expected Josh and Evie for the following Sunday dinner, but they must be respectful.

"I've never liked your dad. I'm sorry, but you had to deal with a lot growing up."

"Yeah."

Jack gesticulated energetically. "He's trying to mess with your head, and I don't like it. You must have been on edge after that. Well done for finally standing up to him. You had to explain your history with Lulu to Evie though?"

"No, I didn't say anything. How can I tell Evie that I killed my teenage girlfriend? And that I am terrified of dating her because she's feisty like Lulu?"

Josh tapped the lip of his glass with his knife's tip as he considered how to start that conversation. Finally, Jack yanked the knife from his hand. "For the last time, you didn't kill Lulu. Maybe you should tell Evie the truth."

Josh shrugged. From a corner of the café, a child stared at him. The respect of the kids was one of the best bits of being a rugby player, but it didn't distract him from his melancholy for long. "She has secrets she won't share, making it hard to trust her with mine. She says she can do everything herself, and it's hard not to be needed when I want to be there for her."

"Don't give me that bullshit about secrets. You both have secrets. We all do."

"What are your secrets?" Josh asked with a knitted brow, but Jack waved the question away.

"My secrets aren't important," Jack replied. "Do you care about Evie?"

Even the clatter of glasses couldn't distract him from his answer. "Of course I do."

"Do you want Evie?"

Josh sighed loudly and dropped his head to his hands before locking eyes with Jack. "Yeah, I'm like some sort of pussy bandit when I'm around her. Well, I want to be."

"Did you say that? Mate, that was too much information. And did you have to stare at me like that when you said it?" Jack joked before taking a sip of his water. "Does Evie know about your lack of experience?"

"She must. I'm clumsy when we get intimate."

Jack raised his hands skyward. "Pussy bandit to intimate? I have no idea what you're going to say next."

"Shut up." Josh laughed. Jack threw his head back and bellowed his laughter. Josh shook his head, but his smile was broad. Life was more entertaining with Evie in it, and he didn't want to change that.

Once he'd finished laughing, Jack said, "It's time you confided in her, buddy."

"And what if she never wants to see me again?"

"Even with the way you've treated her, which you have to admit is shitty, especially considering what she's been going through—"

"Which I didn't—" But Josh shook his head. "True. I made mistakes and hurt her. So why do I keep trying to justify my behaviour?"

"My point is, has she ever given up on you?"

"No," he replied. "But what if my secrets push Evie away for good, and what if I can't deal with her secrets? "

"Trust in Evie, your friend, and trust me."

"I have no idea where she is. And I still worry about her being in that flat."

"Because you care. But where she lives isn't your decision. I'll let you into a secret. There's a small place on the outskirts of town called The Tavern. Once you've led the rugby workshop for the kids at the charity, go there."

"Okay." Josh shrugged with a knitted brow. As they

stood, the child staring at him jumped up and ran towards them.

"No way, it's you! You play for the Bulls." The kid bounced around Josh.

He rubbed his beard, trying to hide his grin, before responding confidently, "Yep, I do."

"Mum, it's The Destroyer," the kid shouted before running and fetching his bag. "Would you sign my T-shirt, bag, pencil case, and basically everything I own?"

Jack giggled as Josh awkwardly fumbled a nonsensical signature on the boy's bag before excusing them from the situation.

"I don't look anything like fucking Gavin! I am not The Destroyer. I have way more class than him, for a start, not to mention my charm and—"

"Probably time for a new style." Jack laughed as they headed to the charity.

"Go fuck yourself," Josh grunted. But maybe Jack had a point. Was it was time to make lots of changes?

Josh reached The Tavern after an afternoon at the charity.

The children ran around the playing field until breathless and still asked Josh to throw the ball as high and far as possible. Their laughter was infectious, and Josh struggled not to bounce around as he walked up to the pub. It was like he was winning his first try all over again. The kid's screams of delight made rugby fun again. Why had it stopped? Because his dad made it less about playing the game and more about him and winning.

Josh shook his head. The run-down local pub that Jack had mysteriously sent him to severely lacked charm. Dirty cream paint flaked off the walls, except where someone had daubed thick graffiti about Stacey's ass and what Phil would like to do to it. Someone had tried to scrub it off, but they must have gotten bored quickly. Grey curtains, which might have been white once, hung in the windows on the first floor, but if the aim was to create homeliness, it was failing miserably. The whole place reminded him of a horror movie set with a minuscule budget.

What if he couldn't deal with what awaited him on the other side of the peeling red door with the grubby frosted window? Evie had to be keeping it a secret for a reason. What if it was a pub and a strip club? If it was, then so be it. Evie needed to make her own decisions. The door opened in front of him with a painful scream of its hinges.

"You going in or what?" asked an old guy with white whiskers springing from his chin. His expression quickly transformed from frustration to surprise. "You play for the Bulls, don't you?"

"Yeah, Josh King," he mumbled quickly before the stranger incorrectly guessed he was Gavin "The Destroyer" Burke.

"But everyone calls you Kong because you're a hairy ape."

Josh glared back before pushing past the stranger and stepping through the door.

"No need to be rude," the grumpy guy replied.

Josh huffed back, but the man had already gone. Suddenly he saw Evie. Even from where he stood, the dark circles under her eyes and her pale skin exclaimed her exhaustion. But still, his heart beat a little faster, and his palms were sweaty. Her beauty was indescribable, even under the dank lighting of the pub. Did they stand a chance of having a future if they couldn't trust each other?

Chapter Twenty-Two

Evie hadn't noticed him, and he capitalised on the moment to take her in. Her tinkling laugh as she gossiped with patrons carried across the whole bar, slicing through the gloom and filling the room. The happy sound would have made it easier to ignore the unpleasant reek from the toilets trying to infiltrate his nostrils had it not been fake. It may have convinced the punters who shared in her cheer, but it was a hollow laugh to Josh. Why were they forcing her to work when her nan had just died?

As she sat with a group of older ladies and listened to their chatter, Evie smiled in the right places and offered a comforting hand when the situation called for it. His heart swelled.

"She's quite a woman, isn't she?" The old guy who'd made a dig when Josh arrived had returned, bringing a whiff of cigarette smoke with him. "She's brought new life to this place. I can't believe she only started working here a couple of months ago. It's like she's been a part of our pub family for ages. Everyone loves her, especially the grumpy landlady, Angie."

Josh nodded, unsure what to say. The guy continued, oblivious, "Don't get me wrong, Evie is no angel, especially with that mouth of hers. We often joke that she makes a gang of builders sound like a schoolgirl trip to church. But she makes everyone feel special, including the oddities like Maud over there. See her?"

Evie listened to a poorly dressed woman with messy grey hair. The lady's boots were faded, with the heel barely staying on as she tapped it restlessly against the chair leg. Evie placed a hand on the woman's worn sleeve.

"Yep."

"She's probably moaning that she's out of money again. We all know, including Evie, that she's wasted her monthly pension on her shitty son and his drug habit, but watch Evie sneak her a free pint later. She does it every time Maud comes in looking destitute. Angie pretends not to notice, but we all see it." The old guy turned to face Josh and squared up to him in the process. He came up to Josh's shoulder, but he had enough power in his wisened poking finger to bruise Josh's chest. "Are you the reason she's out of sorts today?"

Before Josh replied, the guy added, "Actually, don't tell me. But don't hurt her, okay?"

"I wo—" Josh attempted.

The guy poked again, and Josh forced himself not to wince. "Because if you do, you'll have us lot to deal with. Herbert over there used to be a boxer and will knock you out. You'll have to deal with Angie too, and no one should willingly get on her bad side." He leant in conspiratorially. "Rumour is that she likes to whip her guys."

Josh was left with images he didn't want as the guy sloped off with a chuckle. Evie stepped away from Maud. Surreptitiously she wiped a tear from beneath her eyes before returning Josh's gaze. Instantly she swivelled on her heel, not sparing him a glare, and positioned herself behind the bar.

Stepping up to the worn wood, he waited.

Evie busied herself with jobs that Josh suspected didn't need doing. She polished glasses, cut slices of fruit that were clearly out of place, and scrubbed the bar like she was trying to rid it of any remnants of varnish. The half-eaten bowl of peanuts at the other end of the bar turned his stomach as someone returning from the toilet swiped a couple. Why didn't the punters fear the facts about urine-covered pub peanuts?

Josh waited patiently as Evie topped up the nuts. You have to be more patient than she is stubborn. But as he sat at the bar, he knew it would be a close-fought contest.

"Evie, serve the handsome gentleman," a leathery-skinned woman called out from the other end of the bar.

"We don't serve bellends who have no business being here," she hollered with eyes so tight it was like her pupils were lasers burning through his chest. Josh kept his fake smile, torn between making his presence unavoidable and winding her up. Toying with her was quickly becoming a delight.

"We wouldn't have any customers if we had that rule. Now serve the man."

Evie slammed a pint glass down on the bar in a "silent" protest. Reflections of nosey men peered in their direction, their faces appearing between bottles in the mirror behind the bar. "And don't break my glasses in the process, or I'll dock your wages."

"You can't legally do that."

The older woman with the giant wilting beehive on her head looked up from her newspaper. "It's my bloody pub, Evie, and I'll do what the hell I like."

At Evie's dramatic huff, Josh's smile widened.

"Here you go, sir." She thrust the glass closer to him.

Beer slopped over the sides, covering the bar before finding the edge. The slow dripping sound from his drink as the excess liquid hit the floor was a temporary distraction from Evie's attitude. "A pint of knobgoblin, I mean Hobgoblin. Please enjoy and then sod off."

Her glaring face appeared over the edge of his glass as he took a savouring sip. Her vitriol should have left him uncomfortable. Instead, his cock stirred with renewed vigour. "I like the taste," he said with a wink before gulping down the ruby liquid.

Her eyes widened at his sass, causing his smile to broaden in glee.

She slammed her hands down on the bar. "What are you grinning at?"

"You. You're fucking sexy when you're angry." The corners of her mouth wobbled as she fought back a smile.

Josh popped the empty glass in front of her. "I'd like another knobgoblin, please."

"Aren't you worried that the alcohol will make you horny?" she huffed as she snatched the glass away and began pouring him another drink.

Josh took a deep breath and softened his gaze. He wanted her sexually—it was undeniable—but her friendship meant everything to him. Why had it taken him so long to realise it? "I came to say sorry. I'm sorry for trying to make you move in with me and for not trusting you with what happened between Dad and me. I'm sorry for being impatient. Your secrets are that. If you don't tell me them, it's because you have your reasons. I'm here for you no matter what, and I will continue to be for as long as you let me be." He squeezed his lips together. What else could he say to convince her of his support?

"Oh, right." Evie exhaled. As she stared transfixed at

his apologetic face, beer overflowed from the glass she poured into, running across her fingers, dripping onto the metal drip tray.

Josh's hardening erection was making his trousers awkwardly tight. He shifted in his seat surreptitiously. She wouldn't believe him if she noticed he was rock hard. He took a deep breath before adding, "I have a favour to ask, though."

She raised one of her eyebrows, and her mouth soured. "A sexual favour? I should have known." The way she said sexual between the licks of her tongue while she removed his sticky beer from her fingers made him flex his buttocks to control his body, but it was fruitless. His cock was not respecting the situation.

"No," he said between gritted teeth, willing calm.

"Are you okay, Josh? Have you got lockjaw?" she asked without a trace of attitude.

He took a loud breath. "I'm fine. It's the wrist injury," he lied. "Anyway, the favour I need involves your skills and something battery-operated."

Delight rippled through him as she squeezed her lips into all sorts of positions to stop laughing, but it was a losing battle, and delight jumped from her mouth even as she shook her head. "Fine. I've a few hours left of my shift, but then I'm all yours."

He beamed back. His dad's comments about her tried to cloud his judgement, but as she sneaked a drink to Maud while the whole pub pretended to avert their eyes, his smile obliterated all his dad's shit. Evie was incredible. He'd do everything to be there for her for as long as she needed him.

Soon they were at Josh's place, giggling about everything and nothing. Angie let Evie leave early. Josh hadn't let slip what she was going through, but Angie picked up on the odd tear or how distracted she was. Evie explained as they flopped on the sofa at Josh's that she'd been messing up orders all shift.

"It turns out that an Irish coffee isn't whiskey in a coffee and that you should never mistake a no-alcohol lager with The Captain's favourite two o'clock pint of Stella." Evie winced. "And you should never offer to put a lime slice in to sweeten it up."

Josh threw his head back and laughed. The Captain was the one he'd spoken to at the door. No wonder the guy was grumpy.

Evie turned to face him. "Tell me, how did you find me at the pub?"

Today she wore a nearly transparent leopard print blouse. The scarlet bra beneath it was impossible to ignore, but Josh fought to keep eye contact. Her never-ending legs stretched beneath her frayed denim hotpants, and his fingers itched to touch her skin. Josh thrust his hands beneath him.

"Stop avoiding the question and stop fidgeting."

"Jack told me," he confessed. Evie's stern face made him yearn to pull her onto his lap, but he needed her help first.

"I'll kick his ass when I see him next."

Josh rushed to Jack's defence. "Go easy on him. He knew how important it was for me to see you. Besides," Josh joked, "I told him I was a pussy bandit. He couldn't resist helping me after that."

Her explosive laughter was endearing, although she was laughing at him. Her breasts heaved with every breath, and he wanted to hold her, especially as she nearly tumbled off the sofa with her body-shaking guffaws.

But, eventually, she stilled, and he capitalised on the mood to ask a difficult question. "It's none of my business, but why didn't you tell me you had a job at the pub?"

Evie sighed, but Josh cupped her cheek to hold her gaze.

She offered a half-hearted smile. "I needed the money for Nan's care, and if I told you about it, you'd try to give me money or force yourself into the situation." Of course, that was precisely what he'd do. Josh pulled his hand away, but Evie grabbed it and threaded her fingers through it. "Besides, we weren't talking at that point."

"Because I pushed you away when we were messing around, wrestling, on my floor." They both looked to the floor as they continued to hold hands.

Watching her in the bar had done inexplicable things to his body. It wasn't only that her frayed shorts displayed her lower bum cheeks whenever she bent over or the shirt clinging tightly to her breasts like a second skin. It was how she spoke to people, the respect she gave everyone, including those who society would deem unacceptable with their missing teeth and mysteriously stained clothes. Evie brought blessings wherever she went, especially when she bantered like a wizened old soldier. Only Angie bossed her around, which seemed to be with a mother-daughter kindness.

The cheeky winks she'd given him whenever she'd caught his eye, or the teasing kisses she blew across the bar, had him rigid. And he wasn't embarrassed. If they hadn't been in public, he would have paraded his manhood and shown her that she aroused his mind and body. But was it time to share some secrets about Lulu?

"So what was the favour you wanted from me?" Evie's blushes were nothing compared to her gaze flicking to his swelling erection before returning to his face. "Joshua, I do believe you're blushing."

"Well, Evangeline, you are too." He raised his eyebrows suggestively. "I guess you're not too cool after all."

"The favour then," she replied as she cleared her throat noisily.

Was she nervous? He wanted to jump on the sofa and dance, but it hadn't worked for Tom Cruise, and he'd probably fall off and damage his other wrist. "I would like you to trim my beard and hair. I'm fed up being a mess."

Her silence was unnerving. Josh shifted awkwardly and tapped his feet against the carpet as she gawked at him. "Stop staring at me like that."

"I was wondering why now. Why do you want to change your look when you've spent years refusing to?"

He shrugged but replied honestly, "Some kid thought I was Gavin, and one of your pub guys said I was an ape." He expected her to laugh, but instead, she studied him.

"So what? Who cares about other people? You're you, Josh. Fuck 'em. You don't need to be anyone else. You're gorgeous and the best person I know."

He was as flushed as a teenager at a school disco. The lack of a beard would make his blushes more obvious, but it didn't deter his plans. "Thank you. I guess it's the right time to make a change. What do you think about my beard and my hair?"

The flick of her tongue across her lips had his erection throbbing again.

"Your beard is a mess, although I'd love it between my legs," she said casually. "But you're hot to me no matter what's going on with your hair. And it's not thick enough to hide your blushes from me."

His laugh echoed from his belly to his mouth. "How do you know what I'm thinking, woman? You're terrifying." He wanted to kiss the grin right off her lips, but instead, he added, "Let's give it a go, and if I hate it, then it will grow back in no time. What's the worst that could happen?"

Her devilish smile wasn't the answer he needed.

Evie treated him like he was Michaelangelo's David under her touch. There was an unexpected freshness to the cut; if not for the other emotions rushing through him, he would have wiggled his bum in glee. Somehow, having her trim his beard had become one of the most sexual experiences of his adult life. Repeatedly, she ran her fingers through his hair. Then, as she deciphered what mass of hair she'd trim next, she grazed her nails lightly across his scalp or stroke his skin.

When she pulled down little tuffs to "check the length matched," he'd had to swallow hard to distract himself from his craving. Her face was inches away from his as she appraised him with a nibbled lip or as turquoise flecks danced in her green eyes. If he hadn't forced himself to swallow or tapped his fingers against his thighs, the temptation to lift and pin her against the door as he nibbled her lip for her would have been difficult to ignore.

Her finger against his Adam's apple made him swallow so hard she told him off for distracting her work. His cock pulsed at the reprimand. He eased a breath, hoping the moment spent between her hands would never end, yet he was equally desperate for her to finish so they could find another pastime.

The scummy bathroom didn't detract from his arousal, although the scent of bleach from his intensive bathroom cleaning while he'd made her wait downstairs burnt his nostrils. Unfortunately, cleaning couldn't improve the paint-flecked walls and the stain-rimmed bath.

Finally, Evie held her scissors in the air with a satisfied smile. Before the cut, Josh had changed into his rugby shorts to stop bits of hair from sticking on his nicer clothes. But the tenting from his hard cock was impossible to hide under the normally baggy shorts. Josh stood quickly, grateful that her back was to him.

He attempted to slip out of the bathroom without Evie noticing his erection, but she shouted, "Sit back down. I'm not finished with you yet."

He groaned his frustration. "Can't we leave it like this? I'm sure I look great."

"You asked me to do this, and I'm going to do it properly. So sit your sexy bum on that chair."

He rolled his eyes, exasperated, but her demands made his dick judder.

Evie moved behind him. A breath of warm air crossed the nape of his neck.

"What are you doing? Are you trying to torture me?"

"Calm the fuck down. I'm getting the hair off your neck." Her breath swept across his skin. A shuddering sensation travelled from the tip of his cock to the goose pimples on his arms, and beads of sweat appeared on his forehead.

"One last thing." She straddled his lap without warning. "Bloody hell, Josh, you've got a massive plank of wood down there." Josh grimaced as she wriggled in his lap. "I need to see what I'm working on. Keep still, Josh."

Josh lifted his head to find a smiling Evie, although she kept trying to hide it by twisting her mouth.

She teased the top of her lip with her tongue as she attempted to focus. Josh groaned, adding with a raspy voice, "But you're the hottest woman I've ever met." He'd fantasised about being good enough for her. He'd wanted her since Aidan had told him in the bar nearly two years ago to take care of her, but denied that part of himself. "I don't care how cheesy it sounds, but I'd follow you to the ends of the earth."

Casually she continued to work on making his beard even, but her smile was getting trickier to hide as it widened.

"You're only after me for my body, then?" she asked in a faint voice that clouded her meaning.

"No, I want you to talk about butterflies and the French renaissance and whatever you've been reading about recently," he replied genuinely. "I loved watching you in the pub earlier, caring for everyone. I even love it when you insult and banter with me."

She paused, and her grin slipped from her face. The change saddened Josh, as did the anxiety laced through her question. "So why did you push me away two months ago? Why did you reject me whenever I got close?"

He spoke before self-preservation kicked in. "Because, amongst the other things I'm deeply ashamed of, you're the first woman I've slept with in eight years."

CHAPTER TWENTY-THREE

Evie's hand stopped in mid-air. It wasn't what she expected, and yet it made sense. Why was he ashamed of that? He closed his eyes as if trying to hide from her. Or was he hiding his soul like he always tried to do?

She resumed trimming the last sections of his beard. The short hair lightly scratched her skin. "Fair enough. How come?"

At her words, his eyelids fluttered open. His eyebrows knitted together. Had she not stilled his head with the palm of her hand, he probably would have tilted his head like a confused puppy.

Clearing his throat, he made her jump slightly in his lap before he followed it by taking a deep breath and slowly exhaling. *This is going to be big. Keep your emotions in check, Evie.* He'd stop otherwise.

"I had a serious girlfriend when I was eighteen, and things were abysmal at the end. A lot of arguments and other things that, well—it was horrendous. I didn't want anyone after her, and I didn't want to hurt anyone again or be hurt." It was a struggle to keep up with his quick speech. "And then I guess I was too scared to in case anything went wrong or I got laughed at and humiliated. I hate being humiliated, but over something like that? I might not come back from that." His honesty was a shock.

"That's not everything, is it?" He averted his gaze and, in doing so, answered her question. "Do you want to tell me those things right now?"

Josh shook his head.

"Okay. It's scary sharing the past, isn't it?"

Josh smiled gently, understanding the subtext about her insecurities.

"So, one step at a time. But please answer this: what now? What does this mean for us?"

His smile was tentative, but it gave her hope. "Evie, I can't stop wanting you. I was tipsy when we had sex that night after our meal. I wasn't close to being drunk, but after we'd shared some of our fears, I convinced myself that I should do what I wanted instead of what my fears stopped me from doing. I stopped worrying that you'd laugh at me or see that I had no idea what I was doing, and instead, I enjoyed myself. But I don't know what I'm doing with sex, and I know you've noticed."

Evie tucked her closed hand under her chin and sighed. The pressure to say something dishonest to make him happy was appealing, but this moment was as significant to their possible future as it was to Josh's mental health and understanding of himself. So don't fuck this up.

"It does explain a few things. I was worried you were disgusted by your attraction to me or maybe someone had damaged you. But you shouldn't be ashamed of anything. You're pretty fucking awesome at sex. I still haven't found the brain cells you screwed out of me," she said, attempting something light-hearted, but he responded with a hollow laugh. She should tell him that she never stopped yearning for him, even when shouting at him was a better option. "I haven't stopped thinking about having sex with you again, but I was scared."

His brow furrowed, and his legs trembled beneath her. "You were scared?"

A dripping tap temporarily distracted her, but Josh's wincing face pushed her to continue as her heart beat rapidly and sweat dripped down her back. "Because I like you, Josh. More than I've liked anyone. But that gives you the power to reject and hurt me, so I was scared. If this were just sex, it wouldn't matter, but this thing between us has the power to break us."

"Okay," he replied, drawing out the word as if waiting for the punchline.

"In terms of sex, you need a bit more experience and direction. But even with a new partner, the most experienced person learns new techniques and skills. Every person is different. Worry and fear are probably your biggest barriers. Inexperience is easy to overcome."

"So, what now?" he stuttered, hurting her heart.

"Are you keen to learn? Because not everyone is. Some people know what they like, and that's it. Are you some people, or do you want to learn how to pleasure someone, specifically me?" Evie held her breath. What would she give up to be with Josh?

"I want to pleasure you and watch you come apart. I want to learn everything you can teach me," he answered with the exuberance of a puppy trying to earn a treat.

"Shall I be your teacher?" His cock shuddered beneath her, pressing against the crotch of her shorts.

"I'll take that as a yes." The irresistible combination of sheepish guilt and bursting pride on his face tore at her heart. "I'll finish up here first."

As she trimmed, she slowly ground her pelvis against him. The soft massaging of his erection brought a release of endorphins that zipped up and down her spine.

"More torture?" he asked.

"Foreplay," she whispered, revelling how his eyes fluttered closed.

Evie tidied the last part of his beard before marvelling at her handiwork. The shadow created by his thick bottom lip called for her tongue, but she resisted. The worry lines on his forehead reminded her of all the fears and damage he carried. But maybe that's why their friendship usually worked. Josh's nose had a squish from too many rugby ball collisions, and she longed to trace it with her fingertip, but his newly trimmed beard claimed her touch first.

"You're so fuckable, Josh." His cock jolted again, and she groaned as her fingertips danced across his stubbly jaw. Every graze brought a twitch to his face and an extra throb against her crotch. She ground against him in time with his push against her.

Her lips brushed against his in a teasing kiss, and his hands threaded through her hair.

She leaned back slightly. "Oh no. I want to play with you first." Then, smiling mischievously, she stood up and beyond his reach. Josh lent forward, desperate to pull her closer.

"Hands by your sides."

"But—"

"Trust me. It will be worth the wait."

As he tracked her movements, he grumbled in frustration, but the squidged-up smile revealed more than he realised.

"Are you secretly enjoying how I'm taking control of your pleasure?"

His big grin as he shrugged made her giggle. She

prepared for him to struggle with his control due to his lack of experience. Mind-blowing sex took practice, but she was eager to be his guide and teacher.

"I'm going to make sex your new addiction, baby," she teased.

"Fuck," he said through one slow breath.

Locking eyes with Josh, she said, "I'm going to build the tension. I'm going to make you extremely horny and hard, to the point that you can't focus on anything but my legs wrapped around you, riding you. You'll want to move inside me, slowly at first, your cock stretching me as my wetness covers you." He groaned with lust, but she continued, though it tested her resistance. "That's why you have to be patient."

Josh's eyes swept up and down her body as he breathed her in before his hands fell to his side, displaying his submission and trust.

Evie flicked open the button on her denim shorts and slid the zip down.

"Watch me," she demanded. Then, pushing the hot pants over her hips and down her legs before kicking them to the side, she relished how Josh stared at her nakedness.

"You're the sexiest woman I've ever seen." The words left his mouth with a strangled sound.

Evie grinned as she turned. Had she ever been worshipped like a goddess rather than treated like a human sex doll? Josh empowered her.

A zip of joy filled her belly at the sound of his strained laugh when she wiggled her bum for his delight. He could have stood up at any point and taken what he wanted, but he complied. His willingness to be vulnerable made her trust him more than she'd trusted any guy before. She looked over her shoulder at him. "Shall I take my shirt or my thong off next?"

"Your shirt." His response was immediate.

"Tell me, Josh," she said, teasing the buttons of her blouse and turning to offer him a glimpse of her midriff. "Have you stroked your cock to naked pictures of me?"

"Yes." His Adam's apple jumped as he swallowed hard.

"Did you come when you did it?"

"Yes, hard. Very hard." At the words "very hard," Evie stripped her top off. Standing in front of a salivating Josh in a scarlet lacy bra and thong, her confidence surged. She swayed sexily to the music in her head. A slow dirty beat made her want to writhe and stroke her skin. Her white teeth dragged sensually against her lip. Deleting the guys from her past that had caused her pain, she focused on Josh's hungry stare.

Their sexual tension created a fire that could have melted steel when they stared at each other. Effortlessly Evie skimmed her finger across her shoulders before pushing her bra straps down. She looked at Josh with heavy-lidded eyes, her finger teasing the clasp on the back of her bra.

"And when you saw my breasts and came hard, were you imagining anything?"

He closed his eyes when she over-pronounced the words "breasts" and "hard."

"Yes." He gulped.

For each honest morsel from his tongue, she gave him a gift. This time it was a flick of the clasp of her bra. Evie held the lace against her skin, not ready to give him what he craved yet.

The build-up drove lust through every limb of her own

body. The lace thong clung to her crotch, already saturated by her wetness. Undoubtedly, the sexual torment had to be destroying Josh too.

"What did you imagine doing?" she purred.

Her hand fell away when he started mumbling nonsensical words. Evie's bra dropped to the floor, and she kicked it away. Awe transformed his gaze as he stared at her breasts.

He stuttered through his answer. "I was licking your nipples. Sucking and tasting them and making you cry out. You moaned against my mouth." Josh closed his eyes and threw his head back. Was he remembering his fantasies or struggling with control? Evie took advantage of the moment, stripping off her knickers and quickly straddling his lap. His dark eyes whipped open.

"Shit."

"You don't come until I say."

He clenched his jaw and ground his teeth.

"Do what you imagined with my breasts." He feasted on her nipples in the way he'd described. His technique changed every time she praised him and moaned his name. It was as if he was learning how to worship her body to heighten her pleasure.

Suddenly a finger stroked across her clit.

"Bloody hell, Josh."

"Do you want me to stop?" he grunted as he stared at her breasts.

"No." She writhed against his thumb, showing him what to do. His compliance increased her lust as much as his finger did against her clit. "Like that."

Quickly, instructions became unnecessary. So attuned to Evie's responses and keen to feed her hunger, he kissed and sucked her burning skin while rubbing her clit.

She panted and moaned his name until, suddenly, he pushed two fingers inside her.

"You are a pussy bandit." She kissed him hard and revelled in the scratches of his trimmed beard against her face.

"I'm so close," he groaned between kisses, although the thrust of his fingers was unrelenting.

"Then fuck me, Josh."

He lifted her off the chair and carried her to the bedroom. He tripped and dropped her on the bed. Evie dragged him down on top of her.

Rolling him onto his back, she shoved down his shorts and reached for a condom. Ripping the foil between her teeth, she quickly slid the rubber down his throbbing cock while greedily licking her lips.

"Whatever you're considering, don't," he begged.

She grinned back. "What do you mean?" She'd enjoy sucking him later.

Lifting slightly off the bed, Evie positioned his cock at her entrance. Josh's jaw was tight, and his hands were in fists. Then, when she was about to push him inside, he thrust his pelvis forward, quickly penetrating her.

"Bloody hell," she whispered in one breath, seeing the wide grin across his face. Her eyes rolled back in her head, and she attempted to regain composure.

"You're going to be in trouble for that," she said with a strained voice. She threw her head back. His dick filled her, and she wanted to hold on to the moment forever, but he was so close.

"I wanted you, all of you," Josh replied with a groan that seemed to rumble in her belly. It was said so earnestly that it stilled her. He was the revelation she'd needed in her life.

"Make me come," she replied. Emotion filled her throat, increasing every time he shared his soft eyes and a tentative smile. Tears welled in her eyes as they set their rhythm. His thrusts met her bounces as he penetrated her, and his muscles rippled with each push. He was fucking gorgeous. As her breasts jiggled, he stared in wonder as if he'd finally reached the pearly gates of Heaven after a lifetime of suffering.

The speed was building, and both quickly teetered on the edge of climax. She was riding him hard. Josh's skin was hot under her hands as she dug her nails into his chest. His mouth was open, and his grunts rose from his depths. She wanted to lick his abs and bite his flesh, but she focused on the orgasm beyond her grasp. Suddenly her legs wobbled, unable to meet the power of his thrusts. The depth he thrusted inside her each time compelled her higher and higher. She was close to the edge of release but needed one more push.

Josh's thumb returned to her clit and took her to climax. She screamed as she came. Lights flashed behind her eyes. The pleasure was like an avalanche, and with each second, it grew until she wasn't sure if she was breathing. Her orgasm was like nothing she'd had before. Her mouth opened in a glorious O shape as her walls tightened around his cock. Suddenly he roared as his body shook. He came with a shout of her name, but he barely took his eyes off her. They shuddered together before she collapsed against his chest.

Tears brimmed in her eyes, but she pushed them away. The moment's intensity had taken her to a vulnerable part of herself she usually refused to acknowledge, and his rewards had floored her. He brushed his lips against her hair.

Eventually, when he found his breath, he whispered, "That was incredible. I've never come like that before."

"Me neither," she admitted.

Josh held her at arm's length and locked eyes with her. "Seriously?"

"Seriously," she replied, her eyes raised as she tried to guess his response.

His grin was a surprise and endearing. "Give me a bit, and I'll see if I can beat it."

She kissed him deeply before resting on his chest with a smile.

Chapter Twenty-Four

Josh repeatedly blinked as he attempted to open his eyes.

Sunlight filled his room from the curtains he'd been too distracted to close. Evie took him to heights he never knew existed, but it was more than that. The ice that had formed around his heart over the last eight years was melting. With Lulu, in the months before she died, every encounter between them involved manipulation or arguments, but with Evie, it was pure and without judgement. She was patient as she taught him about her pleasure. Who knew how fucking glorious it was to witness her orgasm. He stretched out a hand to hold her close, but the bed was empty.

Her jeans and sports bag were still bunched up in the corner. His butterfly tattoo caught his eye as he popped a pair of shorts on, but it was different. When before it had been a searing reminder of his past, it was now like a memorial. It was time to tell Evie about Lulu. The anxiety of finally sharing something that had the power to destroy their tentative relationship left his heart thudding. Of course, his dad would tell him not to, but Evie had coped with the rest of his secrets.

As he crept down the worn carpeted stairs, her louder-than-necessary voice revealed her location and drowned out the groaning stairs. Josh prepared to jump into the kitchen and surprise her, but Max's deep timbre caught his attention.

Stirrings of worry pricked Josh's skin as he sneaked a look into the kitchen. Evie wore a tight pair of pink leggings and a wrap over top that barely covered her breasts. They hadn't said they were officially dating yet, but Josh would fight for Evie to be his. The vehemence with which he declared it shocked him, but he was adamant. He toyed with the idea of storming into the kitchen, tossing Evie over his shoulder, and grunting at Max, caveman style. But nothing would piss her off more.

Should he head back to the bedroom? The creaking stairs might give him away. Again he reminded himself that he needed to work on the house so it would be a nice place for her to visit. He'd been stewing in his problems for too long. Josh perched on the stairs and waited until Max and Evie made enough noise for him to escape. He sang classic pop songs in his head to drown out their private conversation, but Rihanna's hits couldn't conceal Evie's voice.

"Family is important, Max, but don't let it stop you from being who you are. Don't let anyone make you feel guilty or wrong for what you're going through." As usual, she offered help and support. Why hadn't he noticed something was going on with Max? It was as evident to him now as the dark marks on the bannister woodwork that he fingered absentmindedly.

"But what if I lose my dad forever?" Max queried. What was so terrifying that he couldn't tell Coach?

"And what if you don't? Try giving him a chance to hear you out. Your mum is on your side and will stand by you, whatever your dad says." Evie's no-nonsense response made Josh's heart swell.

"But Dad won't listen to her. They've had other partners and lives since they divorced."

"But she is there for you. I've met your dad several times, mainly when he used to throw me out of the club for distracting the players." Her laugh made Josh smile. "But he was always fair and good at listening."

"Not to his son," Max replied grumpily.

"Is that true?" She wasn't letting him get away with anything.

"Maybe not, I guess, but I'm scared he'll never speak to me again," Max replied, his voice wobbling. Josh wanted to burst into the kitchen and hug him, but he held fast. Evie would know what to say.

"Then he'll be the idiot and in the wrong. Any parent who banishes their child, a child they should love unconditionally for who they are, doesn't deserve to be a parent. And if I have to speak to your dad and tell him that myself, I will. Parents have to love their children."

"Do you see much of your parents?"

"I don't have any parents. That's what they told me the last time I saw them."

What did that mean? The clink of the metal spoon against a coffee cup was the only audible sound.

"Josh, come in here," Evie called out.

Sheepishly he entered the kitchen, searching for her anger.

"Don't give me that face," she said, shaking her head with a smile that put Josh at ease. "If you listen to private conversations, you've got to stop wriggling on the stairs. You're a little bigger and clumsier than a sneaky imp! And you need to tell your landlord to sort out this house. Those steps creek like the whole of your team is jumping up and down on them."

Josh's mobile vibrated in his hand with a call from Max's dad, or Boss Man, as all the players called him.

Josh listened carefully to the statements hurled at him through the earpiece. Then, in his eye line, Max thanked Evie with a hug.

"Anytime," she replied softly before Max slid past Josh and up the stairs.

As Boss Man barked his goodbyes, Evie's green eyes flashed with turquoise sparks before travelling slowly down every inch of his body and resting on the tenting of his shorts. He swallowed hard.

One look, and she's got me. He would happily drown in that look.

"That was Charlie. He demanded to see me in a couple of hours," Josh explained.

"Why?" she replied, her gaze fixed on his hidden erection.

"I dunno. You know how cagey Charlie can be. He might terminate my contract."

She locked eyes with him. The heat in her stare hadn't dissipated. "I doubt it." Evie leaned against the countertop and exhaled, the air puffing out her cheeks. "Sorry that you found out about my parents like that. I wasn't sure how to tell you, but I knew you were listening."

"Did they really tell you that you weren't their child anymore?"

"Yes." Her curt answer told him she wouldn't answer any more questions about them. Not yet anyway. So they stood in silence, the ticking clock the soundtrack to their musings. "I suppose I should tell them about Nan. I might visit them Sunday afternoon."

Was she suggesting he should join her? He remembered everything he'd learnt about her, especially over the last week. Evie wouldn't ask straight out—she probably wasn't comfortable doing that yet—but maybe this was her way of asking for her support.

"Would you be okay if I came along? I could drive," he said, testing the waters.

"That would be nice. Thank you."

Silence descended again, and she watched him with an impenetrable gaze.

"You get how sexy you are in those shorts, don't you?" Evie said, prowling closer and causing his cock to twitch. "And you were right about tidying up your beard and hair. You were gorgeous before, but I reckon I'll have to fight other women for you."

He grabbed her face and kissed her hard. She panted as he replied, "It's no contest. Even if you couldn't kick everyone's arse, which you can, you don't need to. I don't want anyone else."

The rippling smile across her face was like joy in its purest form. Josh delighted in the flush of red creeping up Evie's cheeks. Maybe the ice around her heart melted a bit too.

Ice on nipples.

Where had that come from?

"You just thought something dirty, didn't you?"

He inhaled air between his teeth. "No. But out of curiosity, how could you tell if that was the case?"

"Apart from admitting it, your expression went from soft teddy bear to filthy fucker in a flash."

"I guess that's why I don't play poker anymore."

"And I felt your erection against me," she replied,

slipping her hand into his shorts as if to drive her point home.

"That never happens in poker," he said before releasing a groan.

The laugh she gave him was filled with happiness, but there was intrigue in her eyes. "So what were you thinking? I'll torture you if you don't tell." She rubbed her palm up and down his cock.

"That's no threat. Your brand of torture is fucking sexy."

"Think how much fun it would be if you shared your thoughts." Her thumb rubbed the head of his cock.

"I was thinking about ice," he gasped.

"And where was this ice?" His eyes dipped, of their own volition, to the V of her wrap-around cardigan. "My nipples? You're blushing again."

The mixture of humour and arousal was like a tickle of joy across his skin. Evie was his drug of choice: beautiful, hilarious, and intelligent. "And now that you know what I'm thinking?"

"Well, if we use ice, you'd better make me come before it melts and you get wet sheets, although that might still be a problem, as I'm soaking at the prospect of kissing your body with ice in my mouth."

"I'll see you in the bedroom then. But you'd better be quick because I'm thirsty," he teased, reaching into the freezer for the ice tray. He laughed as the usually well-controlled Evie scampered up the stairs, nearly tripping with excitement.

CHAPTER TWENTY-FIVE

Josh licked his lips as he sat in Boss Man's office.

Slowly he recalled how Evie came undone against his mouth. His newly trimmed beard left his mark on her thighs, and as significant as this meeting might be, a part of him hoped it was short. He was desperate to rush home and soothe her skin with his lips.

"You look like a soppy sod," Charlie grunted. His glares had followed Josh around since he'd arrived at the rugby club, including at the medical assessment on Josh's wrist and the first practice Josh had been allowed to participate in that week. Charlie asked the team doctor many questions, and Josh was in no doubt that this week might be the last of his career.

Although Charlie didn't suffer fools or problematic players gladly, he was an award-winning coach. He was consistently aware of his player's needs and had a strict attitude regarding the team only playing when they were right to and was suitably rewarded with their loyalty and trust. He wasn't perfect though, and when he was out of earshot, the team joked about his cocky dictator ways.

"Cat got your tongue, Josh?" Charlie tested him. It gave him the sensation of nails scraping his skin.

"No. My tongue is doing well. At least, that's what I'm

told. But your concern is always appreciated," he finished sarcastically, unsure how to deal with Charlie.

"Ah, he does answer back. I've been waiting for years to see more than a yes man who never steps out of line."

"What?" Josh reared back, nearly toppling off the vintage beechwood chair that added another layer of class to a beautifully designed office. Most rugby offices were a mixture of worn leather sofas spoiled by sweat stains and broken armrests. Rugby players were notorious for breaking things with their oversized bodies. But Charlie's had style, which ensured that all players were nervous and on their best behaviour when called to a meeting. You didn't want to scratch the one-of-a-kind desk or scuff the cream rug he'd picked up during their rugby tour of New Zealand. Josh lifted his feet and did a surreptitious check of the bottom of his trainers as he waited.

Charlie folded his hands and leaned back in his chair as he eyeballed Josh. "You're always disciplined and controlled. You've never done anything wrong until last weekend." Josh tapped his fingers against his thighs anxiously. Was this when he told him he was dropped from the Bulls for good? "And it was about bloody time." Charlie's sly grin was disarming.

"Huh? But that's what you wanted us to be."

"You have no fire. Don't get me wrong, I'm not keen to have you raising hell all the time, especially if you're going to sprain your wrist when you do, but I've wanted more from you for a long time. You're a great player, but you could be a brilliant one. You do the right things—train, eat right, and get lots of sleep—but there's no passion when you play. On the other hand, the Josh I saw practising this morning had a fire. You were ruthless, especially when you went for Gavin."

"The guy's a dickhead," Josh snapped.

"I'm well aware, but he's also a great player. No one is as desperate to win or as hungry to be the greatest. Unfortunately, he damages other players on the pitch, but that's a problem for me and him to deal with."

Josh sat up in his chair, and his brows knitted together. "But why did you punish me by stopping me from coming to practice this week?"

Charlie leaned forward and jabbed the desk as he made his point. "It wasn't punishment. With a sprained wrist, you're useless to me. But I was curious. Maybe you'd decide your time with the team was up or want it more."

Josh laughed awkwardly. "That could have backfired."

"I had a feeling." Charlie eased his elbows onto the desk and clasped his hands together. His stare was unwavering. It was like he was a master chess player with consequences considered and nothing risked for long. "It was also nice not to watch your dad treating you like shit after practice. We all needed a break from that. However, he's continued to hassle me. Aren't I lucky?"

"You're kidding?"

"No. Your dad has phoned a couple of times this week. Obviously, I've ignored the calls, but the messages he left with my secretary were enlightening. First, he scolded me for not supporting you, but it was you he went to town on." Charlie left the comment hanging in the air. "He also insisted that I promise to keep you on the team next year."

Josh exhaled slowly, causing air to escape his puffed out cheeks. His dad was treating him like a child. How did he think it was acceptable to call his boss?

"I called him once and told him to mind his own fucking business and to leave me the fuck alone. Then I hung up on him." Charlie shrugged with a smile.

Josh's chuckle sprang free.

"I like that you found that funny," Charlie replied with no hint of sarcasm, "although I should have ignored him. Nothing pisses your dad off more."

"But—"

Charlie held his hand up. "I can handle Robin. He always tried to get one over on me at school but never managed it. Well, almost never."

"You went to school with my dad?" Life was revelation city at the moment. What was next? His dad rarely talked about school except when peacocking about how impressive he was at rugby before choosing another route for his life.

"And your mum, although she was a couple of years below us. I was closest to her, but that's the old days. The last thirty years have gone quickly." There was a faint wistfulness when Charlie mentioned Josh's mum. "Anyway, there's a reason why we're having this meeting, and it's not your mum. Firstly, you're fully healed, and you will be playing tomorrow. So I expect to see your fighting spirit against the Dragons."

"I will bring it like never before, Boss."

"Good lad." Charlie nodded. Josh preened his chest. Was this how support felt? "But you're really wondering about your contract."

"Yes." *There's the blindside.*

Charlie stared at him blankly. Seconds ticked by, and sweat dripped down Josh's back. His throat was sandpaper dry, but there was no way to moisten it. Sometimes bottles of water perched on a side table, but searching them out would mean breaking eye contact. Even with the shouts from outside as players practised their last drills, Josh didn't move an inch.

"Do you want to stay, Josh, or is this another thing your dad has forced you to do due to his failed career?"

Failed career? "I want this more than I realised. This team is who I am," Josh replied quickly. He was surprised at his passionate response.

"Good, because we're signing you for another three years. But try not to punch Gavin again. Bring that fire to the pitch instead."

"But—"

"Don't lie to me about hitting him. You're guiltier than my dog when I caught its head in the biscuit tin."

"Okay," he replied sheepishly.

"And tell your dad to stay away from my practices."

"I'll try, but he doesn't listen."

"He's always liked to throw his power around. But don't worry, I'll tell him too. I'll enjoy pissing him off today."

What had happened between them in the past? Josh stared at Charlie. Whenever they went to the pub, his dad's mates talked about how amazing his dad was. But Josh trusted Charlie, and if he saw his dad like this, then maybe everything wasn't Josh's fault like he'd been convinced it was.

"Why are you sitting there? You've got a contract to prove. Fuck off and get back to practice." The authority was there, but a smile teetered on his lips too.

"Yes, Boss." Josh jumped up and rushed for the door.

"And Josh?"

"Yes, Boss?"

"Evie is good for you. In the past, she's driven me to despair with her attention-seeking ways. But she's done something right with you." Josh's face heated quickly, but he refused to hide it. Charlie knew everything. "One last thing. I wouldn't normally ask this, but what's up with Max? Actually, don't worry," he quickly followed up with a sigh and a head shake. "I'll sort it out eventually. Damn, I love that boy, but I can't sleep with worry these days."

Josh waited at the door. Charlie was never this soft.

"Sod off then, before you get as old as I feel."

Without delay, Josh ran, excitedly recording a voice message to Evie on his phone as he bounded to practice.

Chapter Twenty-Six

"Game day," a stranger shouted in the crowd as Evie and Jack entered the grounds. Her heartbeat was rapid and her breath tight in her chest.

"What is up with this weather?" Jack moaned beside her.

The chill piercing the air brought uncontrollable shivers. The cold was accompanied by a fine drizzle that clung to skin, hair, and clothes. The bright spring day that welcomed her with open arms of streaming sunshine as she'd enjoyed her Pilates class that morning was now marauding as an autumn headache.

"Stop moaning about the weather. You didn't have to come. But maybe you were hoping to enjoy someone's rucking skills," Evie teased.

"I don't understand what rucking is. Is that a rugby thing? Rugby is a bunch of men running around, trying to beat the shit out of each other, but pretending it's in pursuit of a weirdly shaped ball." Jack wore a designer raincoat with the hood tightly pulled up. Had anyone this stylish attended a rugby match before? His dad, a staunch rugby fan, would have given Evie a cuddle for getting Jack to his first adult match if he'd been alive to see it. His dad had been rough and ready, and everyone at the pub missed him.

"Earth to Evie." Jack waved his manicured nails in her

face.

"Sorry, I was a bit distracted."

"By a certain hairy rugby player?"

She smiled. "Josh tried to remind me of the rugby rules last night, but we were preoccupied with something else."

"A night of rucking, I presume."

"Maybe…" She drew out the word saucily. Jack was a friend she'd not known she needed until she'd started working in the pub.

"That smug grin tells me all I need to know." Jack rolled his eyes. "You deserve to be happy, but do you have to be this good at it? I'm within my rights to seethe with jealousy."

He gave her a friendly shove, pushing her into someone who didn't budge.

"Sorry," she said in the direction of the grey-haired guy beside her.

"So you should be," the man grumbled. "Hold on. Is that you, Evangeline?"

His fingers reached for the hood of her waterproof jacket. "Robin? It's fine. I can do it."

But he proceeded to lower her hood until she stepped out of reach, colliding with Jack.

Robin grinned. "I'm surprised to see you here. You should stand with me. I'll keep you safe, and we can be alone together." A wink accompanied his smug smile.

"Evie isn't alone. She's with me," Jack thundered and stepped to her side. "We're heading to a different section. It was nice to see you again."

Robin's eyes narrowed. "Again? I'm sorry, I don't recall meeting you before," he replied disdainfully.

"I was friends with Josh at school."

"Josh didn't have any friends like you at school." The snake revealed its true nature. "You know, boys not into sports, boys like you."

"Hold—" Evie jumped in, but Jack silenced her.

"I was very close friends with Lulu too. You remember Lulu, don't you, Mr. King?" Jack raised his brows as he stared at Robin. The already cold temperature around them dropped significantly further.

Robin's mask slipped briefly, revealing a hatred that flummoxed Evie further. She spied Jack's head held high out of the corner of her eye.

"Not really, probably one of Josh's many school flings. He had a lot at that age, as I suspect the girl did too, sleeping with anyone that turned their heads. You're aware of what teenagers are like? They have no respect for others." He fixed his face with a conspiratorial smile as he nudged Evie as if sharing a private joke with her.

"Unlike the loyal adults around them." But Jack's dig was lost or ignored as Robin returned his attention to Evie and took her shivering hands in his.

"Well, you, sweet lady, are welcome to join me. I'll explain the rules, although I'm sure you're intelligent enough to be able to recite them to me."

Even with her numb hands, she tensed as he drew circles on her wrists. When Josh did it, she felt adored, but with Robin, it was a violation. It was like when Peter touched her, and she shook violently at the memory. "Oh, you're shivering. I should get you a glass of wine to warm you up."

"As I said, Evie and I are heading to a different section. Come on, 'sweet lady.'" Jack threaded his arm through hers, leading her away from Robin's manipulation.

Evie looked over her shoulder. Robin's stare followed

them until the crowd swallowed them, but the sickening impression of his fingers remained on her skin.

"He's a toss weasel with sociopathic tendencies," Jack said with unheard-of vehemence.

"What was all that abou—"

But her question was interrupted by the loudspeaker announcing a couple of interviews and a competition. The fans jostling each other as they waved at a barely cheering crowd was unexpectedly calming. Jack's comments about the Dragon's players, the home team, helped too. As he shared gossip from his years visiting the pub and his celebrity website obsession, Evie locked Robin and memories of Peter into a box. The visiting team were announced and ran onto the pitch.

Desire flipped her stomach, pulling it to the base of her belly before throwing it up and tossing it again as Josh ran onto the damp grass. His arms rippled as he jumped and danced in the air. Her heart stopped briefly, and she held her breath as he searched the crowd for where she'd told him she'd stand.

"He's hotter than I remember. Nice haircut and beard trim, babe," Jack commented.

Evie swelled with pride. As Josh's eyes locked with hers, her man grinned and gave her a wink. She beamed back before screaming her support.

Josh's away kit in black and crimson somehow added to his tanned skin. He turned and started running. His legs pumped his body across the pitch, and his hard chest rose and fell. Josh was preparing for an epic battle. Evie nearly told Jack about the love bite she'd given Josh the night before when he'd been fighting with his need to come. His rugby shirt collar hid it well.

"You need to be full of passion for your game. Abstinence will help that," Evie had teased. The love bite, although a little teenage in their moment of need, had been a reminder that she would be ready and waiting for him when the game was over—but only if he displayed his prowess on the pitch. "You have to perform at your best and bring the fire that Charlie wants."

She smiled at the memory until the home team was heralded over the loudspeaker. Jack grumbled loudly, but it was all good-natured. A couple of minutes later, the announcer spoke of a former Dragon's player that died that week. "Please join me for a round of applause in honour of our fallen hero and member of our Dragon's family, Owen Sother."

The fourteen thousand–strong crowd united with the players, and clapping reverberated around the stadium. Evie's sadness was unexpected. She hadn't heard of Owen until today, but the faces of the fans reminded her of the grief she'd compartmentalised. These fans were a family, and they showed love. A pull at her heart that had continued to get stronger since she'd sat at her nan's deathbed brought tears to her eyes.

The clapping began to subside, and suddenly the game was underway. Evie shook herself, but the sadness stayed like a shadow of her experience and a reminder that something was missing.

The game resembled anarchy, with players hurtling into the air, clutching at the ball before tossing it to team members who sprinted down the pitch, oblivious to those around them. But it wasn't chaos. It was an organised and beautiful performance displaying presence and precision. Every touch was purposeful, each turn resembling a pirouette to set in motion moves that could lead to a try and bring the team closer to victory. It was like the butterfly effect. Evie smiled to herself.

The day remained an unseasonably cold and wet April, made more ominous by the dark clouds that imprisoned them in the stadium and forced their adrenaline higher.

Occasionally the ball, glistening with rain, slipped from a player's hands, bouncing along the turf before the opposition snapped it up.

Damp was in the air, and Evie drew her hood around her face to keep it out but to no avail. It was inevitable that she'd be a frizzy mess. Robin's comments sneaked through her consciousness. What was he after? But the action on the pitch enraptured her once more.

The players crouched down in a huddle. Men from each team faced off, standing their ground while forcing the other team to back away. Brute force united with teamwork, and steam rose from the players at the energy and heat expelled. It was like the game was being played in a fantasy realm as mist shrouded the warriors, fixing them in motion as they planned their attacks. Suddenly, fast and fraught play returned to the pitch. All the players were running, and carnage ensued. The shouts and praise from the fans brought an unexpected swell of pride. She'd not had anything to be proud of since her days of ballet performances. Fans heralded Josh's performance, especially as no one had seen him play with such aggression and dominance.

A seed of hope that she was good for him, and his dreams, began to grow.

In the last minutes of the match, Evie couldn't tear her eyes off Josh. Rain pelted the players, making every run and catch a risk, but Josh fought on, his eyes gleaming with fire. Wet clung to their kits, defining every muscle in their second-skin shirts. Mud splattered their uniforms, and the fantasy of stripping Josh's from his weary body grew each time he made an impassioned dive for the ball. His dog-like panting as he stood in the rain when the referee paused the game because of an injured Dragons player gave Evie ideas she yearned to act out. Moisture from a mixture of sweat and rain collected in his hair, darkening it and seducing her further.

The Bulls won with a clear lead. Josh had been a significant reason for that success. Even the Dragons players reluctantly praised his performance.

Jack dragged her to a fan bar in the stadium, and they reviewed the game with some new friends who were also Bull fans. The mood was jubilant, and Evie's heart blossomed with pride. Josh was incredible.

"Is that your phone?" Jack asked as his sonar-like ears, usually tuned to gossip, picked up a sound.

Evie answered without checking her screen, as one of her new friends lauded them with stories of the excellent cup win of 2006.

"You're wet, which is exactly how I like you." Josh's voice on her earpiece had her toes curling with desire. "Don't say anything, not yet."

She turned her head left and right, but his hulking form was nowhere to be found.

"Can't see me, can you? I can see you, and that's a very sexy grin on your face. I reckon you're having filthy thoughts about me." His burgeoning confidence was a massive turn-on. "Nibble on the tip of your finger if you're thinking about your promise to reward me if I played well today."

Evie slipped the tip of her finger between her lips. Instantly she was rewarded with a groan of pleasure down the phone.

"I love it when you do that." The pause was unnaturally long. "I played an exceptional game today. Do you agree?"

Knowing he was watching her ramped up her desire. With a teasing suck of her fingertip, she nodded, unsure if Josh would let her speak but unwilling to relinquish all control.

As if reading her mind, he responded, "Say yes. I love hearing you say it."

"Yes." She quivered.

"I like that. You said it in that sexy way when I licked your clit yesterday." The depth of his voice was like kisses between her thighs. "It's time to collect on your promise. Are you ready?"

"Yes." Lust controlled her. It was as real as if his words were fingers drawing lazy circles down her naked back.

"Do you see the green door to your right?"

"Yes," she replied with a telltale tremble to her legs.

"Tell Jack you'll be gone fifteen minutes. Then walk through that door and make your way down the corridor," he commanded huskily. "You're going to come so hard for me, baby."

CHAPTER TWENTY-SEVEN

The corridor was empty except for champion shirts and photo memorabilia. Past achievements lined the walls, but Evie didn't stop to look closely. Where did this corridor go? She rolled her shoulders back and took deep breaths, but excitement ran through her like multiple electric shocks. Evie paused, but there were no shouts or whispers in the empty corridor. Fans would be leaving from the main door when the bar closed. What had Josh planned?

Her heeled boots clipped the stone floor as she meandered down the corridor. Sweat dripped down her chest under her Bulls rugby shirt, and she slid out of her waterproof jacket before tucking it under her arm. Josh gifted her the shirt that morning. The back was emblazoned with the name King in bright white. It'd given her a swagger all day. She wasn't any guy's property and never would be, but she was proud to be in a partnership with Josh and for everyone to know it.

Need hit in waves between her thighs. This tantalising game was a new side of Josh. Every day he blossomed with a bit more confidence. She didn't want to change or mould him into a different guy, but witnessing a Josh that was happier in his skin was incredible. Suddenly heavy footsteps sounded behind her. Her legs shook. Every ripple of adrenaline was accompanied by a thrill of lust, turning her on and heightening her arousal each time she sucked a breath. Before she turned, a hand grabbed hers and pulled her into a smaller tunnel off the corridor.

Josh's eyes glinted. "Do you surrender, Evangeline?" he said so deeply that his voice was like a hand coaxing her pussy. It was like that moment in his room two months earlier. They locked eyes.

"Yes, baby," she whispered. His eyes blazed with a hunger that matched hers.

"You're so fucking beautiful."

She willed him to kiss her. But instead, he pushed her against the wall in one fluid movement and pinned her arms above her head.

She opened her mouth in a moan, and he instantly took advantage of her parted lips and sucked at the lower lip before pushing his mouth against hers with unexpected zeal. He explored her with his tongue. Goose pimples covered her skin, and she writhed against him. Josh was in his soaking rugby uniform, his body pressed against hers. Her clothes sucked up his wetness while a sheen of sweat and moisture from his kit covered her skin. The kiss was hard and fast. Desperate sensuality consumed them as pent-up desire controlled his moves. Watching him command a field of fighters had done nothing to dampen the passion she'd woken with. Evie ground herself against him again. His hardness aligned with her pussy.

Her moans spurred him on as much as her grinding. Josh lifted her shirt, biting her nipples through her bra before sucking them and adding pleasure to the pain with caresses of his tongue.

"Yes," she groaned.

"Say it again." He smiled around her nipple before

resuming his kisses.

"But we need to hurry," she whispered. "We might get caught."

"I'll tell you when we hurry," he replied with authority, although his sheepish grin suggested he had the same concerns. "I want to be deep inside you. I haven't stopped thinking about it since I left you in bed this morning."

Evie reached for his shorts. She forced them and his boxers to the floor before he argued. His cock was thick and ready.

"Oh, you want to be in control?" He flicked the button on her jeans and shoved them down. "No knickers? Dammit, woman. Whenever I can't want you more, you do something like this." His erection rubbed at her pussy as he teased her. He slowly sheathed himself with a condom even as she hurried him. She kicked her jeans off although they tried to catch on her boots. Overwhelmed with arousal she refused to waste time removing her footwear.

Evie wrapped her leg around Josh to speed him up.

"Don't you want foreplay?" he replied with a wink. He thrust inside Evie before she back-chatted his cheek.

Josh smelt damp and musty, yet it encouraged her lust for him, reminding her of the man she'd witnessed at war in the match. The smell of hot dogs and burgers dissipated after the rugby match, while other scents collected around them. Every game she went to in the future, she'd remember this moment. Her hunger for him went beyond starvation. The fierce way he fucked her barely took the edge off her famine. Evie gripped his biceps through his shirt. His muscles swelled in her hands as he strained against her. They fought their climax. She wanted this moment to last forever, even as she battled the prospect of getting caught. His kisses were hard enough to make her lips sore, but she kissed him back with as much intensity. Josh drew back before slamming hard into her again.

Evie's head lolled in the crook of his neck as he fucked her with abandon. Finally, unable to hold herself up any longer, he took the weight of her body. Josh lifted her and pinned her against the wall. Her legs wrapped tightly around him as her heeled boots pushed against his arse. He went deeper with each thrust and penetrated her as she forced him further inside of her.

The roaring inside her head drowned out anything around them. The intensity that accompanied the roar was her warning, and suddenly she was coming hard. Josh clamped his mouth against hers and let her scream of pleasure echo inside him. Then, with a final push, he exploded inside her.

Panting, she remembered the Josh that held her heart gently and the man she saw on the pitch were the same. Instantly she wanted him to come inside her again, but footsteps in the corridor highlighted a need for discretion. He helped her shove her jeans back on, although it was more like a slapstick comedy when her button caught on her boots. He removed the condom, and they yanked their clothes back in place as Charlie's face peeked round the corner, and his never dulcet tones started on them.

"I don't want to know what you were doing."

Josh hid her glowing red face against his chest, gently holding her close. She smiled against his wet shirt.

"Josh, you have three minutes to get changed and get your arse on the coach. There are consequences if you don't."

"Yes, Boss Man."

"And stop smiling like that, because you're making me

jealous. I can't remember when I last had a quickie at a stadium!" Charlie ranted before adding, "Evie, a pleasure as always."

They giggled like naughty teenagers as they raced, hand in hand, down the corridor before departing to their destinations.

"Stop wringing your hands," Josh said over the Foo Fighters blaring from the car speakers. His drive through the country was as gentle as when he leaned over and squeezed her hands.

Not that it was gentle when Charlie almost caught them yesterday. As Josh fell asleep in front of the television after the match with a big grin, she was sure he was relieving every second.

"I didn't realise I was wringing anything," Evie replied before taking in the spring views from the passenger window. With Evie driving, they'd have been there by now, and she'd have had the distraction she needed.

"I'm not going to drive above the speed limit," he grunted, reading her mind.

"I didn't think you should," she lied.

"You might need to tell your foot, as it keeps hitting the imaginary accelerator pedal underneath it."

"I know these roads better than you. I learnt to drive around here."

"Tractors can't take corners that quickly," he teased.

"I learnt in a proper car."

"Did you recognise a roundabout before you moved? I bet you had to keep stopping to tip cows."

He was winding her up to distract her, but he had a

point. All she saw for miles were fields of emerald greens. Lambs bounded, and trees swayed in the breeze. It was like a picture postcard of bliss, but it was an illusion. They were close to the location infused with suffering. Lies resided at its core. This was where her heart had been crushed, and the pain had remained with her since.

Glimpsing Josh's cheeky face, which failed to hide the worry behind it, her fears ebbed. "Thank you for coming with me. I'm not sure I could do this otherwise."

"You're never alone, Evie. I'm always here, and you only have to ask."

Relief and happiness combined to nudge away, rather than hide, the darkness. Each time Josh showed her love and respected who she was, a little more light came in. A lot was needed, as darkness had reigned for too long.

The sign welcomed them to Short Bellington.

"That is a ridiculous name for a village."

"It's a ridiculous village," she said wistfully as they drove down the main street. Evie pointed to the local pub, The Green Man. "This was where we would crown the carnival queen each year. She was always a perfect blonde who would have been a head cheerleader if such a thing existed in my school. She was usually pregnant by a farmer by twenty.

"That's where I drank my first beer." She directed his attention to the run-down park with broken swings and a faded slide. "And where I threw it up about five minutes later. It's also where I had my first cigarette as Aaron Broker cheered me on."

"So that's who I have to thank for the weeks getting you off your addiction," he replied grumpily.

"He's suffering enough. Aaron was appointed head of

the local primary school. So he'll have lots of naughty kids to keep an eye on now." She chuckled.

"Serves him right," Josh replied as they turned into Church Street. "I hope they raise hell."

"And that," she said with a tremor in her voice, "is where my parents and baby sister live."

"Baby sister?"

"Maybe not a baby. She'll be about twenty-two now. When I left, she was fourteen, innocent, naive, like a little lamb." Evie spent so long trying to blank out the past that she'd forgotten who she wanted to keep in her heart. She missed her so much.

"No beer and fags in the park for her, then?"

"No, Gabi—Gabriella was my dad's favourite. She never did anything wrong. She was the golden child and his perfect little angel. But it wasn't her fault. She toed the line, and so did I until…" But she didn't finish her sentence, and Josh didn't make her.

Josh stopped the car outside the brownstone building. The tinges of red through the front façade revealed ominous shadows.

"It's got a bit of creepiness to it, but maybe it was nice when you were a child?" he added, his voice going high. "Why is the house called Manse?"

"Didn't I mention? My dad's the local vicar," she replied, opening the door and easing herself out of the car. It was time to confront the past and hopefully give it a wave rather than the middle finger. "Josh, please stay in the car."

He'd fight her on this, so she made her appeal as she peeked in the car window. "My parents haven't seen me in eight years. I need to speak to them alone and tell them about Nan. I'll shout to you when I need you. And I will need you."

His eyes implored her for sense, but he replied, "I'm here, waiting, and all you need to do is say my name."

"You love it when I say your name," she joked without humour, but it didn't lighten the mood, as nothing could. Still, his forced smile was enough to push her towards the prison she never believed she'd return to.

Evie slowly stepped onto the path she'd once skipped down with her sister. There was no turning back. It was like ripping off a plaster.

Her heart tugged with happy memories, but others shrouded them and suggested they never existed beyond her rose-tinted glasses. Birds called out from the trees to tell her they'd missed the joy she'd always brought to the place as a child. Those days were long gone. All she got as a teenager were screaming arguments, suffering, and guilt trips. Their standards were so high. She apologised and explained, but it had never been enough. And then there was Peter.

Evie's hand was lifted by forces beyond her control. It was as if she was watching her body knock on the door rather than doing it herself, but this wasn't a dream; it was a continuation of the nightmare from when she left. Fear trickled down her throat. It was like the day she had her first communion wine and had wondered if it would burn her gullet because of all the naughty things she'd done that week.

The front door of her childhood home opened, and her mum's joyful face peeked through. It was the smile she shared when caring for the older people in the village or when she sang songs to eager Sunday school children.

"Evangeline." Evie's mum's face dropped as she recognised her. Instead of a hug or a "we missed you," her mum added, "Let me get your father."

Evie shook with the terror that came with the mention of her dad. It hadn't always been a terror, because they'd got on when Evie was younger, but in the last eight years, she hadn't been able to hear mention of him without bile climbing her throat and dread winding like a snake in her belly. Suddenly he was there before she had time to remember the speech she'd prepared. Green eyes, just like hers, crushed any spirit left inside her. Maybe if she'd had a moment with her mum first, she would have said her piece.

"What are you doing here? You disturbed our after-church dinner." He glowered. "Still, I expect Sunday doesn't mean much to you anymore. Although if anyone should be asking for forgiveness, it's you."

Evie froze in front of him as she had as a teenager. How, after all this time, did he carry this contempt for her? She wanted to shout and wail at the judgment he'd reserved for her.

She took a deep breath and squared up to him. "I came to tell you that Nan, your mum, died this week." She hadn't intended to give him the news brutally, but he brought a fit of anger that grew like a beast in her stomach. He'd brought out this side of her since her teenage years. Was she to blame because of her rebellion, or had his expectations made her into something uncontrollable? Her perfect childhood years had been wiped from his memory.

"Is that all you came to say?" he replied curtly.

"Your mum died from cancer several days ago. Don't you care if she suffered or died alone?"

"I know enough. Your grandma corresponded with your mother for years."

Her dad's revelation stripped her of her fury. Had her nan shared details of Evie's life with them too?

Tears streamed down her cheeks before splatting the

pavement in big drops. Was it from her nan's betrayal or how her dad sneered rather than shared the grief she'd been holding tight?

Josh, I need you.

Her dad raised his eyebrow as he pinned her with his gaze. "Please leave my property. I didn't invite you."

Tears continued to roll down her face. "You're meant to forgive. Why are you treating me like this after all these years?"

He folded his arms brusquely as if trying to enforce a barrier between them. "I have forgiven you, although you failed to admit that you lied about Peter."

"I didn't lie," she shouted, fury and pain colliding. But she refused to throw the tantrum that he wanted to see.

"As I said," he huffed as if her presence was a waste of his precious minutes, "I forgive you, but I will not accept the poisonous lies you told about that man. You nearly ruined his marriage and his career. It's his forgiveness you need."

Evie shook with the rush of adrenaline, fear, and anger. How could the man who once read bedtime stories and held her hand when she fed the ducks be full of hatred for her?

"Stop being so dramatic, child. You should have matured by now, but you've not changed from the teenager whose sole aim was to destroy others for her benefit."

Suddenly a hand slipped into hers. Josh repeated the moment when her nan was dying. Her staunchest defender was by her side. The squeeze from Josh centred her. She pulled her shoulders back and glared at her dad. "I shouldn't have come back. You didn't deserve to have me as a daughter. I see that now. You can insult me as much as you like, but I know the truth, even if you're too scared to admit it." Evie's eyes flicked to the pale face of her mum, who hid in the back of the corridor.

"As far as we're concerned, we have one daughter, and it is not you." Her dad continued to berate her existence. "You were trouble from the second you became a teenager. Now leave and never return. You're not welcome here and never will be."

With that, he slammed the door in her face, leaving her violently shaking as sobs wrecked her body.

Chapter Twenty-Eight

Josh pulled her into his arms.

His chest quickly dampened from her tears, and he held her tighter. He had to obliterate the hate her dad spewed. Then, as her sobs quietened, he brushed his kisses to her hair and whispered, "Evie, honey, we can't stay here. This place doesn't deserve you. Let's go back to the car."

He held her close as they stumbled to the car. Gently he tucked her into the passenger seat before sitting by her side. She continued to cry, but he took her hand and held it close.

"Thank you," she whispered as she grabbed quick breaths.

Dumbfounded, Josh stared at her tear-stained face.

"Don't look at me like that." She giggled. "You're like a cute monkey rather than my sexy beast. I'm trying to say thank you."

"For what?"

"For being there when I needed you."

"I'll always be here for you when you need me." But after seeing her parents, her lack of belief in support made more sense. "And I'll be here for you every day to prove it."

At her sweet smile, he puffed his chest out.

"I'm starting to believe you, although you don't need

to be so arrogant about it," Evie replied with a wink.

They sat in contemplative silence until Josh blurted, "Who was Peter?"

"You heard that then?"

"Afraid so." Josh sighed. "What happened when you were younger? If you're worried about how I'll take it, then don't be. It won't change how I feel about you, and I've probably overthought something worse."

"I'm worried you won't believe me." Josh understood that fear better than she knew. He held her hand closer to his heart and waited. "But I do trust you. I care about you, and I want to tell you. But I'm not sure I can."

Josh stared out the windscreen and waited. A little girl crossed the road in front of the car. She held what was probably her dad's hand and a bright pink foil balloon in the other. Her loud singing carried through the gaps in Josh's window. Was Evie like this before she was rejected when trying to find her identity and place in life?

Josh's phone vibrated in his pocket, but he ignored it. It would be his dad. He'd already left a dozen messages and would be furious that Josh had let another one go to voicemail.

The girl and her dad crossed the road. She danced in circles before bounding towards a village green with the balloon clutched tightly in her hand. Maybe their broken relationships with their parents drew him and Evie to each other.

"I used to love to dance," she whispered through silent tears. The scent of her musky perfume filled the space of the car. "I still do, but I don't perform. I used to dance for personal enjoyment, but I don't do that anymore. So I guess that's not important." She was confusing and disjointed, but he'd be patient for her.

"Let me start properly." She sighed deeply, and he fought the need to soothe her. This was her story; all he needed to offer was a safe space. "In my last year of school, when I'd just turned eighteen, I was a keen dancer. I loved dancing more than anything, and it possessed me. I would dance every extra lesson, break, and when I was supposed to be sleeping. I got told off for dancing in corridors and doorways at school."

She chuckled absentmindedly.

"Ballet was the only thing important to me, and everything else was a waste of precious time when I could be dancing. I was hoping to go to dance college when I left school. Dad wasn't happy. He wanted me to go to university and achieve academically, but keeping me motivated was tricky. He bargained with me, and we fought a bit, but I agreed to study hard at school and with a personal tutor three nights a week if I got to dance the rest of the time and follow my dreams."

"Sounds like a fair deal."

"He believed that I'd decide dancing wasn't for me or see there wasn't a future in it. And if I didn't, I'd have a good academic background to take me anywhere. The tutor was a man from his church, a science teacher who taught me at school. Dad was pushing me into medicine."

Josh held tightly onto his surprise. Evie was intelligent enough to be a medic, but it wasn't the field he'd pictured for her.

"Did it go well?"

"Yeah, I was getting the top grades. I loved learning, and I was performing well in shows. All my auditions resulted in the lead roles. My dad was proud. He didn't say it, but he was on my back less and didn't tell me to be quiet when I talked about dancing. Finally, he'd moved away from guilting me over my mini teenage rebellion. I believed everything might be okay between us."

"But something had to have gone wrong. It was sickening the way he looked at you. I wanted to punch him to the floor."

"It was my tutor. Well, it was both of us. The first problem was my boobs started to grow, like really big."

"I wasn't expecting you to say that," he joked, hoping it was helpful to lighten the mood.

Evie laughed, but it wasn't a true Evie guffaw. There was joy around the edges, but happiness hadn't reached the middle. "Sadly, big boobs make dancing more complicated. Lead roles were harder to get. It was less about my skills and more about how I didn't fit the ballerina mould. But it didn't deter me. I fought, trained, and worked harder than anyone else, and for a time, it was enough."

"Then what went wrong?"

Evie refused to make eye contact with him. Josh wanted to cover her with a blanket of love and respect and hold her close until the past faded, but he couldn't remove her history. Instead he held her tightly, taking her hands between his, not revealing his shock at how cold they were. He looked out the windscreen.

"How come you ended up living with your nan?"

Her hands trembled in his, and he held on tighter. "I fell in love with Peter, my tutor."

The car may have been drowning in silence, but Josh's mind was noisier than if he'd been speeding down a motorway with open windows. Shame radiated from Evie. Evie's dad had accused her of lying about Peter, which was the foundation for his hatred. What happened?

"And Peter fell in love with me. That's what he told

me." Evie paused. "Peter was married. He had two children, and his wife was so kind. I'd known her through the church for years. I flirted with him, and my mind was always on him. I'd give him love letters." Hadn't they all had crushes like that when they were a teenager? Something darker was coming. "Then he bought me a secret mobile and told me not to tell anyone about it and to keep it hidden but with me at all times. At first, we'd send each other hellos or jokes, but then the flirting we did in person was replicated in the messages. Over time his messages got a little more sexual, and mine did too. I should have stopped it." The fact she was eighteen was irrelevant. The man had groomed her.

Rage boiled through Josh's veins. "He was an adult and in a position of trust. You were his student. It was on him the whole time to stop it."

Evie held up her hand, silencing him. Josh sighed as he nodded, although every part of him wanted to protect her from revisiting that time of agony. "Eventually, we started talking about fantasies. The messages he sent me were explicit and about his fantasies with me. It was wrong, but when I got nervous, he'd say that he loved me and that I was more important to him than anyone."

The more he heard, the more Peter sickened him.

"I was on the brink of sending him pictures, maybe even sleeping with him, when I found out it wasn't just me. I'd been willing to do anything for him. He seemed to love me no matter what I said wrong." She shoved her sleeve under her eyes to stem the flowing tears.

"What do you mean?"

"Sometimes, I'd whisper something flirty to him at school. The staff and students didn't hear, but he told me that people would call me names if anyone found out what we'd been doing. Apparently, we were keeping it a secret for my benefit."

"Dickhead. You don't still believe that, do you?"

"No, I was foolish, and I thought he loved me. He'd do things like make me dance for him. I was low when our thing started because of trying to fight for my place in ballet. I was scared I might disappoint my parents or prove them right that ballet wasn't a good career for me. I hated my body, but Peter loved me for who I was. He told me that I was beautiful at a time when dancers made me feel freakish."

Josh pulled his hands away and made fists. Angry tears collected in his eyelashes. "It wasn't love. He was a predator. He found your weakness and used it to get what he wanted."

Evie's tears fell like a monsoon. "I know. I was a gullible idiot who fell for his lies. He never loved me, and I was nothing to him."

Josh threw his door open in blind fury.

*****

Sobs jerked Evie's body. Josh had left the car, and she was alone again.

Josh whipped her door open in a frenzy. His arms reached for her. He helped her from the car, pulled her tightly against his chest, and refused to let go. His body shook in what she suspected was anger, but he continued to pin her to him.

"Don't you ever blame yourself," he told her, his voice tight and his tears falling onto her hair. "You were manipulated by an older man who knew what he was doing."

They shook and cried together.

"You're not angry with me?" She hated her weak, childlike voice. The day she moved to her nan's, she'd vowed never to let anyone close and only be strong.

"You didn't do anything wrong. I have no reason to be angry with you."

"But you're shaking and crying."

"Because I'm fucking livid, Evie. That man exploited you. Aren't you angry at all?"

"I was."

"Did you have counselling or any kind of therapy afterwards?"

"I was too scared to go. I didn't want to be judged."

"Promise me you'll research it? Talk to Aidan about counselling. He had someone who helped him with all his medical stuff and anger. Promise me. I'll support you in whatever way I can. I'll pay for it if you need me to or keep you company at the pub if you take extra shifts. What you went through could have destroyed you, and you deserve help to work through it with a professional."

The soft smile she gave him made his tears fall heavier.

She nodded. "I'll speak to someone, I promise. I didn't have anger in those days. I was more hurt than anything, especially considering what happened when Dad found out."

Josh pushed her back suddenly, almost toppling her over. "Sorry, I can't believe I forgot about that bit. Sit in the car."

He squeezed her quickly before helping her back to the passenger seat. Her feet hung out the side where Josh sat on the curb. His face was as readable as the words in a children's book. Love shone from him while concern furrowed his brow and tightened his lips. Hands gently toyed with her calves, unable to reach any other body part.

"I hope your dad beat the shit out of him." She knew he didn't believe it though.

"No, he didn't. Everything came out the night after I'd finished school. At the prom, I saw him talking to another girl. I confronted her in the bathroom and told her to stop flirting with him. She told me they were in a secret relationship and had been for a couple of months. I was livid. She showed me some of the messages he'd sent her. That night I told Peter I wanted to meet him at the bottom of his road. He thought it was because I was finally willing to sleep with him, but that was the furthest thing from my mind. I'd felt guilty about what I might be doing to his family all that time, but I stupidly thought he loved me. Not that it's an excuse." Tears splattered her clothes.

Josh wiped his tears away. "I wish I'd been there for you then. I would have done everything to stop that fucker from getting near you," he whispered.

"You would have?"

Josh nodded. "What happened next?"

"I snuck out late when everyone was in bed, but Gabi saw me. Like a dutiful daughter, she woke Dad immediately. I had no idea he'd left the house until he caught me at the bottom of Peter's road. Dad lost his shit when he saw me shouting at Peter, and of course, Peter sold me to the wolves instead of defending me. He told Dad I'd been trying to seduce him all year and that he had said no, and that he'd been worried about my mental health. Peter said I'd threatened to lie to his wife that we were sleeping together if he didn't meet me for a chat that night."

"What?" Incredulity seeped from his pores. But for Evie, the more she shared, the more she understood how little she'd done wrong.

"Peter told my dad that he'd met with me that night to help me see reason. I was troubled, and he wanted to help me."

"And your dad believed him over his own daughter?"

"Of course. Dad hadn't forgotten my difficult years or the issues with my behaviour. Peter was an upstanding member of the community, a good church man, and a family friend. So why would dad believe me?"

"Because you were his fucking daughter! Didn't you show your dad the texts?"

"Peter told me to delete them every day. He explained that with no evidence, I couldn't get into trouble. But he meant he couldn't get into trouble."

Josh's eyes turned blacker than the barren countryside during an eclipse. "I have no idea who I'm going to kill first, but there will be a massacre in this village."

"At least let me finish," she joked, hoping to calm him. However, her Josh wouldn't physically hurt anyone unless his life was threatened. It was one of the reasons she loved him. But the next part wasn't going to help his fury. "I made Dad come with me to the other girl's house, but she denied everything. I think Peter got to her first. Dad dragged me home, branding me a liar who'd shamed the family. It wasn't enough that I lied about Peter, but by bringing the other girl into it, I'd sullied her name too. I tried to tell him that Peter was lying, but he'd stopped listening. Nan later explained his thinking. She said that Dad refused to admit that someone he'd trusted with his daughter did what Peter had. Dad would have believed he'd let me be groomed and inadvertently encouraged and paid for it. It was too much to see me every day and attempt to manage the guilt. So instead of dealing with what he'd done, he chose a coward's way out and branded me a liar while banishing me from his world."

"It doesn't make it okay."

"Of course it doesn't, and I'll never forgive him, not now. But good men exist. You showed me that." Josh blushed, and a smile covered his anger. "At dawn that morning, he drove me to a train station with fifty pounds and my nan's address."

"Fifty pounds is bullshit, and your dad is a bastard. He left you to fend for yourself."

"Which I did. Nan didn't have much money, and I didn't have any skills for a proper job. So I fell into glamour modelling while attempting to be a waitress. Some guy approached me and offered me money. Then when Nan started to get ill and the bills came in, it was unmanageable. I couldn't cope. I sold lies to the press to pay for her care. I didn't have anyone but her, and I owed her. She'd believed me, and I loved her with all my heart. I'm not proud of selling those stories, but I didn't feel I had choices. Now I know there are other options."

"I wouldn't have guessed any of this. When you were with Aidan, I thought you were a bitch."

"And I thought you were a judgemental wanker," she replied but followed it with a cheeky grin.

"You had a point." He shrugged. "But why aren't you angrier? That guy destroyed your life."

"I guess."

Josh's voice rose suddenly. "You guess?" He cleared his throat and took a deep breath. "Sorry."

"The thing is, it's the only life I've known. I can't say, 'if things had been different,' because who can be sure how things would have ended? If Gabi hadn't seen me, if Peter hadn't lied, and if Dad had chosen to believe me instead of Peter. It's all ifs. You can't base your life on ifs."

Josh remained silent.

"And there are positives too. I got to know my nan. I was there when she needed me and had no one else and..." A sheepish smile was turning up the corners of her mouth. "I got to meet you. That might have happened anyway, and I would have liked a different path to get to where we are now, but life happens, and you do what you can to get through it and not let it fuck you up in the process, although I'll consider counselling. After hiding it all this time, talking about it is kind of freeing."

Josh leaned in and raised his head to receive a kiss.

"I want to care for you and show you how much I admire you," he said against her lips.

"Then take me home and make me dinner."

"For you, Evie, anything." After a quick peck, he closed her door and walked around the car. A piercing screech got her attention, and she threw open the door to a tanned beauty.

"Don't go yet. Please. I need to speak to you, Evangeline."

"Gabi?" She hadn't heard that voice in eight years.

"Yes, of course. I had to see you."

"What if Dad catches you?"

"He's hiding in his study. I think he's in shock from how he spoke to you."

"I'll give him a shock," Josh growled from the side, making Gabi jump.

"No, you won't," Evie replied. "Please get me a piece of paper." She needed a second alone with her sister. "There's a lot I want to ask you."

"Same here." Evie and Gabi were different in every way, each physically taking after a different parent and with polar personalities, but her familiar eyes brought an unexpected ache to Evie's heart. "But I can't right now. I have to go to church and set up for Easter. We've got a big week coming up."

"He's still got you doing that?" Evie kicked herself. She'd enjoyed church when she was younger, but her dad's rules and people like Peter put her off the church.

"Don't be like that. I enjoy it. I enjoy spending time with the children. Just because it's not your thing doesn't mean it's wrong."

"Sorry," Evie rushed to say, but the weariness in her sister's eyes made it clear she'd damaged their delicate relationship. "I didn't mean to upset you. I missed you." Gabi edged away. Evie's rapid heartbeat forced words from her mouth. "You've probably heard stuff about me—"

"Dad never let me speak about you, but I overheard Mum talking to Nan. I'm sorry to hear she died, although I only met her once when she came to stay. I was about five. She was erratic, and it made Dad livid."

"I remember." Evie stifled a giggle. "But she was an amazing woman, and the craziness was the icing on top of her madness sponge. You would have liked her."

They stood, staring at each other. Gabi wasn't as well put together as Evie remembered. Her bun was lopsided, and her cuffs were worn down and scraggly as if she'd chewed them. Gabi stood on the sides of her feet, which was an awkward balancing act. She was always a little uncomfortable in her skin, but Evie couldn't put her finger on what had caused this change.

At a tap on the glass behind the downstairs net curtain, Gabi pushed loose strands of hair from her face. It was the nervous tick she'd developed in primary school when children teased her. Evie fought a lot of kids on her behalf, but the tick remained.

It was a mystery which gutless parent tapped at the window, but it was enough to make Gabi look dejectedly towards the house. "I'd best go."

"Wait," Evie pleaded, chasing after her. "Here is my address and phone number."

Swiping the scrap of paper from Josh's hands, she quickly scrawled across it. It was like she was on a countdown timer. "And this is where the funeral will be. Friday at two o'clock. Please remember, because I'd love to see you there."

"Thanks." Gabi snatched the paper and shoved it in her pocket. "Bye."

"I love you," Evie said as Gabi rushed back to the house. The emptiness Evie had carried before Josh returned.

Evie meandered back to the car. Her head dipped as melancholy filled her veins.

Suddenly a push from behind nearly knocked her into the car. But it wasn't a push; it was a bear hug from her baby sister. "I love you too. And I never believed what people said about you. Take care of yourself," Gabi whispered in Evie's ear before sprinting away.

*****

"Are you okay with going home?" Josh asked tentatively once Evie strapped herself in.

"There's one more place I want to go, and then we can head home," she replied. Although they'd recovered from their crying, the power of making themselves vulnerable brought them closer. Was this what came with honesty and love? The confidence to share his whole story rose. When the time was right, he'd talk properly about Lulu.

Soon they sat outside a newer house than the manse. It resembled a typical village new build, with generic brown bricks and windows in precisely the same place as the houses it was sandwiched between. The front door looked like it was purchased from Homebase and screwed in that week. It was bland, the opposite of the beauty beside him.

"Should I wait here? Will you be long?"

"I need you with me, Josh, holding my hand and reminding me I'm not alone." He tried not to push his chest out with pride. "You're my boyfriend, after all."

They'd never said the words boyfriend or girlfriend before.

"Yes, I am," he agreed with a grin.

Josh took Evie's hand, and soon they were hurrying to the front door. Keeping up with her forthright strides was a challenge. She was a purposeful woman who had conquered and achieved a lot in her life, but this screamed of being a defining moment.

The name Haven was etched into a house plaque on the side of the door. There was something pretentious about the name, and the door knocker in the shape of a lion was another unsightly addition to the copy-and-paste house.

"Arse," Evie whispered. Which feature drew that astutely given insult? His glimpse of the bristly welcome mat answered his question.

Welcome, Lovely People

She squeezed Josh's hand tightly.

"Where are we?" he asked. Evie thudded the door knocker. It echoed around the sleepy street.

"Peter's house." Josh's anger bubbled, and he gripped

her hand tighter. "This isn't your fight, Josh. There are things I need to say to him. And stop squeezing my hand so tightly. I won't be able to give you hand jobs again at this rate," she added, but her attempt to lighten the mood didn't stop Josh's wrath.

Evie knocked on the door loudly again, impatience rising with every second. "I must do this, but I need you by my side. You're here for me, which means not starting a fight on my behalf."

Maybe his evolution hadn't finished; the caveman was in his depths. The vengeful ape in him demanded to snap and rip heads off as he declared his alpha role.

Surreptitiously he took in her trembling form. But it wasn't what she needed from him. He loved her too much to make it worse.

Shit, I do love her.

The door opened.

CHAPTER TWENTY-NINE

Evie sucked in a breath as the demon of her past confronted her.

Peter was the epitome of a school science teacher, kicking back with black-rimmed glasses, a smart polo shirt, tailored jeans, and white trainers. Out of the corner of her eye, she caught Josh's sneer.

Her confidence was a distant memory now that he was in front of her. They waited like performers in a drama who'd forgotten their lines and had no prompt to aid them. Warmth retreated from her body, and vomit rose from her belly. She couldn't do this. The man had ruined her life and destroyed her relationship with her family.

"Can I help you?" Peter stuttered.

Josh squeezed her hand gently, and she juddered back to life. The anguish that she'd pushed down all these years, the anger that she'd let rule her when modelling, and the pain that had stopped her from living fused and forced themselves through her limbs. She squeezed Josh's hand back and lifted her shoulders into her fighting stance.

"Is that all I get? Not a 'hello, how's your life been since I destroyed it'? Or 'I'm surprised you survived after I made your dad banish you'? Fuck, you didn't comment on my 'beautiful body,' which you wouldn't stop talking about when I was eighteen."

"I don't know who you are." The lie was as transparent as his face was becoming as the pale pallor settled on his skin. Still, uncertainty made her tremble, but fight or flight suddenly kicked in, and with Josh by her side, adrenaline roared through her.

"Don't fucking lie to me, Peter. You recognise me. I'm the girl you cheated on your wife with. Well, one of them. There were so many of us that it must be hard to remember who's who."

Peter dropped his head.

"You should be castrated."

He shook his head. He resembled one of those wobbly-headed dashboard toys. "What are you talking about? Please leave here."

"Why? So you can pretend you never groomed me? You should be in hell, but you tried to send me there instead. It didn't work, and my life has ended up okay."

"You became a glamour model," he said, stumbling over his words.

How dare he speak to her like that. Josh leaned forward, and she found her voice again.

"I got this, Josh, but thank you," she said gently, willing him into silence.

"So you do recognise me, and you've followed my career?" she replied like a viper set on destroying its prey with a snap of its jaw. "You tried to ruin my life. How many other lives did you destroy with your grooming and lies?"

"What is happening out here?" a woman's voice called out from behind Peter.

"You have to go before you bring more shame on your family," Peter said between gritted teeth as he tried to close the door.

"Or shame on you?" Evie replied.

"Peter, who is at the door?" Evie recognised that voice now. Penny, Peter's wife, suddenly appeared by his side. "I know you, don't I? You're Evie Draper. I haven't seen you since you left to go to the city about…"

"Eight years ago."

"She popped by to say hello," Peter bumbled, trying to close the door.

"The fuck I did. I popped by to see if your husband had got his comeuppance."

"Excuse me?" Penny snapped. "His what?"

Josh wriggled next to her but still stayed quiet.

"His comeuppance. I left the village because I had an affair with your husband, and when he denied it, my parents kicked me out and refused to speak to me." Evie rushed through the words before Peter shut the door in her face.

Penny's brow furrowed.

Peter shook his head violently and turned his wife to face him. "Evie was kicked out for being a silly teenager and falsely accusing me. Now she's back and trying to do it again. You know I'd never do anything like that." He turned back to Evie. "Get out and away from my house," Peter spat at Evie before returning to his wife. "You can't believe this thing over me. She was a porn star, for God's sake."

"Glamour model," Josh dived in, "just to clarify."

"And who are you?"

"I'm Evie's boyfriend," he replied, "although that's not hugely important right now."

"It's important to me," Evie said, squeezing his hand before turning to Peter's wife. "Penny, I'm sorry. I never meant to hurt you. I never slept with him, although I doubt that's a consolation. I thought I loved Peter and that he loved me. I wasn't the only one he did this to."

"More lies," Peter stuttered.

Penny wrung her hands. "There was a rumour about a girl from the school and a teacher."

"Nina Palmer?" Evie offered. There could be lots, based on Peter's history, but it was worth a shot.

Penny's eyes widened. "Yes. That's her. She had a baby but wouldn't name the father. The rumour was that an older man was the father, but no one knew who." Penny rounded on Peter. "Was it you? Are you the father?"

Evie stood back. Should she and Josh go? It was like she'd dropped a bomb and was leaving the aftermath.

"Of course not. Don't be so silly."

"I always thought the boy reminded me of someone when I saw him in the village."

"You're being ridiculous. You always get jealous like this."

"Ridiculous? Well, let's go and see Nina, shall we? Let's have a nice little chat with Nina and her son. You've got nothing to be scared of, because you're so innocent and I'm so ridiculous," Penny replied. The intensity of her words suggested this wasn't an unexpected revelation about her husband after all. Maybe she'd suspected something about his behaviour for a while.

"Come on now, darling. You're getting carried away and riled by this pathetic girl here."

"I'm a woman, Peter. I know you prefer them younger because they're easier to manipulate, but call me a woman, you twat," Evie hit back.

Penny pushed past Evie and strode down the path. "I'm going whether you come or not, Peter," she shouted back. Peter pulled the door closed and ran after her, desperately trying to soothe her, but the woman was on a mission.

Evie's eyes were wide, and her mouth turned down at the edges as she swiveled to Josh. Had she destroyed the family because of her need to deal with the past? Then, as if Josh read her thoughts, he said, "Don't blame yourself for any of this. It's all on Peter, not you. He groomed you. Don't forget that."

"Should I report him to the school board and the police? I partly thought it was my fault, so I… What should I do?"

"It's okay, Evie. You don't need to decide right now," Josh said as he gripped her hand tightly. "Do you want to go?"

She nodded. "There's nothing we can do now." Evie stared after Penny and Peter.

"Let's go," Josh said. He grabbed her hand and scooped up her emotions as they returned to the car.

*****

"I was certain he'd ruined my life," she said as Josh drove them down country lanes and away from the village. "But I guess I'm stronger now. And I wouldn't have recognised a good man if it hadn't been for him. It took a shitty one to see how amazing you are."

"You don't have to go to the police or anyone else until you're ready. Too much has been out of your control because of Peter. You are in control of your life."

She twisted her hair around her finger as she said, "I will go, but not today. And I will try a counsellor too. It's silly that this makes me think of the butterfly effect and how it took a long route to learn about amazing men. The butterfly wings don't always make an immediate change, but I don't want him to hurt anyone else, and I need help to talk through everything that happened."

"You're the wisest woman I know. And nothing you say sounds silly." He didn't always understand her analogies or ponderings, but he didn't need to. Contemplative silence gripped them for a moment. "Can I ask you something?"

"Always."

"How come you gave your sister my address and not your nan's?"

"Because I want to move in with you." Her smile shone, eclipsing any darkness that resided from their trip. "You and those smelly boys. If you'll let me."

"Let you? You try and stop me. I'll ensure you have all the drawers in the house, a walk-in wardrobe, a throne in the living room, and everything else you want or need."

Josh yanked the car into a parking space and kissed her smiling lips until they were red and sore. "And I'll kick those smelly boys out. You don't need to be their mum," he said before resuming his manic kisses.

"Josh." She giggled, pushing him away. "Won't that be too much money? I have to pay my way, but I'm not sure I can afford that. Maybe we should rent somewhere smaller."

"Evie." He took her face between his hands. "The Josh you know is careful to the point of insanity. I'm careful with money too. I own the house mortgage free."

"Oh. But surely careful Josh is worried we're moving in together too soon," she teased.

That was what his dad would say. Evie stroked the lines that formed on his forehead. She didn't ask for an explanation of why they'd appeared but smoothed them away like she tried to smooth his worries away. "Yes, but I'm trying not to listen to him anymore because he doesn't want me to be happy. I want it to be our place."

"Okay, but on one condition."

"I'll go down on you every night?"

The giggles began, and she struggled to breathe through them. "If you insist. But I was going to ask to wait until after Friday, after Nan's funeral?"

"Of course. We'll wait until you're ready. It's probably best to wait until after Saturday. Once I've played the last game of the season, the big match, then I can be all yours." He gave her a cheeky wink, making her giggle. He couldn't wait to be all hers.

Josh gave her a quick last peck on the lips before they continued their journey.

"Why is the match the big one?"

"Boss Man let it slip that the England coach is attending because they're old friends. It's not a scouting trip for talent, but Boss Man said that if the coach sees something or someone he likes, maybe he'll consider them for an international game."

"That would be fantastic. Do you have a shot? I think you do, but my bias might be blinding me," she added. "You're incredible on and off the pitch."

He shrugged before pulling back onto the road. "I do if yesterday wasn't a fluke."

"And do you want to play for England? You haven't always talked about rugby with a lot of passion."

Josh paused. "I know, but do you know what? I've never wanted this more. Yesterday proved to me how much I love playing. When I was running that pitch, it was like I was alive and wanted to play for the rest of my life. I don't get it, but something has changed in me. I want to play for my country and kick so much arse."

"Then I'll keep everything crossed for you."

"Not your legs, please not your legs," he teased, squeezing her thigh.

Evie's responding laugh brought a flutter of endorphins to his belly.

He drove them out of the countryside and towards a place that might become their home soon. Josh sighed as they neared town. "It's also an important game for Lucas. We're playing his old team."

"Is that unusual? You've already played them this season."

"True, but the rumour that Lucas refuses to deny is that he slept with his ex-coach's wife. My friend has hinted that the wife might be coming to the game."

"But surely, she'd avoid the match if people discuss those rumours? Although if she's anything like me, she'd be more likely to go."

Josh chuckled. "Ain't that the truth? But I hope she doesn't come. From the things Lucas says when he's drunk, I can tell there's more to their story. He's hurting, and it would mess him up if she came. The guy will go far if he learns to control his emotions. But something from his past has a hold on him."

"Everyone has their secrets."

That quietened him. Conversations with his dad resurfaced, burning holes in his soul and burrowing their way into his hidden fears.

CHAPTER THIRTY

"Morning, sexy." Josh snuggled up to her proudly, the big spoon against her body.

There was already a stirring in his groin. Josh kissed her neck, trying to blot out the nightmares that bullied him into silence. For the last couple of hours, he'd lain awake. Josh almost woke her a couple of times, intending to bare all, but whenever he came close, he remembered the texts his dad had sent.

Dad: Your mum misses you, Joshua. I presume your new woman is the reason you're too busy to call us. What if she's another Lulu?

Josh: Please leave this alone, Dad. I am allowed to have a life.

Dad: And who gave you that opportunity and every opportunity by keeping your secrets? I'd hate for her to find out about your past.

Josh: I'm going to tell her about Lulu. I want to move forward with my life.

Dad: You're a fool if you think she'll still love you. You'll lose her.

Josh: She'll understand. She's got a past too.

Dad: What's her past? I don't want anything to get in the way of your future.

Josh: It's none of your business.

Dad: I know you're reluctant to share, but you can tell me anything. I'm the one you can trust.

Josh: Don't worry about it. I will tell her about Lulu.

Dad: She'll hate you, and you'll never get her reaction out of your mind. I'll be here to pick up the pieces, as always.

Josh: I have a good feeling about her.

Dad: You barely know her. Trust your dad, Joshua.

Josh sent a brief message to his mum to ensure she was okay. She'd instantly replied to tell him to continue doing the things that made him happy and that she'd like to see him one lunchtime. He'd take her for a birthday meal that week. Would she tell his dad? When he'd wept with Evie outside her parent's house, his dad's voice whispered that real men didn't cry. But he had cried and was okay with that. He was someone's boyfriend, and she made him realise that anything was possible.

His dad left voicemail messages, saying Josh needed to keep up his training due to his poor season but that the weekend's match was a testament to Robin's hard work and that Josh couldn't have achieved it without him. But it was Charlie, and the team, that had enabled him to do well. It had nothing to do with his dad. His dad had been the problem for a long time. Evie was his muse when it came to the pitch too. He nearly kissed her face off when she'd said it was all him and that all she did was believe in him.

"I like your kisses," Evie purred, causing Josh to shudder. Evie used the palm of her hand to stroke his cock. What stirred before was hardening quickly. "Maybe you can kiss me somewhere else, or do I only get to collect on that promise once I've officially moved in?"

"What do you mean?" he replied coyly as he scooted down the bed, his lips caressing her naked skin. He brushed his mouth over her nipples before he travelled lower. Intent charged his body, and sensuality covered his lips like moisture.

"But first, I need to ask you something," she said seriously.

His jaw tightened even as he rested his chin on her stomach. What if she knew about Lulu? He needed time to explain it adequately before she heard it from anyone else.

"I was wondering…" A sliver of bile hit his tongue, and he held his breath as her green eyes fixed his gaze. "Would you meet me somewhere near town this evening?"

"Sure, where? Are we going out drinking?" She didn't know his secret, but his tight chest remained, and a dull ache arched around his forehead.

"Nothing like that. I have a secret plan, but trust me, because I'm pretty sure you'll like it." Her blossoming grin reduced the ache instantly. If his past didn't destroy the relationship, his overthinking might. "I'll text you the address. But we've got an hour before you have practice, so I'd like you to resume what you were doing."

"Not even a please?" he teased.

"No. Get to it," Evie growled.

In a fit of rebellion, he licked her nipples. Josh grinned when they hardened against his tongue.

"Josh," she warned. The heat between her thighs branded her on his chest while her hips wriggled against him to force him lower.

"Evie," he teased back, "I will lick your pussy when

I'm ready. It's my turn to play with you." But trying to resist the pulse of her clit was useless. The smell of her arousal burned his flaring nostrils while her juices covered his skin. There wasn't enough time in the world to enjoy her how he longed to, but he'd give her an orgasm that would leave her quivering all day and unable to focus on anything but him.

Maybe he'd give her two. Josh's chest flamed as he dipped his head and flattened his tongue against her clit.

Later that day, Josh made his way to the location Evie had finally texted to him. His fingers tapped restlessly against his palms as he crossed the road to an old red-brick shop. Was this the mysterious place she went to when she wasn't working at the pub? And why wasn't she asking him questions about his past? He took a deep breath and forced the overthinking away.

Evie cared about him no matter what and would eventually be okay with his secrets. But they had no future if he continued to hide it. And what if his dad said something before Josh explained what had happened with Lulu? Josh was starting to see his dad through the eyes of others.

Memories of Robin's controlling and manipulative actions were hard to ignore. Unfortunately, other deeply buried memories started to surface too. Seeing him with Evie and meeting Peter reminded Josh of his dad flirting with Lulu. But he'd been teasing her, hadn't he? That was what he'd said.

Evie wasn't the only positive in his life. Rugby was

going well, and practice that day had been outstanding. Boss Man had been full of praise; at least, that was what "You weren't *just* shit" translated to. But even with that positive, Josh struggled to ditch his secrets and forget his dad's behaviour. Only Evie's mystery location gave him respite from his stresses.

"Will she care that I'm half an hour early?" he mumbled.

He opened a door next to a mobile phone shop. The sign beside the door proclaimed "AXIS" in a baby pink font. As Josh cautiously walked up a clunky set of stairs that led above the shop, he searched for clues, but the walls were blank and the stairs badly carpeted. A vague smell of dampness filled the air. What if Evie had returned to glamour modelling? He had to be okay with it because she made her own choices. The sounds of chattering children distracted him from his worry. The children's voices stopped suddenly at Evie's commanding yet soft request.

Intrigue controlled his movements until the tinkling keys of a piano stilled him. It was like the music bounced from the room into his path. He glanced through a door and gasped, but no one in the studio turned. There, in front of him, was Evie in a black leotard and gauze skirt. Sunshine eased through the window and gave her an ethereal glow that added to the sight that left him frozen. His jaw hung down as he counted the children, mostly little girls in candyfloss pink tutus and leotards, surrounding her.

Was this what she wanted him to see? For several minutes Evie gave directions to the children. Josh remained hidden in the doorway as the children skipped and danced. Evie threw encouragement to all the children. One girl floundered as she tried to skip in time with the others, but Evie didn't criticize her. Instead, his goddess took the tiny girl's hand and danced with her.

Were there any limits to her layers? Each one that peeled off made his heart want to burst from his chest. That morning he'd taken Evie to climax while she writhed on his tongue, yet now he imagined how their babies would look. Josh rubbed his beard as he contemplated what their future could be.

"We have a latecomer to our class," Evie shouted to the children. Twenty sets of eyes stared in his direction and pinned him in the doorway.

"I'm an observer," Josh replied, but Evie coaxed him to the middle of the room. His feet wouldn't budge, but his heart wanted to be by her side.

"We don't have observers. Miss tells us we only have students," an angelic-faced girl hollered with a tone he imagined Evie used on the children before. The child was probably quoting her.

"We also don't shout things out without being asked, do we, Polly?"

"Sorry, Miss Evangeline." He experienced a tug of desire at the name Miss Evangeline.

"But Polly is correct. You must join in if you're in the ballet room and a class is in progress. Maybe it serves you right for being early," she teased. "Now, come here, Josh."

The children giggled as they tracked him. "But I can't," he protested. "I'm not dressed for it." Heat rose in his cheeks.

Evie raised one eyebrow as her gaze travelled over the rugby shorts and shirt that he hadn't changed out of after practice. "I don't have a tutu in your size, but you'll be fine like that."

"But I'm not a dancer, and I've got two left feet, and

I'm in trainers," he protested as he fisted his shirt.

Evie addressed the class. "Can he dance with us dressed like that, students?"

"Yes," the kids chimed, grinning like little trolls as they stared at him. Twenty-one against one, and all of them cheeky like their teacher. He didn't stand a chance.

"We were about to practice pliés. So you can join us in that, Mr. King," Evie stated professionally, although her eyes glinted under the bright lights of the dance studio.

"Fine," he grumbled. But as he joined the group, a glow filled his belly that Evie shared this part of herself with him. "How do you do it?"

She made a tsk sound and held up her palm. "Stop. Mr. King missed something important. Can anyone tell me what he's doing wrong?"

Twenty hands shot up immediately. Each eager-eyed child wanted to share their knowledge or embarrass him. A couple of children giggled behind a hand while others used their spare hand to hold their raised one at the bicep as if it made Evie see them above the other children. Their pink tutus bounced with excitement.

Evie surveyed the room before pointing at the girl who'd struggled when the group skipped. "Tilly?"

Her voice was as cute as fluffy pink puppies. "He needs to do his stretches."

The children stopped giggling long enough to show him how to do them while Evie added encouragement or suggested minor changes. She'd taught them well.

Over the rest of the lesson, Evie demonstrated a series of ballet positions with a kind authority that drew him closer to trusting her while ensuring he was enamoured.

She'd tasked Tilly with caring for him, especially during the complex moves. The little girl glowed under the responsibility that Evie had gifted her. Josh wasn't a dancer, which was evident to the whole class, but instead of laughing at him, which he caught other children doing until Evie berated them, Tilly patiently showed him every nuance of the dance moves. On several occasions, the gentle character knelt as her pretty tutu rested on the floor and moved his feet into position. While tiny in comparison to him, Tilly treated him like an equal. She wasn't scared like some young children were of his ogre-like appearance. Instead, she ensured he was allowed the opportunity to reach his potential.

Eventually, the class came to an end. Josh sat in the corner as Evie gave praise and personal homework to each child before they said their goodbyes and bounded to their parents.

Observing Evie had ensured she'd won his heart for life. Admiration for Miss Evangeline flowed through his blood like glitter, and now that they were alone, he was lost for words.

"Aren't you going to say anything?" she asked with a cheeky smile.

"I don't know what to say." Her smile dropped. "You must see how awestruck I am? But nothing I can say would do you justice. I don't have enough words to describe you, Miss Evangeline," he added, stumbling over his praise.

Her face blossomed with each word until she beamed at him. "Maybe I should give you the surprise I invited you here for originally. Sit down," she instructed as she pointed at a seat in the corner. Josh sat without question, and his eyes travelled down her body as she fingered the remote.

CHAPTER THIRTY-ONE

"**B**efore I start—" Evie's voice quivered as she stood in the dance studio and stared at Josh. "I wanted to say that last summer, I decided to return to what I loved and teach ballet. I couldn't face dancing and performing again, but I wanted to teach it without struggling with the shame and hatred Peter had instilled in me. Teaching started to fill the hole that had been inside of me since I left home."

Josh didn't move a muscle, transfixed by her words.

"After every lesson, I would stay behind in the studio and dance for you, although you never saw it, and our friendship started to heal me. Of course, we've had ups and downs since then, but when my nan died, and you supported me, it gave me something that had been missing from my life for years. I don't fully understand what, but I don't need to. You being there for me changed my life."

"I'll always be here for you," Josh whispered.

She raised her shoulders proudly. "I haven't performed for anyone for years, but you inspire me, so I choreographed a dance for you. Thank you for everything."

Green sparkles held him still. The music filled the room, and he recognised the song instantly. Radio 1 had played it a lot the previous year. The tune had a low beat that reached deep inside him and vibrated every muscle, yet there was also something delicate that transcended sexuality. The simple melody over the beat carried a beauty that stunned him but not as much as the woman dancing for him.

Evie's lithe body showcased the texture of the music as it inspired her into moves that he wouldn't be able to recreate even after a lifetime of lessons. One moment, her arms would flow as her legs turned and swept her around the floor. Next, everything would still except one leg arching as high as her shoulder. Each stretch of her thighs and flick of her foot was for him, inspired by him, and he was mesmerised. The sensuality of her graceful caress of the music enraptured him.

Her precision when she pointed her feet transfixed him, so he couldn't even smile when she wriggled her body while on her toes. However, nothing was amusing about her elegance when she moved. Her beauty swept effortlessly around him, and with each twist, she hypnotised him and left him dazed.

A passionate fire raged from her soul as she leapt across the room and showcased splits in mid-air. She displayed beauty in each aspect of her performance.

The music began to slow, forcing a thud deep within his belly. His limbs ached with need. The turns and flicks became more delicate but no less enthralling.

The leotard clung to her body. The curves she probably hated as an eighteen-year-old dancer, which had left her in tears at auditions, increased her desirability and beauty and made her dance more powerful. Evie was a goddess.

The need to have her captured him. As he gazed at her pirouette, he fantasised about wrapping her strong legs around him as he bent her low and held her still as she climaxed in his arms.

Josh shifted awkwardly in his seat when she turned away from him. Each move aroused him more, but he didn't want the dance to be about that. She was more than a sexy woman; she was a warrior that owned him. His respect for her blistered his soul as lust drove through him. He wanted to honour her skin with his lips yet admire her beauty all at once.

Suddenly Evie spun in front of him. With each twist, she came closer, yet her green eyes never left his. Instead, she spun faster and faster, displaying a skill that blew his mind until she stood panting in front of him.

"I want you," she declared as her chest heaved with every suck of air into her lungs.

Swiftly Josh stood, grabbing her bum and pulling her into him. Her legs wrapped around him, and he ripped off her flimsy skirt.

"You're wet for me," he growled as he gripped her bum and pushed his erection against the crotch of her leotard.

"Don't make me wait," Evie pleaded.

They were partners in their sexual adventures. Evie gripped his biceps with her long fingers as he walked her towards a solid wall in two strides. She kissed fire at every place she reached. It was as if she pulled at the nerves across his skin before transforming him into a blaze.

Quickly he pushed the piece of material that covered her pussy to one side. Thank God they'd had the contraception talk the day before. He freed his erection from his shorts and rubbed his dick against her lips.

"Stop teasing me," she cried. Her voice was like liquid yearning.

Josh responded with a laugh that rumbled through both of them. He relished her clinging to him. It was as if he stopped her from drowning in herself, yet she had saved him in ways she didn't know. Their nights spent caressing each other's souls when the barriers went down were among the many things he adored about their time together.

Evie's begging moans brought out an animalistic part of him that he'd kept buried for a long time.

"Please," she cried. Josh thrust into her before she'd finished the word. His lust eclipsed his fears.

Her cry of pleasure obliterated the last of his thoughts temporarily. Their bodies fused instantly, finding a rhythm that played to each other's strengths. They had power that rose from their core and gave birth to a passion that enabled her to meet each slam of his body. Evie pushed his buttocks with her heels, pressing him deeper still. Reflections of their feral fucking were played from every angle in the mirrors of the dance studio.

Evie's echoing screams revealed she was already close, and he grazed her neck with his teeth, tipping her over the edge as he went as deep as possible inside her. Evie's mouth opened in a magnificent O shape.

Witnessing the woman he adored orgasm around him forced his long-awaited climax. His heat flowed into her, and the release was as intense as the build-up. Josh wobbled as his legs shook with exhaustion. Adrenaline poured out of him, and sweat covered his forehead. Gently he carried her and lay her on the floor.

Josh observed her panting face and reached for the shoulders of her leotard as he covered her with kisses and readied himself for round two.

*****

"**You** had sex at the dance studio?" Jack's eyebrows raised with a mixture of jealousy and admiration.

"It was a full-on session," Evie replied before crossing her arms and grinning proudly. The sun warmed her skin as she lay on the picnic blanket. There was no point hiding her excitement. Even as she sat in the park with Jack by her side, it was overpowering. Children laughed as they flew down slides and hit the skies on the swings somewhere in the distance, but all she thought of was Josh. "I could barely walk yesterday. I forgot to do my after-dance stretches."

The breeze carried a scent that was a mixture of sweet chocolate, fruit cakes, and freshly cut grass. It tousled Evie's hair while birdsong competed against the laughing children.

"I'm sure many other things got stretched though."

"Jack! That's the sort of thing I would say."

"Either you're rubbing off on me or I have to be dirty, because you're ridiculously soppy right now."

Evie laughed with him. He had a point, but she quickly returned to her dirty form. "I know someone you'd prefer to rub off on you. Josh told me he'd seen you and Max chatting after practice."

"Max has volunteered to help at the charity. There's nothing more to it, so don't start suggesting otherwise," Jack replied.

"You'd better not be holding out on me. I can't be doing with any more mysterious men." Jack's instant block of a Max-related chat threw her.

"What do you mean?"

Evie suspected something was happening between Jack and Max, but interrogating him was pointless if he was adamant about keeping his secrets. She'd give him a reprieve. He knew she was there for him if he needed her.

"Josh is acting like there's something he needs to tell me."

Jack's silence added more to the mystery. "And when his dad texts, Josh gets edgy. That man has a hold on him."

"Listen to me, love. Don't trust his dad, not in any way. That man is a snake. He's manipulative and destructive, and the sooner Josh realises, the better." Robin had sent her a text, asking to meet her, but she had no intention of replying.

"There was one thing amazing about the other evening at the dance studio," she said, avoiding the reference to Robin.

"Just one thing? Josh needs more practice." Josh's practices were unnecessary. He'd learnt what to do and how to satisfy her. No lover or partner had come close to how Josh understood her body. And all she had to say was "Miss Evangeline," and he'd jump her. The role-play kink was quickly becoming their greatest pastime. Evie blushed, which caused Jack to roar with laughter. "Evie the hard ass is going bright red. I never believed I'd see the day."

She laughed along with him, although she rolled her eyes. Evie tossed a cherry tomato at Jack, but it missed, accidentally smacking a cheeky bird that had been sneaking in the direction of their lunch. "We're practising enough, thank you very much. But the amazing thing was his behaviour with the kids. He's a natural."

"He's the same at the charity. The kids adore him, and he never gets frustrated, however many questions they ask or times they demand he performs one of his jumps."

She smiled softly. "There's one little girl who's attended my classes for about a year. She hasn't made any friends and gets anxious, but he was gentle with her. She whispered to me as she left that it had been her favourite lesson and asked if he'd be there every week."

Jack threw his hands in the air. "Are you thinking what Josh would be like as a dad? Do you want long-term? Bloody hell, E. You've been dating a week."

But their relationship had been forming for longer. "I'm not hoping to get pregnant soon, don't worry. I never believed 'the one' existed, but I'm starting to. But—"

"But?"

"I need to learn what he's hiding before I can trust him completely. And how do I cope with his dad in the long term? Because he'll force himself between us forever. Josh is different when his dad is involved." They'd gone in a conversation circle due to her fears of Robin. "Does the name Lulu mean anything to you?"

Jack's work mobile rang, diverting their attention. "Saved by the bell," he mumbled. "Sorry, babe, I've got to take this and head to the office. Thanks for lunch. Take care of yourself and stop worrying."

Evie's polite smile wobbled as he kissed her on the cheek. As he rushed off, her phone beeped with a text. A thrill gripped her, but the message replaced her joy with a chill that filled her blood.

Robin: Hello Evangeline. I'm not sure if you got my last message. We should meet to discuss Josh. I believe he's keeping secrets from you. I suspect he wrongly thinks you're not clever enough to see through his lies, but you deserve better. I look forward to hearing from you. Robin x

Evie deleted it before tossing the phone back into her bag. The screams of angry seagulls fighting over the cherry tomato mirrored the wrath inside her head.

"Leave me the fuck alone, Robin. Josh will talk to me when he's ready. And I'm not fucking stupid," she whispered to a sky of greying clouds.

The darkness was coming. Would she come out the other side alone?

Chapter Thirty-Two

Plates clattered around them, and mundane chatter reached their ears. But the smell of garlic and softly melted cheese made Josh draw a deep breath. The restaurant he'd found for lunch with his mum was busy. She watched the bustling wait staff in wonder as smooth jazz played in the background. The frantic pace made it tricky to relax, but the smile on his mum's face made up for it. The shabby chic style and dimmed lighting reminded him of a rugby trip to Paris. His mum was affectionate for French culture, although she'd never visited the country. Josh's dad didn't believe in paying for foreign holidays. A wet, windy week in Wales was good enough for him, and they could go to rugby games too. Wales was lovely, but sometimes, when it was the two of them, she mentioned how she'd like to travel but that Robin wouldn't let her go without him.

"I'm glad you were free, honey. I've missed chatting with you," Rose said.

"Sorry. I've been swamped, but that's no excuse. I should have come to the house more." Her excitement at the café didn't hide her weary eyes. Were her crow's feet always so obvious? As an adult, he'd been so distracted by his ghosts he'd not seen his mum turning into one in front of him.

"Don't apologise for that. I'm happy that you're happy.

I haven't seen you like this in a long time, and I only want what's best for you, sweetheart." Her smile softened when she gazed at him.

Josh snapped off the top of his brittle breadstick with his teeth and enjoyed the satisfying crunch that echoed around his mouth. But there was a chill to his skin when he took in his mum's distracted stare and how her mouth occasionally turned down at the edges. Women were such a mystery to him. At least Evie always said what she was thinking. A smile formed on his lips, and he wrinkled his eyes.

"You're joyous." Rose broke into a beaming smile, but her glassy eyes confused him. Tears slipped down her cheeks. "Thank goodness."

"Mum." He wrapped her hands with his. "What's wrong? You can tell me anything, but please don't cry. I've said the wrong thing, haven't I?"

Josh tried to soothe her but was at a loss. Taking direction from when Evie cared for those in the pub, he waited in silence as he tenderly held her.

"I've worried about you for a long time. There were days I wondered if you'd ever be okay," Rose said so quietly he strained to hear her over the music.

"I don't understand."

"After Lulu died, you changed. You closed yourself off to people, and I worried I'd lost my slightly rebellious, fun-loving boy forever."

"I'm here, Mum. I've always been here but needed someone to help me find that side of me again. My Evie accepts all of me, the good, the bad, and the ugly."

"She's your girlfriend?"

"Yeah, she is. We've both had complicated pasts, but

no one makes me happier. Evie doesn't need a man by her side, but we're getting to a point where she wants me there." Josh told his mum of their trip to see her parents, although he kept some aspects confidential. It wasn't his story, but his shoulders softened at sharing a little of the experience, and he breathed slower. "She's a strong woman who cares about people."

"She's had difficult experiences, especially with the death of her nan. I'd like to come to the funeral tomorrow if that's okay. I'll come alone, though."

"Not with Dad?"

"I refuse to let your dad be there with me." There was a sudden edge to her voice. "Don't let him near Evie. Hold on tightly to her, emotionally and physically, when he's around."

The conversation raised more questions than it answered, but at that moment, the waiter brought their food. He eased down plates of delicately prepared salads with sumptuous, spicy chicken on skewers. Saliva collected on Josh's tongue at the wafts of bacon and avocado.

"To my birthday," Rose called out with a rare glass of wine. She usually avoided alcohol, although that was when his dad was around. How many years had it been since Josh and his mum spent time as just the two of them?

"To your birthday," he responded, tapping his fruit smoothie against her glass. The big match loomed closer, and he was fighting fit. He was missing tomorrow's practice for the funeral, but the end of the season was within his grasp, and he'd relax his healthy habits then. He would give everything he had Saturday to impress the guy scouting for the England squad. He wanted to be the best and chase his dreams. The resurgence of passion for the game was a shock he was still managing.

Knives tapping against forks dragged him from his daydreams, and he tucked into his meal. But a gremlin scratched at his brain. What had his mum alluded to about his dad, and why shouldn't he be near Evie?

The numerous patrons weren't enough to distract him from his past, and Josh reluctantly recalled the night Lulu died. Robin had picked at Lulu. He'd relentlessly given his opinion on the relationship many times, but that evening it came to a head with a raging argument. They had been close to wading in on each other with fists when his dad shouted in anger, "Lulu isn't the type of person that will be satisfied with one man, and she will be the destruction of you. She's already been a bad influence. You need to see some damn sense, boy!"

Josh defended the relationship but not enough.

"Sometimes," his mum said, her wistful voice pulling him from his barrage of guilt, "I wonder what my life would have been like if I'd stayed with my first love."

"Wasn't that dad?"

They'd devoured their lunches, and only a tornado of thoughts distracted them from chatter.

"No, not really. There was another guy I loved. But once your dad decides he wants something, no one stands a chance. I was one of those decisions. The one thing he couldn't achieve with a decision was a premiership rugby career. Your dad never got to play professionally because he wasn't good enough, and he was jealous of you for that. That's probably why he wanted your international hoodie from when they chose you to be part of the England team a couple of years ago. It was just a piece of clothing, but it reminded him that he was a failure, and it was another thing of yours he decided should be his."

"But he said he chose a different path in life, not that he'd failed to make a squad."

"He never could admit his failings. Do you know, I always wondered if you actually loved rugby or if he just pushed you into it," Rose said. There was a softness to her gaze that pulled at his heart. "I only wanted the best for you, and your dad said that was rugby."

"I wasn't sure either. I kept that hoodie and hid it from him."

Rose smiled a cheeky grin. "I know."

"But I think it's because I was proud of what I'd done. That I'd achieved that and not because of him. I love rugby so bloody much. The last couple of weeks has reminded me that I want to win trophies and get the team excited. I want to be the best and maybe even be legendary. Does that sound cocky?"

"It sounds amazing." Rose beamed.

"Having a cosy chat, are we?" A shadowy figure loomed above them. "What are you two talking about without your dear old dad and husband?"

Rose quivered, and instantly Josh's heart went out to her.

"How did you learn we were here?" She may have been trembling, but her tone suggested annoyance too.

"I saw Josh's car." Robin glowered at Rose. "I guess I'm not the favourite parent anymore."

Josh cleared his throat loudly. "We were having a great meal, actually, Dad. There was no passive aggression or veiled digs."

"Someone's increasingly insolent these days. By the way, how is your girlfriend, Joshua?"

"She's fine." His mum's earlier cautions were like a strobe in his brain.

"I've learnt some things about her, and I should warn you because I don't want you to get hurt. She's a glamour model."

"She was a glamour model. She doesn't model anymore," Josh replied with forced nonchalance. "Not that I'd have a problem if she returned to it if it was something she wanted to do."

His dad glared at being caught but sneered as if not finished. "I presume you know she's sold stories about her many conquests."

"Yes, but it was in the past." Robin's smug smile faded. "And she had her reasons, which are none of your business. Not that you'd be rude enough to ask."

His dad's narrowed eyes pinned him while his tight lips communicated brutality. "We don't keep secrets from each other, boy. Wasn't that our deal after Lulu's 'accident'?"

"You'd better not be blaming Josh for that," his mum returned with an intensity that surprised the King men. "We're both aware of what was happening at that time."

"Rose, this isn't relevant to you." Robin dismissed his mum. Vomit clawed up Josh's throat before Robin turned his attention back to him. "You are important to me, but I need to learn everything about Evie to keep you safe. You're susceptible to manipulative women. We need to plan what we do when your career is over, which will be soon if you stay with her."

"Josh, I need to speak alone with your dad. I will give you a call tonight."

"But, Mum, I—"

"Please, honey, just trust me," his mum begged. "I need to deal with this myself."

Josh's hands shook as he grabbed some cash from his wallet and threw it on the table. Should he stay and ignore his mum's request or trust that she had this in hand?

Josh bent and locked eyes with his mum. He blinked a couple of times at the anger clouding the whites of her stare when she looked over Josh's shoulder at his dad. But with the rigid set of her jaw, she appeared more resilient than ever. "Mum, I'm always close if you need me. I hope to see you at the game, if not before." He lowered his voice at the last part. The idea that his dad might turn up at the funeral made him sick. "I love you."

Josh hugged her and dropped a kiss on her cheek, waiting to see if she'd tell him to stay, but instead, she directed her comments at Robin, "We need to talk."

As Josh walked out of the restaurant, a sudden realisation unnerved his stride, causing him to stumble. He'd left the car at home. How had his dad found them?

Chapter Thirty-Three

Standing at the side of her nan's grave, Evie held her breath as the minister shared verses on how life was like a series of seasons. Josh's words as he took care of her that morning settled her trembling heart.

"This is your day to mourn in whatever way you want and need. It's not about anyone's judgements. You said you've grieved her for the last couple of years as she faded, but today might bring up stuff you weren't expecting." He'd pulled her against his chest as they lay in bed. The care and respect he'd shared with her in those brief moments had been challenging. People rejected her and didn't love her unconditionally, except for her nan, and she'd never forget all that they were to each other. But maybe life was changing in a good way. It was heartbreaking that her nan wasn't there to see it, but perhaps she instigated it as she left this earth. "I'm here for you however you need me to be, whether holding your hand, giving you drinks, or telling you jokes. If you want me to stay at a distance, then I will."

Josh's kisses had feathered her body, and their precious moments in the silence of his room led to gentle lovemaking that enabled her to manage the day.

The day was beautiful. The sky was a cloudless bright blue and reminded her of the nights her nan dragged her to the hills to scream. It was a therapy her nan stuck to from her teenage years when her mum died, leaving her with emotions she couldn't handle.

"Life can be a bigger bitch than those dancers you trained with. When it is a bitch, and it gets us down, we don't hide under the duvet and wait for it to get better, because that won't happen. Instead, we go to the hills and scream all our anger and pain out. Once the wind picks it up, it's gone. Then we eat bacon and get the hell on with our day." Gabi had been right. Their nan was crazy, but she was the best kind of crazy.

The insignificant wind around the graveyard was evident when skirts fluttered or the leaves in the trees teased their dance. At least with the addition of the bright sun, Evie hid her tear-free eyes from the other attendees behind dark Jackie O sunglasses. Her lack of tears wasn't because she was free of sadness. Sometimes it was as if her heart had been torn from her body. The pain was there and always would be, but there was joy too. Her nan had lived an exciting and mostly enjoyable life based on her choices and not on the decisions of others. Evie may have remained stoic to others, but her mind shuffled. However, pride at having known and adored such a strong role model and loving person eclipsed most ramblings.

Evie gazed around the graveside at a mixture of faces from her past, joined by those from her present. The policeman Hamish, who'd tried to give Enid roses, which had resulted in their break-up, stood with tears streaming down his cheeks while the minister shared a message of sadness. He clutched red and white roses tightly in his hands and shook with a grief beyond anything Evie had witnessed.

Evie stepped closer to him. Eyes were on her back, but

she ignored them and instead offered Hamish a tissue and a hug with a tentative smile.

"I loved your nan," he whispered between sobbing gasps of breath. "She loved me too, but she couldn't bring herself to trust me."

Evie suspected that her grandad was a nasty man. The rumours were that he'd bullied his family, especially Enid, until she stormed out of the marriage and forged a life without him. She'd brought up Evie's dad alone, but Enid refused to talk about the past. There was the odd occasion Evie got snippets, but she'd cemented most secrets to her soul.

"Don't let love get away from you," Hamish said between snivels, unembarrassed by his sadness. "I'm honoured to have loved someone with my full heart even if nothing worked out."

Josh's mum suddenly stepped out of the group and gently took his hand. "We'll get you a nice cup of hot tea," she whispered. "You can tell me about Enid. I'd love to learn more about her."

Rose offered Evie a smile that revealed her stunning blue eyes before walking the man towards the church. It was difficult to believe that she was old enough to be Josh's mum, although he'd let slip that he'd been born when she was eighteen.

"Her husband was cruel to her," Hamish said before they were out of earshot.

The minister paused with a gentle smile and allowed her to return to Josh before continuing the theme of loss.

The group watched silently as the coffin was lowered and the minister committed Enid to the ground. The silence perforated her heart.

The service finished with a prayer that made Evie yearn temporarily for the security of her childhood, of her family's love. They'd been happy and close once, but life and judgement had gotten in the way. During the service, she'd glimpsed a stranger hiding behind a tree. Wisps of their dark hair rose in the faint breeze, reminding her of how Gabi's flew when they ran around the park as children, but when Evie looked again, there was no one.

Evie took some earth from a pot and dropped it onto the coffin. It made a noise like pebbles on a carpet, a dull thud that would reverberate through her memories for years.

After telling everyone how welcome they'd be at the wake and shaking more hands than everyday life dictated, Evie said goodbye at the grave. The plain maple coffin in the ground held a body that in no way reflected the life her nan had led.

"I'll never stop loving you, Nan, and I'll hold you with me always. You taught me a lot, especially to be proud of my decisions, who I was, and that we all make mistakes. I wish I'd taught you that it's okay to accept love from others. You can still be you but in a slightly different way. I'll make sure I bring you roses regularly. I may sneak some from Hamish too, because you loved him really." Evie took a deep breath, wishing her nan had learnt how amazing love from a genuine, caring man was. She didn't need love to be whole, but when it came to her door, she didn't have to lose who she was by leaving that door open. "I'll love you always."

At the wake, Josh left her side only to get drinks or ensure everyone was okay. She couldn't have asked for more from him. Strangers and friends told stories about her nan and some of the escapades she'd gotten into. The afternoon flashed by, but Evie held on to each story as if she were a memory box. She tucked away every tear shed and chuckle made into her heart as a reminder she wasn't alone but carried her with her.

As the evening came to a close, Evie overhead Rose saying her goodbyes to Josh.

"Speak to her," Rose whispered, probably believing Evie was still at the bar, raising a glass to her nan. "She will understand. Trust me, darling."

Josh caught Evie's eye as she stood behind Rose. Her brow furrowed as his eyes suddenly darted away. He'd been on edge all afternoon, and frequently she'd caught a hollow look in his eyes. The hunch of his shoulders reminded her that he carried the world on his broad form. The hornet's nest in his mind was evident, but the detail behind it was a mystery.

He'd barely slept the last couple of nights. But it was more than the funeral and the big match. Did he know about Robin's texts? They were becoming more frequent and threatening, interspersed with comments about how he could help her grief. Rose appeared robust and capable without him by her side. But Josh faded fast. As she joined him, his trembles against her body and his glassy yet empty eyes ensured many questions.

As the sun set and the last person at the wake disappeared, Evie reached for Josh's hand, and they slowly walked home. They didn't speak, both caught up in the busyness of their brains. What had Rose meant? What secrets was Josh keeping from her after she'd shared so much with him? Their meandering took them past the graveyard.

"What are you keeping from me, Josh?" Evie demanded. The words had risen like a bubble in her throat.

"Not today, Evie. Today is your day, and I'm here for you."

Evie rounded on him. "And you have been all day. But I need to know what your mum meant. I have given you everything of me, and I can't go on knowing that any second you might hurt me or that you're lying to me."

"But you've been through enough this fortnight. I can't."

"Josh." She shoved him, but her hands bounced off his muscles. "I can't. You need to tell me, because all the possibilities of what it might be are killing me. I don't trust easily, and I can't deal with this anymore."

"Today was about you," he pleaded.

"Then let me have this."

The pain in Josh's voice ripped a new hole in her heart. "But there's something I have to tell you, and once you hear it, you won't love me anymore. You won't want to see me again."

She took a deep breath. "Then fucking tell me, because if you don't, we might not have a relationship for much longer anyway."

Josh's shoulder's slumped in defeat. "Fine. Follow me." He held his hand out to her before sluggishly leading her deeper into the graveyard.

Was this the end of their relationship?

Chapter Thirty-Four

Josh sat on the damp grass in front of Lulu's gravestone. Evie was by his side, but shame stopped him from looking at her.

"There's a butterfly on her gravestone," Evie said. "Is that why you have a tattoo of a butterfly?"

His selfishness in telling her the story the evening after her nan's funeral was like a violent kick to the face, stifling him. But she'd demanded it. The secret that had lived inside him all these years was swallowing him whole. Evie's hand slipped into his.

The gentle, loving act enabled him to speak, although his voice strained. "I was going to tell you this, probably next week, but I was. I should have said sooner, but I was terrified."

His head dropped to their linked hands. He sighed loudly, hoping she'd butt in and end his speech, but she didn't. She was too bloody patient, and he adored her for it.

"If you listen to what I say and don't want me around anymore, then at least I'll know, and I won't torture myself or you any longer. If you can give us a try, we can start with a fresh slate, no more secrets, with the past behind us."

Josh took a deep breath and said the words that had haunted him for the past eight years. "This is Lulu's grave. I loved this woman. Lulu was my first love and my girlfriend until the night I killed her."

*****

Evie gasped, but she held tightly to his hand. "How?" she whispered. Her heart's thudding reverberation was enough to splinter her rib cage.

"She was in a car accident." Eventually, he continued after a long pause that doubled her trembling. His words were stilted and cold. "One night, she was driving around country lanes and lost control of the car. It was partly due to not wearing her seatbelt and, according to investigators, the adverse weather conditions. The force of the impact made her brain smack against her skull with such a force that it caused fatal ruptures. That's what kills people in car accidents like that, the internal brain injuries. I spent much of my life researching it to find out if she had a chance."

"You're not making sense. How can the crash and her death be your fault if she was driving alone?"

Josh turned away, although he didn't let go of her hand. "Because I stressed her out. We had a nasty argument before she left, and I got her into such a state that she wasn't safe driving. If it hadn't been for me, she wouldn't have been out, and if I hadn't said the things I said, she wouldn't have driven the way she did. I killed her."

Her thudding heart calmed a little. "Josh," she said forcibly, demanding his attention as she tried to gather understanding, "I want to learn the whole story, but can we sit on a bench rather than on the damp grass?"

They found a rickety wooden bench close to the grave. Evie beckoned him closer. Josh's head turned to the little green gate in the corner of the graveyard as if he were planning an escape, but their burgeoning relationship and friendship demanded the truth if it was to survive and grow. The last vestments of trust between them were like rickety foundations.

Evie sucked in the misting air as he thumped down on the bench. "Tell me about Lulu. What was she like, and how did you meet?"

Josh winced. His deep breath filled the air as he breathed life into the past. His stare fixed on the gravestone as if he needed to see it to share his pain.

"Lulu was trouble, but she was the best kind of trouble," he replied with a winsome smile. "We met at college and had the sort of relationship that eighteen-year-olds with raging hormones have. I spent a lot of time training and studying, but every other moment was spent with or thinking about her. Sometimes we were reckless. We'd skip school to head to the beach for the day or sneak into the rugby club at night and get wasted on the pitch. A couple of times, we went to that high bridge over the river and jumped in naked. It was so dangerous, but I felt alive with her. My dad was worried that I was risking my future. I was on the cusp of being signed to the Giants under-twenty-ones team, but I didn't care because I had a sexy girlfriend who made every day fun and exciting."

Evie stirred with a tinge of jealousy for Josh's first love, but she flung it away. Then, turning, she let her right leg hang listlessly from the bench while tucking the other underneath her. The story was getting darker and was as physical as the tensing body by her side. "But something changed?"

"Lulu lost her sparkle. It sounds stupid, but it's the only way I can describe it. At first, she was edgy around me. We always found time for each other, but suddenly she got swamped, and when I asked what she was doing, she'd kick off and tell me to mind my own business."

Like I used to when he asked me.

"I couldn't do or say anything right, and she was always angry with me. Lulu hated coming to my house, but she refused to say why. She suddenly put loads of effort into her appearance, caking on make-up and wearing minimal clothing rather than the stuff that she found comfortable or the clothes that made her happy. Nothing she owned and nothing from the past was good enough anymore, including me. She was so sexy when she wore her favourite baggy jeans, but she suddenly hated herself in them. Lulu was beautiful and confident, but she complained that she wasn't attractive and became desperate for reassurance. However often I gave it, she'd say she was ugly."

Clues hit Evie's synapses like electricity switched on and travelling around a circuit. Connections formed and dragged her closer to the truth, but it was out of her grasp.

"When life got out of Lulu's control, she'd stop eating. I'd help her through it as best as a bumbling eighteen-year-old could, and sometimes it was enough for me to remind her that I was there for her when she needed me. She was always okay after a couple of days, as if she'd reset, but not this time. For a while, I presumed it was an out-of-control moment because of exams or whatever."

"But this time, it lasted longer?" Evie attempted to soften her voice, conscious that Josh was reliving his past by sharing it.

"Yeah, it was weeks after exams had finished, and she was kicking off when I asked if she was okay and if I could do anything. There was someone else," he blurted out. "Shit, why hadn't I considered that before? It was when I started talking that it became obvious."

"Maybe it's because you've never really talked about it?"

"Yeah." He clasped her hands tightly. "Dad told me not to speak about it but to move on. And when I spoke to Jack, he got weird. Jack was friends with Lulu too. But if there was someone else, it explains this butterfly necklace she had. I found it in her bag when I was looking for a pen. When I asked her about it, she lost her shit and said if I didn't trust her, I should end it. I didn't understand. I guessed it was a trinket from her parents or something because Lulu loved butterflies."

"Is that why you got your tattoo near your hip?"

Josh looked down as if he was penetrating his suit trousers with his stare.

"Kind of. But I got it for me too. It reminded me that I shouldn't be spontaneous or out of control again. I needed to remember that I should only have controllable things in my life because, otherwise, bad things happen."

"Then you got the wrong tattoo because it's impossible to control butterflies. If you put them in a jar, it's not unusual for them to batter themselves repeatedly against the glass to get free. In many ancient cultures, butterflies resembled a person's soul or reincarnation, like a rebirth. Butterflies are mystical creatures, and you can't cage or control them without killing them."

"I'll never get tired of hearing you share your knowledge. You're like a butterfly. Evie, you're my butterfly."

Evie blushed. "Tell me more about what happened the night Lulu died. The night you said you killed her."

"I did kill her." Josh's mood darkened quickly. Josh

had waited too long for this revelation, and it hung like an albatross around his neck. Had he been able to share this with someone who listened with an open heart, or had it been shoved down inside him repeatedly and left to rot and poison his entire body?

"At times, our passion made us unstoppable teenagers, but sometimes, like that night, it turned us into these monsters who'd rip each other to shreds. We had a shitty argument. There was no love, or maybe there was too much." He shrugged. "I don't know."

"What was the argument about?"

"It started with a conversation I had with my dad."

"No surprises there," she replied flatly.

Josh's eyes widened before he continued, "Dad had told me Lulu would destroy my career, that she was worthless and I was too stupid to see it. He called her nasty names, and I should have defended her. I loved her feistiness, and we were madly in love. I should have told him that, but I was gutless and cared what he thought."

"You can't blame yourself." But her words were lost in his grief.

"I was worried my relationship with Lulu was falling apart because of insecurities and behaviour. Dad made me admit she was losing it and that I didn't like how she looked these days. I meant I was worried that she was harming herself by not eating, but if she'd been happy, then I would have been happy, but that was when she walked in. She was out of her mind that I'd said such awful things about her. She bolted. I tried to run after her, but Dad stopped me. He said she needed space to cool off and that if I trusted him and his knowledge about women, he would talk to her for me. I believed him when he said it would all be okay."

Josh shook violently as he experienced the fight all

over again. His pain was in lines across his face. She listened carefully, but he wasn't with her emotionally. Instead, Josh's past took him somewhere darker and unreachable.

"Trusting Dad may have been a mistake. After he'd seen her, she was angrier than ever. She screamed about how I always took my dad's side and didn't see what a bastard he was. I stupidly shouted back. I shouldn't have done it, but I hated how shit she made me feel. I thought, in my naivety, that nothing could come between us. So when she screeched at me that she wanted to break up, I laughed at her." Josh quietly wept. It was as if he'd stored that argument and used it to flog himself daily. "I told her to do what she wanted, that she was easily replaceable, and I never loved her. I laughed that she'd been fun and attempted to hurt her like she hurt me. I raged that my dad was right about her, and when she asked me what he'd said, I snapped with something he'd said the night before. He'd stated she was a worthless, ugly tart that wanted to ruin my life. That was the last thing I said to her before she left. I'm the worst person in the world, and I deserve to suffer for what I said to her."

It was as if a physical fight was raging next to her. Josh had said unforgivable things but was a teenage boy with an emotionally abusive dad. Did he realise the significance of his dad in this?

"I had no idea where she was heading, which made it harder to find her. It was dark, and the rain streamed onto the windshield. I barely saw past the whining flip of the wipers in front of my eyes. I searched all the local roads. I was petrified that she'd done something stupid. And then I saw her car." Josh's pause seemed to last a lifetime. Large salty tears dropped from his eyes as his grief turned to sobs.

"Lulu's car had hit a lamppost before it flipped and slammed into a wall at the side of the road. She must have been speeding when she lost control. I ran to her because I knew CPR and believed I'd make it okay, but she'd died from the impact. There was nothing anyone could do. I killed her. If I had been controlled or dated someone sensible, maybe everything would have been okay and she'd be alive now."

Josh's body shook, and Evie pulled his head to her chest and rocked him like he was a little child. Finally, he gasped for air and pulled it deep into his lungs. "Let it out, honey. You need to let it all come out," she said tenderly.

Eventually, the tears began to slow. His face was white, and terror raged behind his swollen red eyes.

"Josh, I'm going to be honest with you." He recoiled, but she didn't let go. She refused to let her fears stop her from saying what he needed to hear. "Yes, you hurt her, but you didn't kill her. Deep down, you believe that. You were a teenager in love. You didn't have the maturity to deal with that situation and made mistakes, but that doesn't mean you killed her. Teenage break-ups are like teenage relationships— passionate, intense, and so full of emotions that they can be destructive. But you didn't set out to hurt her like that, and you must forgive yourself. You couldn't have controlled yourself, or Lulu, like you can't control any human. You tried to control our situation, and that never worked, did it?"

"I pushed you away all those times because I believed I needed the opposite of Lulu, someone sensible and not feisty that I could keep safe. It sounds so fucked up now. I thought I'd destroy you like I did her. Or maybe you'd get to me first and destroy me."

He dropped his head, but Evie forced him to face her. "But you fancied me and were fighting that."

"It was you I wanted. You're all I've thought about since Aidan first told me to look after you, but I was scared of what would happen if I was myself. In reality, it was never about you but about me."

"And it is you, the real you, that I like. The controlled side of you can be fun, but you have lots of layers. You're a sexy onion."

His laugh released the tension she'd held tightly.

"I've been called worse," he joked.

"But please don't think you need to be with someone you don't want. It's unfair to them and you. It will cause more hurt."

"My dad said you might destroy me as Lulu did. He told me I had a hand in her death."

"I'm going to be honest, Josh. I don't like your dad. He is the most controlling, manipulative person I've ever met, more than Peter."

Josh froze against her. Shivers replaced the tears and acted like a catalyst for his words. "I'm starting to see it, but I'm struggling to believe it. I'm worried about Mum. How do I help her? And I'm scared he'll come between you and me like he did with Lulu. I can't lose you. I want you to be the real you, but sometimes it freaks me out."

"And I'm going to keep freaking you out, but you need to explain to me when you're freaking out and why."

Josh nodded. "You're very wise, Evie."

She smiled, but her mouth turned down as she contemplated Josh's family. "I'll do whatever it takes to stop your dad from coming between us. I don't know what to do about your mum, but we'll think of something." She stood, attempting to pull him with her.

Nervously she waited for him to stand by her side.

"I thought you'd hate me."

"Josh, throughout our friendship, you've given me loads of reasons to rage at you, but this isn't one of them. Now let's go home, as you've got a match tomorrow."

He rose like a fighter. "You're the best thing that's happened to me. I owe you everything."

As they walked hand-in-hand towards Josh's house, Evie digested his fears. What were they going to do about Robin, and did he have the power to destroy their relationship? The big game was tomorrow, and Robin would be there. All the players in this weird game of emotions would be in attendance, and she was terrified.

Chapter Thirty-Five

Josh wolfed down his omelette as he prepared mentally for the match, but on the other side of the kitchen counter, Evie perched on a stool and picked at her food.

So this would be their house soon. He'd emptied his wardrobe in the prospect of her moving that week, although she'd made him put everything back in, as apparently he needed somewhere to keep his clothes.

"What's in your head? Did I make the wrong breakfast for a dancer?" he asked. Was their moment at Lulu's grave the day before continuing to fester?

"Why are you standing there in just your boxers as you ravish your food on game day? You've forbidden us from sex before matches, yet you're like a fuck siren, dragging my pussy to the beach on your hard rock! We can't screw because you'll lose your mojo or something, so why are you doing it?"

He laughed, relishing how much he loved her horn-filled anger.

"Who says we're not?" he teased, swaggering around the counter with a grin. He growled from his gut at Evie's legs, on show beneath her long rugby shirt. Need coiled tightly inside him as he contemplated sliding the tip of his finger from her ankle to her knee before replacing it with his tongue as he reached her inner thigh. She had the smoothest skin, and her legs were pure muscle.

"You said last week we're not allowed." Evie wrinkled her nose when he winked at her. "Don't walk towards me with your shorts on your hips and your 'come fuck me' eyes."

"You're telling me not to, but I believe your beautiful green eyes are twinkling, Miss Evangeline."

Evie's laugh was strained with desire. "They're angry like me, but you can't tell because you're the one twinkling."

"Your cheeky grin is giving you away too." His teasing was relentless.

"That's the face of frustration."

"Sexual frustration," he growled as he reached for her trembling hand and held it against his heart. Her fingers teased the hair around his nipples while her palm pressed hard against his chest.

"Do you feel that?" The skin-on-skin contact made his heart beat impossibly faster.

Evie swallowed loudly, and his cock lurched. "Yes."

Josh's voice deepened. "That fire is always with me. If I have you now, I'll need you straight away again. I want all of you, all the time, and nothing dulls my need for you."

Her nails lightly scratched his chest. "So it doesn't matter how wet I get for you then, because it doesn't make you desire me more?"

Josh's grunt echoed off the countertops.

At Evie's sly smile, he flexed his abs. She dropped her voice too as she added, "That's good then, because right now I. Am. Soaking."

He groaned, and his erection throbbed. "Shall I prove to you that nothing makes me want you more?" he asked as he reached for her, but Evie jumped off the stool and out of the room.

"You'll have to catch me first," she said between laughter.

She pelted up the stairs as his well-honed rugby skills kicked in. Even as the queen of misdirection, she was no match for him. Josh barrelled up the stairs and found her waiting on the top step. Through giggles, she uttered, "You've captured me."

Josh crawled up her body as his lips caressed each inch of naked skin. He lifted her arms and pinned her beneath him. Her grin was wide, and she moaned her yeses as he rubbed himself against her flimsy knickers. Josh trembled at the idea of being inside her as she opened her thighs. It took no effort to rip her underwear off.

The ageing carpet had to be rough and the stairs uncomfortable, but her moans continued as his hand slipped under the hem of her rugby shirt and cupped her breast. He raised an eyebrow as he flicked and ran his fingers around her nipples. Evie's returning stare reminded him of a volcano on the precipice of eruption: dark smoke and promise burned in her eyes.

"We can't do this here," she whimpered between lengthy moans. Evie leaned her head back, and he took the opportunity to kiss and suck her neck, grazing her with his spiky stubble. His dick was as hard as a rock.

"Are you sure, baby, or is the idea of being caught by my housemates turning you on?"

Her back bowed, and she moaned before making her demands. "Fuck me here, right now. Don't stop," Her guttural cries were pure gasoline to his fire.

Taking her lead, Josh shoved up her shirt and bit her

right nipple before sucking on it. He was starved, and she was his mirage in the desert. Their soft lovemaking the previous night hadn't quelled his need to pleasure her and to have her moan his name.

"Open your eyes," he commanded.

She spied him warily. He returned her suspicious stare with a cheeky smile as he ran his finger across her wet clit. Her teeth tore at her lips as he worked two fingers inside her.

"I want you to see what a man who worships you looks like when he makes you come. Because I fucking love every part of you. I love how you throw facts at me when I least expect it, challenge me, and never put up with my shit. I adore your cheeky laugh, your care for everyone, and your determination. You're a fucking force, and I love your body, your tits, how wet you get, and how your pussy grips me. You're everything, Evie."

A tiny cry left her mouth when he pushed his digits deeper, curving them slightly to rub her G-spot while his tongue continued to lather her nipples.

Suddenly a bedroom door opened above them.

Evie clamped her hand over her mouth while they waited to hear where Max or Lucas would go. The temptation to make Evie scream spurred him on, and he continued to thrust his fingers inside her. The combination of desire and frustration as her body lifted to meet his fast fingering was irrepressible.

Footsteps reached the bathroom door above them.

Evie forced down his shorts. "Hurry, because I need you inside me."

"I wouldn't dare disobey you," he replied before quickly penetrating her.

They screwed on the stairs like horny students as every

thrust of her body forced his cock deeper. For years he'd been too scared to embrace the risqué side of himself. She brought out so much of him that he'd buried but loved. Joy blossomed as desire tried to reign inside him. The danger forced his arousal to increase, and he sensed the rumbling hints of his climax. Her legs held him deep as he repeatedly pushed inside her. Heavy breaths shook him. The sound of a hurricane from the pressure inside him deafened him to anything but their relentless sex. She breathed heavily and whimpered as they neared orgasm. Her telltale noises and shakes spurred him on to fuck her hard.

"Come, Evie. I want you to come hard on my cock, knowing that anyone might catch us fucking. I love you, beautiful. Now come for me."

Immediately Evie came apart. She writhed wildly and spasmed against him as a spectre of sexual mystery took her breath.

Blood rushed around him and culminated in an orgasm that ravaged every limb with force. They clutched each other tightly, riding wave upon wave of orgasm as the stair carpet burnt their naked skin. The marks would act as a reminder for days of their exploits.

It took longer than expected to regulate his breath, and as his body quivered, he studied Evie, but it wasn't enough to see her; he needed to touch her everywhere. Panting against each other with wild grins, they kissed softly. The bathroom door opened again, and footsteps trudged to one of the bedrooms.

"Just so you're aware," Lucas called out, "I know exactly what you're doing, and I'm fucking jealous. I haven't had sex in ages." He slammed his bedroom door to the sounds of their hysterical laughter.

*****

If there was any worry about their exploits that morning and the effect it might have on Josh's performance, Josh put it to bed in the first five minutes of the match. Evie watched in fascination as Josh totalled player after player from the Giants' team. The rush from witnessing him beat down every opponent that attempted to pass or conquer him was nearly as enthralling as when he came inside her. Her thrills became physical and transformed into goosebumps.

"That's my man," she whispered before cheering with a sound that rose from her depths, joining the crowd shouting honours to their gods.

In the past, when she'd seen him play, he was another inconsequential player, like a cog in a wheel that barely fought to justify its purpose. Now he had a presence bolstered by strength and tenacity that drew attention.

Even Jack, with his limited rugby understanding, stared. "What happened to Josh?" he asked in the second half.

Evie blushed. *I happened.* But this version of him always existed. The last two weeks had been a catalyst, and he revealed himself as the man and player he truly was.

Players from the opposition would run at him, but with brute force, he'd challenge them and toss them to the side. Josh was an impenetrable wall. The crowd praised his moves and chanted his name while jostling their pints. A home game, especially the last one of the season, was always a special event, but this was significant. As the roar of the Bulls went out, Evie ruptured with passion.

The one thing dragging her mood was the escalating shadow of Robin. His presence hung in the air like the flags waved by exuberant fans. She'd had three missed calls and an answer machine message from him before the match.

His voice turned her stomach, and the manipulation behind his words made her wretch.

"Evangeline." Robin made her name sound grubby. "Why are you avoiding my calls? You can come to me about anything. Life hasn't been easy for you, especially with your nan dying, but I can be your confidant. Josh isn't mature enough to handle what you're going through, but I'm wiser. I can help. He's a lovely son, but he's broken. I don't want you to feel unattractive or unable to measure up to the other females Josh has had in his life. You're a beautiful woman who deserves love, and I'm here for you when you need me."

Evie attempted to focus on the game. Josh may have been having a game that would make rugby pundits lord over him, but it wasn't plain sailing for all of his team. Lucas couldn't score a try or kick a ball in the right direction. He was on the edge of his patience, and the jeering from the Giants fans wasn't helping. The pressure or the presence of his former coach and his wife was getting to him. With each failed attempt, he was more likely to do something stupid.

But the drama didn't distract Evie from Robin. Her phone vibrated with more texts from him. The jostling rugby fans around her made it harder to breathe. It reminded her of the claustrophobia Peter had instilled in her. She pulled at the collar of her rugby shirt, but she couldn't suck enough air into her lungs.

"Jack, I need a drink." Her best friend knew that she hadn't drunk alcohol in months. At his narrowed eyes, she was imprisoned. She threw a question at him to divert his potential queries and plastered a fake smile across her face. "Can I get you anything?"

"No, I'm good, but hurry back, babe, okay? You need to be here at the end. I bet your beau will be searching for you in the crowd." Evie nodded and made fists with her hands to stop from trembling.

As she walked towards the undercover bar, whistles and angry shouts came from the pitch. Was a fight breaking out? Maybe Lucas had reached his limits.

Footsteps followed her as she walked under the stands towards the bar. There were thousands of people at the game, but she'd have space here. The match was reaching its climax, so most people wouldn't leave it. Away from the crowds and alone in the tunnel, Evie's stress eased. Together, she and Josh would devise a plan and help his mum. They'd be a team against Robin. She let out a slow breath when suddenly a hand grabbed her by the shoulder and spun her around. Robin's face loomed into view. She stepped back against the tunnel's stone wall.

Chapter Thirty-Six

The stone wall of the tunnel was hard against her back as Robin leered closer.

"Fancy seeing you here, Evangeline. Surely you're not bored with the game already? Are you having second thoughts about Josh?" He sneered before hiding it quickly. It brought bile to her throat.

"Did you follow me?" she snapped.

"Don't be stupid. I was walking to the bar." His eye twitched. "I'm here for you, Evie."

A softer, gentler smile replaced his intimidating gaze, but it was an act.

"Don't pretend you care about me, Robin. Empathy can't find space inside you because you're so full of shit."

"That's no way to talk to your boyfriend's dad. However, I do like this feisty side of you."

He stepped closer as if to pin her against the wall, but she shoved him away. "Stop trying to intimidate me. Besides, you don't like Josh being with feisty women."

He froze. "Who told you that?"

"Josh did when he told me about Lulu."

Robin's laugh twisted with anger. "Did he tell you everything about him and Lulu?"

"Of course he did, because he trusts me." She

shrugged, refusing to show weakness.

"I bet he didn't tell you he killed her." It was a blow she easily deflected.

"Are you unable to listen as well as being a vindictive piece of shit? He told me everything." She overemphasised every word of the last sentence. "And we're both well aware that he didn't kill her."

Robin raised one eyebrow, reminding her of Josh when he was confused or curious. But he was nothing like her man. His mouth was in a hard straight line.

"You let him believe that. You're a manipulative sociopath and don't deserve to have him as a son or spend any time with him."

"Neither does a stupid, cheap tramp like you," he countered. "You can't believe he loves you. He pities you. And when he's bored, he'll ditch you and find the woman he wants to spend his life with." Again, Robin found her weakness, and he was getting under her skin. "You're a bit of fun. Someone well versed in sex who can teach him things before he moves on."

She closed her eyes, warding off his punches to her confidence, but Robin hit his mark. Her inner strength was depleting.

"It's obvious to all of us, and Josh said as much to his mum the other day. He's already tired of you and wants an intellectual equal. You're a vapid, messed-up glamour model."

"I'm more than that," she whispered. The sour combination of Robin's burger and beer breath wafted towards her.

"I see your beauty and kindness and can make you feel special. You should trust me and let me help you." Robin eased closer. "You care about Josh and don't want to harm his career. So it's best if you listen to me, Evie. He's not enough of a man for you, and he doesn't understand how to treat a woman like you. I'd buy you jewellery and take you to nice places."

"You'd buy me a necklace?" Jewellery was significant. Suddenly she was making connections through the fog of memories.

"If that's what you want. I would buy you anything you asked for."

"I bet you bought that butterfly necklace for Lulu." It was obvious. Placing her palms on his chest, she pushed him hard and forced him to retreat. "I bet you told her all the things you told me."

"I don't know what you're talking about." Robin's face was motionless, but it silently screamed the need for control.

"Lulu didn't want to hurt Josh, but you groomed her." Evie shoved him again. "She thought she was damaging Josh's career. You were sleeping with a vulnerable teenager and your son's girlfriend. What the fuck is wrong with you? Is it because the vulnerable ones are ripe for your manipulation, or were you jealous? After all, he was successful at rugby. Josh was going places and had a beautiful girlfriend who cared about him, and what were you? You had a gorgeous wife and a son to be proud of, but all you saw was your failure. You're the fuck-up."

"Josh told me you were stupid, but you're ridiculous," he sneered.

With each lie dripping from his forked tongue, her confidence grew. The truth was as evident as Josh's love for her. "And he fed you the information you needed to manipulate her. He trusted his dad and went to him for advice. Instead, you shamed him for dating her while manipulating his fear. Did you orchestrate her walking in on your argument with him, or was that blind luck?"

"I bet you've been talking to Lulu's friend Jack. Did he make up some drama?" Robin attempted a casual gait as he stepped away. He was convincing, but Evie held firm.

"Jack knows?"

"There isn't anything to know. I've been accused of things before, but that was due to jealous people trying to ruin my life. You, of all people, should understand what that's like. I know about your past."

She saw the lies for what they were, an attempt to distract and confuse her. Josh had told his mum a little of her past because he'd asked her permission first, but Robin didn't know the details, or he would have used it against her.

Evie walked back towards Jack. There was nothing left to say to Robin, but he followed her, continuing his digs and scrabbling for power. Robin was losing control of those around him.

"At least Josh has parents who love him. What do you have, Evie?"

Something inside her snapped, and she rounded on him. Robin didn't flinch.

"All this time, you let your son believe he'd killed his girlfriend while you were the reason she was upset that night. You killed her."

"But because of it, he became a better rugby player. So I did him a favour." He shrugged.

"Are you fucking kidding me? Do not pretend you brought good things to his life with your lies. You nearly destroyed him. You're a fucking psychopath who doesn't understand how amazing Josh is. You don't deserve the love of another human, not ever. You deserve to suffer like those you've hurt with your games. You're fucking twisted. Now ask me again what I have. I dare you, Robin."

He stood, stony-faced, and met her glares. Emotion barely registered on his unmoving face.

"Too chicken?" With every word, her voice increased in volume. Passion led her vehemence. "Fine, then I'll tell you what I have. I have a soul. I have regrets and hope. More than that, I have your son's devoted love. You won't be able to say the same once I tell him what you've done."

"Not if I speak to him first and tell him that his glamour model girlfriend tried it on with me," he replied with a coldness that reached her bones. Then he walked away, leaving her frozen. She'd been in this situation before when the "adults" decided her future, and her dad kicked her out.

What if Josh didn't believe her?

*****

What a match. Josh swaggered into the changing rooms like a hero returning from war. Boss Man hugged him after the game, telling him, "It's not over yet, Josh. You've got more, and your best rugby is ahead of you."

It was the performance of his career. *So far.* His inner voice no longer sounded like his dad's. He needed to find Evie and celebrate with her.

Many players had packed up, but Josh sat on the wooden changing bench, staring at the disarray around him with joy beyond anything he'd ever experienced.

A noise at the door startled him. "Dad?"

"Joshua, my son, I need to speak to you." His dad was

deathly pale.

"What's wrong? Is mum okay?"

"Your mum's fine," he replied flatly.

"Not Evie?"

"Yes, I'm here because of Evie. I'm sorry to tell you this, but she tried to seduce me."

"What? Don't be ludicrous. Evie wouldn't do that."

"Are you calling me a liar?" Robin asked angrily, nearing Josh. "She propositioned me."

"No, but—"

"It's been going on a week or so. Evie repeatedly texted and called me. She's hounding me; it was her that told me where you and your mother were eating on Thursday. I didn't want to say anything because you think you love her, but she's not who she says she is."

"But that place was a spur-of-the-moment thing—"

Robin paused briefly before replying, "Oh, well, she must have guessed then. She tried to kiss me while you were playing. Evie told me that you weren't experienced enough for her and that she was bored of you already. She wants a real man."

"He's lying." Robin and Josh's heads whipped around to a shaking Evie.

"What the fuck is going on?" Josh's world was falling apart.

"Who has lied to the papers, tried to sell her sex tape, and has a very revealing past?" Robin implored.

"She told you about that?"

"She told me all about it. She told me she wanted the experience that comes with an older, married guy. I told her you were intelligent, but she said you were a dumb, rugby-playing ape who wouldn't notice."

Tears streamed down Evie's face, but she held her

head high. The green in her eyes no longer sparkled. "Josh, I can't say or do anything to hurt you. Everything I've told you this week and every moment we've spent together made me love you more. I don't want to imagine myself with anyone else or be with anyone else. I love you. Your dad is a liar. There's a lot more he's lied to you about."

Josh ran through everything he believed as the clock ticked loudly. He'd known his dad for years, but it was Evie who he trusted. And although Josh was processing the previous day's conversation at the grave, there were things about his dad that he couldn't ignore anymore. But he needed to speak to his mum and ensure she was safe before he dealt with his dad. Robin would punish her if he couldn't get to Josh. Josh struggled to find his voice.

"I can't stay and wait while you reject me and everything I stand for again. Goodbye, Josh. I'm sorry you can't love me like I love you and that you don't trust me." She walked out before he stopped her and explained his plan. The anger across her features as she'd turned pained him more than any injury he'd had in his career.

"Good riddance," his dad sneered.

"She was the best thing that happened to me, and I'm certain you were lying and not her." Josh's sadness turned swiftly to anger, and in a fit of rage, he grabbed the collar of his dad's shirt and brought his fist up to hit him, but he dropped it quickly.

"Too gutless as usual, and if you were as certain as you say about Evie, why didn't you stop her? You're pathetic."

Josh ran for the door to find his mum and stop Evie. His dad knew how to hurt him, but the insults were easier to deflect. He slammed into a solid chest, colliding with a group he never expected to see together. Charlie, Rose,

Lucas, and Jack each had a face more intriguing than the last.

His exit was barred, and so was his future.

"You need to listen to us," Lucas grunted. "You need to know the truth."

Josh stared at each person in the room in turn. All four faces displayed different emotions: remorse, guilt, anger, and sadness. It was only his dad that continued to carry an ambivalence. He had to go to Evie, but he was imprisoned in the room.

"Your dad is a liar," Jack announced. It was a familiar theme. Josh once believed his dad was his idol, but Robin quickly fell off the pedestal that Josh had put him on.

"I know."

"He told you about Lulu?"

Robin's eyes flickered, and he glared at Jack before he fixed Josh with an unimpressed stare and yawned. The fucking audacity of him. Josh shook his head.

"I never meant to hurt you, but Lulu made me promise to keep her secret. So when she died, I had to honour her. I didn't want her memory trashed, but I let you believe what had happened was all your fault, and I'm so sorry," Jack said tentatively. "But after seeing how little your dad cared and how he was trying to repeat history with Evie, I can't stay quiet anymore. Lulu wouldn't have wanted that."

"What the hell are you talking about?" Josh said, dropping to the bench.

"Lulu and your dad were sleeping together."

"Bollocks," Robin snapped. "The fucking drama on you."

But instead of quieting Jack, it spurred him on. "She confided in me. She hated herself, but it was obvious that he had become her addiction. He manipulated her, found her weaknesses, and used them to reel her in. Lulu made a mistake, but your dad got her to the point that she didn't understand it was a choice. He targeted her because she was vulnerable and used it against her."

"Why would I be interested in the stupid eighteen-year-old girl dating my son? You're embarrassing yourself."

"You hated that Josh was better at rugby than you," Rose tossed back angrily, "You hate someone having something you can't have, especially when that someone is your son. Josh was dating a girl who adored him and was about to be signed to the under-twenty-ones side of a premiership rugby club. He'd already achieved more than you had, and you despised it."

"That's bullshit. I've always supported the boy. You know that better than anyone."

"Only when it made you look good. It was never about Josh. You've never cared about anyone but yourself." Rose stalked him with tight lips and flaring nostrils.

"Rosie pie, don't tell me they've got to you too." Robin gave a charming smile. He had more masks than a fancy dress shop.

"No, Robin, you've got to me. I've tolerated your affairs all these years because I thought it was all I deserved. I believed you returned to me because you loved me the most. But I was your doormat. You came back to me because you could and treated me like I was worthless because that's how you saw me. But knowing what you did to Lulu and how you tried to destroy our son is the last straw."

"Sweetheart—"

"I'm leaving you. I have too much self-respect to be with you anymore. You're a worthless bastard, and I want you out of my life."

Robin's bellowing laugh was intentionally cruel. "Until I cock my finger and beckon you back. You can't cope without me because you need me."

"I don't, Robin, I never did, but you convinced me that I couldn't survive alone. I can't wait until I never have to see you again."

"You're *my* wife. You don't get to say when it's over. What if I won't let you go?"

"Then I will beat you to a pulp like I should have done when we were at school," Charlie growled.

It was like a ludicrous pantomime, but the actors and the drama were real. Clothes littered the changing room, and empty bottles haphazardly found a home in the mess. Yet the group performed an argument worthy of a Shakespearean tragedy in the sweat-imprisoned space.

"You want my cast-offs? She's yours if you want to slum it with her. I have no use for her anymore. You always did have a thing for this sl—"

"I will punch that smile off your face," Charlie roared, but Rose stood between them.

"He's not worth it. He's not worth anything."

"Don't forget, Charlie, buddy," Robin said with a vile laugh. "I screwed her first."

Josh saw red and jumped up. He grabbed his dad by his collar and slammed him against the wall. "You don't speak about my mother like that. You don't get to speak about her ever again."

Josh let go, and Robin crumpled on the floor.

"I need to get to Evie. What if something happens to her? She has no idea that I believed her."

"I'm glad," Lucas piped up. Everyone turned to him. In the drama, they'd forgotten he was there. "I came to tell you that I saw your dad try it on with her, but she pushed him off."

"Where did this happen?"

"In the tunnel." Lucas glanced at Charlie sheepishly. "I threw a tantrum after Boss Man pulled me out of the match."

"Something we'll be discussing on Monday," Charlie replied with a warning.

"Go to Evie," Rose pressed.

"I'll drive," Jack shouted.

"But what do I do about him?" Josh asked. They turned to Robin, who stared up at them.

Rose spoke confidently and clearly. "Leave him to me. He's my responsibility." Josh went to cut her off, scared that she'd take him back. "But not for much longer."

"We'll make sure he doesn't try anything," Charlie said, with Lucas nodding by his side.

"I might need somewhere to live soon, but we'll discuss it later," Rose said, her voice wavering. To be single for the first time since she was eighteen, even if she was getting out of a loveless marriage, was a big step.

Josh held his mum's eyes with his for a heartbeat. "I'm here for whatever you need. I was going to chuck Lucas and Max out anyway."

"Nice way to break the news," Lucas replied sullenly.

"Evie's moving in. Well, she was. That reminds me, we must go via my place before we find Evie."

"Do you know where she'll be?"

"I have a good idea."

Stepping out of the changing room and towards the car park, Josh refused to let hope die.

"Please, Evie, don't give up on me yet," he whispered.

CHAPTER THIRTY-SEVEN

The short car ride was full of revelations. Jack may have dressed impeccably with a fashion sense rivalled by *Vogue* editorials, but his car was messier than the Bulls' locker room. He'd strewn empty McDonald's and Costa coffee cups across the floor, and something sticky on the door handle meant Josh kept his hands firmly in his lap. Josh attempted several times to distinguish the festering smell and considered picking up air freshener when they'd stopped briefly at his house en route.

Josh tapped his fingers restlessly against his thighs, which were out of place in the tiny passenger seat. "Lulu called you the night she died?"

Jack refused to meet Josh's stare as the car rattled through town. "Yes. She told me she'd tell your dad it was over between them. She must have ended the call not long before she crashed."

"It wasn't my fault," he repeated like a mantra. Lulu's death would be part of him forever, and he couldn't change how he'd hurt her.

Tears brimmed Jack's eyes as they stopped outside Enid's flat. Josh took his hand and held it. "I should have told you sooner, but I barely functioned in the weeks running up to the funeral. I'd lost my best friend. You and I weren't close, and I had no idea you blamed yourself. I didn't think learning about your dad and her would help your grieving; honestly, I was scared. Finally, one day, I built up the courage to visit you, but your dad wouldn't let me or anyone else past your front door."

"He said her friends blamed me for what happened and didn't want to see me."

Jack squeezed his thumb. "Not long after the funeral, you moved out of county to play for the Giants. When we met again after Aidan started dating Sophia, I saw your suffering, but I'd left it too long to tell you. I was afraid of how you'd react, and I was gutless. It's a poor excuse. It's a worthless sentiment now, but I'm truly sorry."

"You don't need to apologise. You did what you thought was best." Josh pulled him into an awkward bear hug, but the seatbelts got in the way.

Jack pulled away and looked out his driver's window. "No, I didn't. I did nothing. But promise me that you don't hate Lulu. What she did was wrong, and she knew that, but she was vulnerable too. She hated herself all those times she met with your dad, but he was an adult and manipulated her until he became her addiction. First, he offered her all she needed to feel whole, then he chipped away at her confidence and made it impossible for her to walk away."

"I'm sad for her that I brought my dad into her life." Josh's sigh filled the tiny car. "I can't believe how much we all suffered because of him."

"Years of it," Jack replied, turning back to Josh.

"Do you think my mum will be okay?" Every hour brought a fresh shift to Josh's world. "I've seen glimpses of her strength all my life, but I'm scared of what might happen next."

"She'll have you and Evie to help her."

"I'm not sure any of us have Evie anymore. I don't deserve her, and I keep making mistakes." Josh's head dropped. He studied the bruises and nicks forming on his hands from the match.

Jack shoved him with his shoulder, although with Josh's strength, he bounced back. "Evie loves you. It's obvious to everyone around you."

"Yet she acts like she doesn't need me and can do it all herself."

"Because that's who she is." Jack unclicked his seatbelt and grabbed Josh's shoulders. "It's the little things that matter to Evie. Women like Evie don't need a man to fight their battles. They need someone to be there for them when the battles get bloody, who can tend to their wounds and help them to get stronger and fight again. They need someone to come home for, who is there for them no matter what."

Josh's face sank. "But is that me? The guy who shouldn't have had any part in my growing up taught me to be manly and dominant."

Jack gripped him tighter. "But is that what you believe manly is? Does the idea of being the type of person Evie needs bother you?"

"It worries me," he admitted with trembling limbs. "I like being the one to hold Evie's hand when she cries or the person that has her back. I enjoy making her food and ensuring she eats it when life overtakes her. I get bizarre levels of joy from watching her ravage something I've cooked for her. But having to keep quiet when she's dealing with all kinds of shit and letting her go into those situations without me in front and protecting her seems cowardly."

"It doesn't make her less of a woman or you less of a

man. They're the roles that fit your talents and are fluid anyway. Just because she doesn't need you out front doesn't mean she won't next time. And there are times you'll need her out front for your battles. It works for you guys. Evie doesn't need a knight in shining armour, but she needs respect, trust, and unconditional love."

"She needs me," Josh conceded with a tentative smile.

"You're finally getting it. It's taken you long enough," Jack joked, before getting suddenly serious again. "Don't let your dad hurt your future and your past. You will move on from the pain one day, and maybe Evie will heal you too."

"When did you get wise?" Josh's smile screwed to the side of his face.

Jack's laugh hinted at more secrets and fed Josh more questions, but this wasn't the time to ask them. They sat in the car a little longer. The silence was their comfort.

"Do you love Evie?" Jack asked as he stared through the windscreen.

"Do you need to ask?" Josh elbowed him, causing him to shake in his seat.

"Oi, you." Jack laughed. "I want to hear you say you love her, because if you don't practice, you're gonna fuck it up." Jack winked.

"I don't just love Evie. I adore her."

"Then get out of my car and tell her, because she loves you. Don't let your dad and all the shit he's said to you destroy this. Think of what Evie has said to you. I've seen her love for you every time she's looked at you. We all have."

Josh gritted his teeth so hard his jaw hurt. "But I didn't defend her quickly enough. What if I'm too little too late?"

CHAPTER THIRTY-EIGHT

Josh stood outside the car as Jack revved the engine.

His fear was more potent than anything Jack had thrown at him. The sky had lost the brilliant blue that had surrounded him when he'd played his match earlier. Spring showers closed in on the town, and his feet stuck to the concrete as if he'd rather welcome the heavens than deal with the storm raging in Enid's flat.

"Let's hope it is a shower and not a storm," his mum used to say when she sent him off to practise in the park after school. "You can weather a shower, but it's much harder to survive a storm." He'd always presumed she meant for his rugby playing, but the day's revelations added another dimension to his childhood.

With a shaky wave to Jack, Josh trudged up the urine-soaked steps to Enid's flat. Was this a shower in the relationship's infancy or a full-blown monsoon that would desecrate their future?

Josh's fist hit the door loud enough to wake the dead. Fear turned his knock into a warning of impending war.

She had to be there. He'd considered the dance studio and the pub, but this flat was her home and sanctuary, where she was accepted for who she was.

Thrusting his fist towards the door again, air brushed past his skin. Evie's pinched face and steely glare as she stood in the open doorway spurred him on rather than scared him. He wanted to see her face every day for the rest of his life, even if she never smiled at him again.

"You." Josh's heart quivered from the rage she'd managed to fit into that single word. "What the hell are you doing here? I'm the woman who tried it on with your dad, apparently. I'm a stupid tart, aren't I?"

"I wanted to tell you some things," he stuttered. He swallowed loudly at his impossibly dry mouth.

"Who said you get to be the one who speaks?" she snapped. "Not that you'd listen to me anyway."

Josh took a deep breath. "Can I come in?"

Evie shrugged and held the door open with just enough space for him to squeeze through. He kept his gaze pinned to the ground in case she tried to trip him.

He was safely through the door. *First objective achieved.* Josh froze at the scene in front of him. Evie had tossed clothes in an array of colours around the room. Had it been due to a fit of anger or in an attempt to organise chaos?

Boxes lined one side of the room, and books and shoes covered every inch of seated space on the sofa. A half-filled suitcase sat on the coffee table as if bestowed a definite purpose. Inside it, clothes had been tightly rolled and were nearly brimming out the top. Where was Evie going? And would she have told him she was leaving if he hadn't arrived?

Easing some books to the side, he perched on the arm of the sofa.

"Don't move those. I have a system," she grunted.

Josh placed the books back and stood awkwardly in the corner. Evie returned to her packing and held up two bikinis. She'd worn the one with the sparkly sequins and silver fringing in his favourite glamour modelling shot, and the red one with more string than material was from one of her motorbike photoshoots.

Her busyness was distracting, but he had to try and win her back. "I'm sorry," he blurted.

Evie paused briefly and quirked an eyebrow before continuing with her packing. "Is that all you came to say? Because I've got things to do."

"What are you packing for?"

Evie remained focused on her task. "I got offered a glamour modelling job in London."

"You can't go." Cold drops of sweat found the skin of his neck, causing him to shiver.

"It's not like there's anything to stay here for." She dead-eyed him before continuing her packing.

His whole body trembled as he stepped toward her. Josh fisted his hands and took another deep breath. He'd be out of air soon. "Okay. That's fair enough. But I want you to know I'm beyond sorry for what happened today. I can't believe I didn't defend you, and no matter what, I needed you to know that. But whatever you want to do, I'm on your side. I'll be here when you get back, and no matter what happens, I'm here for you."

"Like you were an hour ago?" Forcing more distance between them, she headed for the pile of tiny underwear in the corner of the room. Picking up material that wouldn't cover a nipple, she joked without humour, "I probably won't be needing these."

Josh stepped closer. He eased the underwear from her grip and delicately returned it to the pile on the floor. He took her hands and held them to his chest like he had that morning. That seemed a lifetime ago. His heart beat rapidly.

"I'm sorry, Evie. I can explain what was going on in

my head, but first and foremost, I should have defended you immediately and not shown a hint of belief in what my dad said. I abandoned you when you needed me the most, and I can't do anything to change that, although I wish more than anything that I could. I will never do anything like that again. I will always be on your side and believe you no matter what. No matter where we are in the world, I know you are the most genuine and beautiful soul, and I'm sorry. I'm so sorry."

Evie refused to make eye contact.

Josh crumpled internally. "I would fight all the rugby players for you if it helped. When my dad said those things about you, I was traumatised for a moment, and I am disgusted with myself that I let him get in my head even for a second. And then I worried about how I could help my mum. But my thoughts should have been instantly on you too. I always believed you and never doubted you."

Josh held his head in his hands.

Evie sighed as she sat on a rustic wobbly stool. "I needed you, Josh. I always need you. Yes, I can be difficult, but I want you on my side and by my side no matter what. Can you do that?"

"Yes, a billion times yes! I will never believe others before you. I know it was too late, but I defended you to Dad, and I will do that to anyone else who crosses our paths." Josh strode to her and kneeled before her. "My heart wants to burst at the idea I might lose you. I bloody love you, Evie Draper." His voice shook as they locked eyes. Her green eyes sparkled a little and grew with every thud of his heart. "Do you love me, Evie?"

"Of course I do." Her trembling voice gave him a sliver of hope. "But it's never been a question of if I love you. First, I loved you as my best friend, and then I loved you like a girlfriend. You're my everything, but I don't know if I can get over that you don't trust me." Evie yanked her hands out of his grip and stormed to a pile of books.

"But I do love you and trust you. If glamour modelling is what you want, I will stand by your decision and be there for you. You've told me you hate it, but if you want to do it again because you love it or miss it, then I will be your head cheerleader. I will follow you to the ends of the earth if you let me."

Evie froze. Her head dipped, and she let out a long breath. "I'm too scared of all this emotion I have for you. What if we hurt each other and can't heal from that next time?"

Once again, he walked over to her and put her hand on his chest. "I'm scared too, but I can't stop how much I love you. I was too scared to admit it for a long time, but I can't ignore it anymore. Before, I tried to make you someone I couldn't hurt and that couldn't hurt me. I had to protect both of us, but I stopped you from being you. But I don't want to stop you anymore. Every mistake we make together means we're better at being in this relationship. I want to give us a go no matter what and let you be you without worry."

"So you'd let me do glamour modelling and make videos with random naked guys?"

"Does that count as glamour modelling?"

"That's not an answer. Would you let me?"

They stood in the middle of the room, her hand on his heart, drowning in piles of packing.

"If you wanted to do that, then yes. I'd be by your side or be at home with a hot meal for when you get back. Whatever it takes. Because I love and trust you." The idea of her with other guys in naked shoots unnerved him, but it was because of insecurities that he'd work through. He wanted her to be her authentic self. "Whatever it takes."

Evie pecked him on the lips. "Good."

"So when are you going to London?"

"I'm not. There's not a chance in hell I'm returning to glamour modelling."

"Huh? Evie, what is going on? I don't understand, and my head hurts from this rollercoaster of a day. It's been long, emotional, and life-changing. I don't know if I'm a fighter who just lost the greatest bout of his career or the winner of the game of life." Evie's fingers smoothed away his frown lines.

"Those are some metaphors. After what happened with your dad, I thought I'd lost you for good. I didn't know if I'd see you again. But I knew as soon as I saw you at my door that you loved me and I loved you. But I'm scared of all of this and letting someone back in, and I want you to reject me, because being with someone I love as much as I love you terrifies me."

"Me too. But the fear of being with you doesn't compare to the terror of being without you. We have to give us a chance, don't we? Nothing compares to how I feel about you. Are you willing to risk the pain and give us a try?" Dread had him on edge. Finally, there was a breakthrough, but it could all be lost.

"Tell me what you love about me?"

Taken aback by her question, he said the first things that came to mind. "Your spirit and your feistiness. The way you say what's in your head without a filter. Your kindness. Your knowledge and wisdom. Obviously you're the sexiest woman alive, but that is just one thing. There is so much to you, and I could sit in front of you all day, listening to your thoughts on the world and watching how you care about everyone from old men like the Captain to tiny girls with limited confidence like Tilly. You're a goddess who I'm lucky to have met."

"I love you, Josh. What happened with your dad wasn't your fault. He'd been texting me, and I should have told you, but don't you ever do what you did again, or I will punch you in the balls," she explained. "And you love that I said that because you've already told me you adore my feistiness."

Josh laughed hard enough to make his abs hurt.

"But I am sorry for walking out on you without letting you catch up with what was happening. If I'd stayed while your dad trashed me, one of us would have done something we regret."

Josh drew her close, taking sanctuary in the beat of her heart against his. Their hearts shared a rhythm. "There was a mini second where I questioned everything, but you were in the right. I'm not perfect, but I have a lifetime of that man's manipulation to work through. So I guess I'll be heading to counselling too. I want you by my side in the joys and when I go to war. Do you forgive me?"

"I do. We've both got a lifetime of shit to work through, but I know you have my back."

"Do you have my back too, even after I fucked up?"

Pulling away, she stared into his eyes. The loss of heat from her body caused him physical pain. "I do, Josh. You must see that."

He shook his head, returning her sadness.

"Look me in the eyes," she demanded, but her voice softened.

"They're beautiful."

"You silly bugger." She giggled. "Hear this, Josh King.

You are all I want and desire. I'm not good at sappy stuff, and sometimes I don't lean on you when I should, but believe me when I say that it's you and only you. You'll be the one I turn to, and you will help me become the best version of myself."

"Like you do to me."

Her smile shone. The warmth that flooded Josh's insides gave him ecstasy akin to when he was inside her. "I got something before the match. It's healing, but I want you to see it."

Evie's fingers teased the buttons on her jeans.

He dropped onto the sofa in front of her. Evie's books smacked against the floor as they fell from the couch.

"My books," she shouted with a teasing smile.

"I'll buy you more. I'll buy you any you want, or I'll let you buy them yourself and carry your books if you let me. Just promise me you won't stop what you're doing." Watching Evie lower her jeans had him throbbing like a man who'd been locked away from his partner for years.

It was torture not to stare at the knickers that clung to her pussy, but she directed his gaze higher.

Evie drew back the protective wrapping to reveal a tattoo on her hip.

"It's a butterfly." Josh leaned forward, keen to trace it with his fingers, but she flinched away.

"It's sore." It was three-quarters of a butterfly, and many intricate little butterflies formed the wings. "It's in honour of all the people and experiences that have got me where I am today. All these things, good and bad, have moulded me into this. Of course, I wish Peter and other things from my past hadn't happened, and I'd come here for another reason, but I can't hide or lie about my past because

I wouldn't be me without it."

"It's beautiful, but why is the bottom of its right-wing missing? Couldn't take the pain?" he asked cheekily.

Evie swiped playfully at him. "You're the biggest pain in my life. That space is for the future. I don't know where it will take me. Maybe it will flap its wings, and I will have kids, or maybe life will take me to live abroad, but whatever happens, I hope I will be with you. Ours is an unfinished story."

"You're starting to sound soppy."

"And you're sounding like an arsehole, as always," she joked. "There are three more tiny gaps for three butterflies in different colours. I'll get them added soon."

"What are they for?"

"One will be for Nan, a purple butterfly because she loved purple. Another will be baby pink to represent ballet. I love ballet more than ever. It's my first love, and now that I've rediscovered it, I want to have a dance school one day."

"Miss Evangeline."

"Stop giving me those horn dog eyes."

"Stop standing there in jeans that cover the place I dream about every night. Take them off completely."

Evie shimmied out of her jeans and kicked them at him. He caught them with a groan of desire.

"Don't you want to learn about the other one? The third butterfly?"

"Of course, although I'm struggling to concentrate on anything but your knickers right now." She stood in front of him, and he ran his hands up and down the back of her thighs.

"It will be a crimson butterfly. Your tattoo is a tribute to Lulu, but it's also honouring who you were once and speaks a little of who you can be. So you will be my third butterfly."

"How do you make me wonder if my heart will explode while standing there in your underwear?" he whispered.

"Because I'm fucking awesome." She shrugged with a beaming smile.

Another book clattered to the floor, taking him temporarily out of his reverence. "Hold on. I need to backtrack. You're not going to London to do glamour modelling?"

"Nope. I always get offered jobs, but I'd never take them. I hated it, and someone out there loves it and should get the work." Evie leant into his caress as his hands continued to roam her skin.

"So why are you packing?"

"Because this place belongs to the council. I'll have to leave now that Nan doesn't have the lease. I can't pretend she lives here. I don't need to be here to have her with me."

"But where will you go?"

"After what happened at the stadium, I wasn't sure. I can move locally, or start afresh abroad, or…"

"Or?"

"You said I could move in once the season was over, but after this afternoon, I wasn't sure if the offer remained. And I wasn't sure what I wanted. So I came home to pack because of the eviction notice and to keep busy."

"Do you want to move in with me? Because that's all it depends on. I need you with me when I wake up. I long for you to be by my side, not just when we go to war, but when we fall asleep too."

The smile at his soppy sentiment turned him into a glow worm, shining brightly for all to see.

"But if you are moving in with me, you've made a big mistake," he added, pulling her onto the sofa and cuddling her.

"What do you mean?" she replied, pushing him away.

"You should have packed all that sexy underwear. I can't wait to see you in and out of it." Evie looked like she was going to try and swipe at him, but he caught her hand, holding it gently in his. "But first…"

He leapt off the sofa and got on bended knee in front of her. Her face went from a smile to wide-eyed terror. "No, Josh. It's too soon. Don't ruin it."

Ignoring her, he reached into his pocket before placing something metal on her palm.

"A key?"

"Well, it's a bit soon for marriage," he joked with a wink. "It's your key. I got it cut this week. You're going to need it if you're moving in with me. I planned a big thing, but this is right."

Evie pulled him up and dragged him back on the sofa before climbing on him and kissing him hard.

"One more thing, although I don't want to move now." He stroked her thighs as she straddled him. "But I left them in Jack's car. Shit."

He lifted Evie into the air and popped her back on the sofa. "Don't dare move a muscle." He rushed to the door, shouting, "Well, I'll allow you to take your top off if you really must."

His heart thudded without pause, but Jack had saved the day and left Josh's flowers outside the door. "These are for you." He froze, seeing Evie in her lacy green underwear, her top tossed to one side. The colour matched her eyes perfectly.

"As you requested." She winked with her hands on her

hips. "Are those roses for me?"

"Yes," he stammered, unable to recall his mini-speech. "They're butterfly roses," he stuttered.

"They're beautiful," she replied, skipping towards him.

"Wait," he finally managed. "You know what Enid once said. If you accept my roses and my love, you have to put up with my shit forever."

"Forever is a long time," she replied coyly.

"I know. Are you sure you're willing?"

Evie snatched the roses from his grasp, pulling them against her nearly naked chest.

The throbbing at his crotch was out of control. "Are you aware, Miss Evangeline, that for the year and a half we've been friends, I've never seen your bed?"

"No man has. Would you like to make its acquaintance?"

"I'd be delighted to, and then we must get you packed up. It's moving day."

"Promise you'll be careful with my tattoo," she called out as she ran.

"I make no promises," he growled as he chased her to her bedroom. "Those butterflies will flap their wings by the time I finish with you."

Epilogue

This was it. Evie gulped.

Josh's strong hand in hers managed to quell her fears a little. "They'll be great, and it will be because of you."

Together they watched the children flutter onto the stage. It was the first public performance of the children from Evie & Enid's Butterfly Ballet School. She'd spent months deciding how to honour her nan, but this was fitting for the years Enid had inspired those around her.

Together, Josh and Evie had spent the last hour calming nerves, rushing children to the toilet for anxious wees, and praying they wouldn't be mopping the floor from vomit-filled stage fright.

For the first half hour, the children danced brilliantly, and now it was Evie's turn to take to the stage for a solo performance. The only sound was from the speakers as everyone held their breath. Evie performed Princess Aurora's dance from *Sleeping Beauty*. This was for Josh. With the hard stage beneath her feet, this was what she'd longed for over the last nine years. Sweeping her arms and pirouetting across the stage, she caught sight of Josh's shadow in the wings. A light flashed across his face, which shone with awe. It was as if he was bestowing her his love and granting her power over him. It spurred her on, and she gave the moves energy she'd been missing in many rehearsals.

Panting hard, she gazed into the crowd as she finished. Figures were hard to distinguish, but one stood out. In the front row centre was Gabi, smiling and clapping hard enough to fill the theatre with her praise.

Joining friends and families of the dancers after the show, Evie pondered how she'd found a loving family when nine months earlier, at her dying nan's bedside, she'd declared she'd be alone forever.

"You were amazing, sis," Gabi called out. "I'm beyond proud. I knew you were a beautiful dancer, but that was incredible." After a fluttering kiss on her cheek, Gabi disappeared into the crowd, probably to congratulate the children. It stunned Evie how much Gabi adored the little butterfly dancers she'd met only five months earlier.

"Who was the babe?" Lucas whispered, sneaking up to Evie.

"Hands off my little sister, you perv. She doesn't need a bad boy in her life, and she's too innocent for the likes of you."

"Evie, you should know by now that what you said is a red rag to a horny bull! Unfortunately, I've got no choice, and I will have to seduce her."

"I'll make Josh rip your balls off."

"I'm afraid he's too busy training for his international games. Josh is the King of England now," Lucas teased a little, but what he inferred was true. The England coach had scouted him, and his skill on the pitch was improving consistently. So now he was being called up to every game

England played. No longer was his nickname Kong. Instead, he was King of England. The World Cup was the following year, and he'd be starting for his country.

"Then I'll rip your balls off myself. I'm very protective of my little sister."

"I've always been more scared of you than him."

"What are we talking about?" Jack bounded up to them with Max by his side. They were the couple of the moment and a perfect match. There had been some adversity, partly from a confused Charlie, as it had never occurred to him that his son might be gay, but things smoothed out, and Jack was a regular fixture at every game and family meal.

"About how Evie will rip my balls off," Lucas replied effortlessly.

"Surely not Evie. She's a tame pussy cat these days," Jack retorted, pressing her buttons.

"Whatever you say, Chuckles," Evie replied with a smile. "He was threatening to seduce my sister."

"Don't go there, Lucas, not if you value your life. Ever since Gabi moved here to start a new life, Evie has become a protective jailer."

"And you've got to get past her new housemate too. So save your efforts for another unfortunate beauty," Max added, smacking Lucas on the back.

"I can sneak past anyone." He ducked down and jumped from side to side. "You've seen my cheeky yet wily skills on the pitch. I'm a fucking sexy ninja. So who is her new housemate?"

"Josh's mum." Max grinned his reply.

He bolted up straight. "Fuck off. How did that happen? A divorcee mum and a sweet ass—"

Evie glared him down.

Lucas cleared his throat. "I mean, sweet girl like that.

What do they have in common?"

"You're an ass."

"Did they get fed up hearing Evie and Josh banging each other's brains out as they did on the stairs that time?" Lucas mused, treading a thin line.

"I hear my name," Josh called, joining the babbling group and towering over most of them.

Although Lucas was a good friend, Gabi had many demons to work through, and a bad boy wasn't suitable for her. Evie stared at Josh, who challenged her daily and ensured that even when they battled, they both won. "Where have you been?" Evie asked, trying to move the conversation away from her sister.

"It's a surprise." He nodded too obviously to Jack.

Evie held back her giggles. Josh was awful at keeping secrets, but he deserved his moment. She'd found his proposal speech and the engagement ring earlier that day in the bathroom when he'd misplaced them. She'd pretended she hadn't seen a thing. But the nervous excitement radiating from him was infectious, and goosebumps covered her arms. Was he really going to propose tonight?

"Maybe Josh's mum got fed up sneaking Boss Man around," Lucas teased, returning to the earlier conversation.

Josh shook his head. "My mum is not having sex with Max's dad. No way. Not a chance."

Max went suspiciously silent.

"They were each other's first loves, remember? So don't be too sure," Evie replied with an encouraging smile while Jack nodded. Jack knew everything worth knowing and saw these things before anyone else.

"Answer me one question about your sister," Lucas requested, breaking the awkward silence.

"Fine, but nothing dirty."

"What does she do for a living? How does she pay for those pretty dresses that—"

"She's a primary school teacher," Evie interjected with a warning glare.

"Oh, she's perfect. It's a red rag to a bull, Evie. I have to get her to go on a date with me now. Fate has decreed it. See you on the other side." He grinned as he headed away from the group.

"We'll save her. I doubt he'd even recognise her again in this crowd," Jack responded immediately, dragging Max off on an impromptu rescue mission.

"You were stunning tonight, by the way," Max called out before he was swallowed up by the many proud parents and excited children overdosing on sugar.

Josh smiled adoringly at her, and she grinned back. If only Nan could witness their happiness and maybe be proud of her too. As she tapped her hip where her tattoo hid beneath her leotard, she knew her nan was with her.

"Which finally leaves me with my goddess," Josh said, drawing her closer for a kiss.

As he leaned away, he focused on something over her shoulder. His brow furrowed. "Will Mum be okay? She's moving out of ours and has a job at The Tavern."

"She's a grown woman finding her place in life. Angie and The Captain will take care of her. She needs to experience life and work out her place in the world. Getting pregnant by your dad at eighteen stopped her from doing things. This is her time to discover what life has in store for her. She got away from your dad, and that was probably the hardest step."

"True, but I worry."

"Of course you do." Evie brushed his forehead lines

with her fingers. "But she's doing okay, and now you can see her become her genuine self without your dad destroying her soul. We'll make sure she's safe."

"Thank you." He pulled Evie in for another kiss.

"What for?"

"For everything." The lips against hers were hard and passionate. "You were incredible tonight. The kids were lovely too, and their performance was great. But the way you danced stopped my heart."

"It must have made an impression." She wriggled against him. "Maybe, if you're really lucky, I'll do a private dance for you later."

"Will I get to see your butterfly?" he growled.

"I might let you kiss it once you've had your fill of my breasts."

"Impossible. It can't happen. There's more chance of me becoming a dancer, and we're both aware I haven't got the twinkle toes for that."

"There's time, but we need an occasion to practise for. Maybe a wedding will come up in the future. Who knows?" She winked before kissing the man she'd one day call her husband.

FURTHER SUPPORT

If you need someone to speak to due to the themes in Stalling in Love, there are places available for you.

UK

Cruse Bereavement Support – cruse.org.uk

Samaritans – samaritans.org

USA

Grief Haven – griefhaven.org

Office on Women's Health - www.womenshealth.gov/relationships-and-safety

Australia

Grief Australia – grief.org.au

Lifeline – lifeline.org.au

ACKNOWLEDGEMENTS

I'm so lucky to have many great people around me who help me with my writing and all the little bits that people don't see, whether chatting through a cover idea, deciphering how to format a manuscript or giving me space to work through ideas.

A humungous thank you to Kathryn Kincaid, an epic writer, beta reader and someone to chat with and run through thoughts with. I've learnt a lot from reading her sexy romance, and I can't wait to see her book, Play Your Part, on my shelf. Sarah Smith and Rose Rayne Rivers were some of the kindest and most helpful beta readers I've encountered. They pushed me in my writing and have helped me improve and evolve. Their books are mind-blowing and sexy as hell. I wouldn't have self-published Stalling in Love without the knowledge, encouragement and support of these three writers.

Thank you to Joanne Machin, a lovely human and world-class editor. I'm so grateful for her patience and kindness. She took my manuscript and made it something I'm genuinely proud of.

The biggest thank you to the readers who stuck by my writing on my website, in anthologies and stories I've self-published. Your feedback, reviews and lovely words keep me going, and I'm honoured that you've taken the time to read an unknown indie author.

To Dawn, a great book designer. It's not easy finding someone to design your dreams, but she took every request with enthusiasm, and I love seeing all the rugby men and feisty women she creates.

All the women in my family who taught me to dream big. Who have watched as I was kicked out of ballet lessons as a child but who helped me pass my ballet exams. They've also tolerated my endless discussions about writing too.

My husband and our fur babies, thank you for putting up with the many hours I've spent in pubs or with a laptop on my lap in front of the television. You have a bounty of knowledge for the random words I can't locate from the depths of my brain.

All the rugby players, you inspire me as a fan and writer. I look in awe at your ability to take knocks and get back up again. No matter what, we have to keep trying.

Finally, a massive thank you to my friends 'in real life' and the ones I've met online, especially Kaz and Gill. Your empowering words and kindness pushed me on when I thought about giving up. I don't know where my writing would be without you and the Twitter community.

ALSO BY REBECCA CHASE

Head Over Feels: Sexy and funny debut contemporary romance

Crave for Me: three short tales of erotic romance

Occupational Hazard: A sexy workplace anthology

REBECCA IS FEATURED IN THE FOLLOWING ANTHOLOGIES

Best Women's Erotica of the Year, Volume 4

Erotic Teasers: a Cleis anthology

About Rebecca Chase

Rebecca Chase is an English rose and a pocket rocket with a taste for drama, romance, love and sex. She adores writing, whether it's a short story with unexpected passion or a novel that takes you through the ups and downs of a blossoming relationship. She's always looking for everyone's next book boyfriend. When it comes to her stories you can guarantee there will be romance, there will be love, and most of all, there will be mind-blowing sex. You'll be desperate for more while aching for a happy ever after.

Connect with Rebecca

Website - www.rebeccahchase.com

Twitter - twitter.com/rebeccahchase

Facebook - www.facebook.com/RebeccaHChaseAuthor

Tiktok - @rebeccachaseauthor

Instagram and Threads – rebeccahchase

Goodreads - 15019280.Rebecca_Chase

Printed in Great Britain
by Amazon